THE FIRST THING
THAT HIT ME WAS THE SMELL.

It was stronger than just plain old funk. Stronger and stranger too. I felt my pores tighten. My nostrils shut down all operations, closed off communications, and I was breathing through my mouth. It was dark in there. The boarded-up windows shut off most of the natural light. I felt around the door for the light switch, and when I found it and clicked it on, the second thing that hit me was that something terrible had happened here. Something had f————————————t was nothing mo———————————s foot through th————————————tronic equipment ————————————holes in others, ar———————————s.

I knew I should have gotten out of there right then and there, but somehow I just couldn't. It was like being trapped in one of those sleep-walking dreams where you have to face all kinds of horrors even as you're fighting and struggling with all your might to wake up. The front door opened into the living room. Every room seemed to have suffered similar abuse. But the greatest abuse was to be found in the bedroom. There, stripped naked and beaten almost beyond recognition, was where I found Raymond. . . .

Terris McMahan Grimes

—◦◦◦—

BLOOD WILL TELL

A SIGNET BOOK

SIGNET
Published by the Penguin Group
Penguin Books USA Inc., 375 Hudson Street,
New York, New York 10014, U.S.A.
Penguin Books Ltd, 27 Wrights Lane,
London W8 5TZ, England
Penguin Books Australia Ltd, Ringwood,
Victoria, Australia
Penguin Books Canada Ltd, 10 Alcorn Avenue,
Toronto, Ontario, Canada M4V 3B2
Penguin Books (N.Z.) Ltd, 182–190 Wairau Road,
Auckland 10, New Zealand

Penguin Books Ltd, Registered Offices:
Harmondsworth, Middlesex, England

First published by Signet, an imprint of Dutton Signet,
a division of Penguin Books USA Inc.

First Printing, January, 1997
10 9 8 7 6 5 4 3 2 1

Printed in the United States of America

In memory of Marilyn Leoma Brown

ACKNOWLEDGMENTS

My heartfelt thanks to Detective Jeff Gardener of the Sacramento Police Department, Herb Tillman of Tillman's Investigations and Bail Service, Susan R. Wyckoff, and John B. Miller. A special thank-you to Norman Lorenz for sharing his insights of human nature with me.

Chapter One

"Don't nobody get nowhere round here 'less they kissin' somebody's ass."

The voice sounded like Brenda Delacore's, the number two person in the personnel office at the California State Department of Environmental Equity, my assistant. But I couldn't be sure it was her, the office acoustics around here are so weird.

I'm the personnel officer. I have a private office with a wall of windows—windows mean a lot when you work for the state. But my office is a jerry-built afterthought, and the walls on three sides don't even go all the way up to the ceiling. They wander to a stop about a foot away. Because of its peculiar construction and the way the air flows, or maybe it's the ratio of negative to positive ions—I don't know—my office has some strange acoustical qualities. It's a kind of noise funnel. I'm always picking up ambient snatches of whispered conversations. The funny thing is, it's the whispered stuff that floats in from time to time, not the stuff spoken in a normal voice.

The voice I heard could have been Brenda's, but there was just enough distortion to keep me from being absolutely sure. However, there was no mistaking the person she was talking to.

"That's just what I been telling you, girl," came the insistent reply. "Let a Nee-gro get some kind of position, any position—chief assistant deputy to the undersecretary bathroom monitor—it doesn't matter. The first thing she's going to do is turn around and mess over brothers and sisters. Am I lying? Am I lying?"

That could only have been spoken by Yvonne Pinkham, the second highest-ranking woman of color in the department. Poor child. I wanted to go out there, put my arm around her shoulders, and tell her to take those orange plastic braids out her hair, and go back to her desk, sit down, and do some work.

The voice drifted off, and I tried to go back to work, but I couldn't. I was angry now. Anger bit at me, distracting me, taking my mind off what I was doing. Whatever happened to black unity? Whatever happened to gratitude, for that matter? Brenda had come *this close* to getting a permanent one-step demotion for a series of her shenanigans during a period when she'd acted for me. I'd fought hard for her, arguing that this was her first offense—actually it was her first documented offense—and a permanent demotion was too severe. I'd prevailed, and she'd been demoted one step for two one-month pay periods instead of permanently. This amounted to a $300 fine spread out over two months. I thought I'd done well. But Brenda apparently didn't. I hear she's been going around the department saying I sold her out. How sharper than a serpent's tooth.

The door to my office opened abruptly, and Miyako, my secretary, stuck her head in.

"He's on the line again. I didn't want to risk trying to transfer him. I might lose him like I did the last time."

"You sure it's him?"

"It's him. Come on."

I got up and hurried to the reception area to take the call. The receiver lay on its side. Miyako pointed to it with one hand and beckoned to me with the other. I picked it up.

"Hello, this is Theresa."

The receiver sprang to life, pulsing with energy. I nearly dropped it.

"Hey there, how you doing?"

"Clarence?"

"Yes, ma'am."

"I understand you're having some problems with your supervisor."

"No ma'am, I got it all worked out."

I looked over at Miyako and flashed her the sign for okay.

"That's great, Clarence. You and he came to some kind of understanding?"

"Yes, ma'am. We did. I'm gonna shoot the som'bitch."

"Clarence, you're joking, aren't you?"

"No, ma'am."

I sat down in Miyako's chair and took a deep breath. None of the training I'd taken at the various management seminars the state had sent me to had prepared me for this. I knew I had to stay calm. A show of emotion could push him closer to the edge. I tried counting backwards from ten, but I just got a bunch of random numbers. Miyako, sensing my struggle, stood tense and alert.

"Clarence, listen to me. Don't shoot him. Do you hear me, Clarence? Don't shoot him, please."

There was silence.

"Theresa."

"Yes, Clarence."

"I got to." He spoke in calm, measured tones as if he'd given the matter a great deal of thought and had come up with the only logical solution.

"No, you don't."

"Yes, I do. I got to. He isn't a man, Theresa. He's just a small, nasty, little animal. A vermin. Something that needs to be smashed."

"Clarence, where are you?"

"I'm sitting right here in his office."

"Is he there with you?"

"No, ma'am. He's probably outside the building taking a smoke, or he's in a meeting somewhere, trying to figure out how to ruin somebody's life."

"Clarence, we need to talk a little more, just you and me. I'm coming up there. Don't do anything, okay? Just wait for me. I want to talk to you. Okay, Clarence?"

I pressed the receiver to my chest and mouthed to Miyako, "Call the police."

She turned to go to another phone. I grabbed her arm. I snatched a pen from the mug on her desk and wrote in slashing capitals on her desk pad, "Find Arvin Gaines. Don't let him go to office." She nodded and left. I put the receiver back to my ear.

"Clarence, you still there?"

"Yes, ma'am. I'm here. I ain't going nowhere."

I hung up the phone and headed out the door.

I crashed into Dot and her mail cart as I rounded the corner to the main corridor. I apologized over my shoulder, but I didn't stop to help her pick up the envelopes and small boxes that tumbled to the floor.

I got to the elevator and punched the up button. I

was on the first floor, and Clarence's unit was on the eighth. The elevators in the Resources Building are notorious for being slow and cranky. I looked at my watch. I couldn't afford to take the chance of waiting just one minute too long. The stakes were too high. I darted down the hallway to the stairwell. I wouldn't have taken the stairs a year ago, but I'd been thirty pounds heavier then.

My muscles started to protest around the fifth floor. They were loud and angry by the time I reached the eighth floor. But the thought of Arvin beating me to his office kept me going. I didn't exactly burst out of the stairwell when I got there, but I didn't crawl either. I allowed myself to pause for a moment to catch my breath and to get my bearings. The Internal Audits section where Clarence worked was at the far end of the hall on the northeast side of the building. I turned in that direction and faced down a long expanse of blinding beige. Beige walls, beige ceiling with fluorescent lights lit to a clinical degree of brightness, and discolored beige vinyl flooring. The unremitting beige was broken up by evenly spaced, numbered doors painted in a color derivative of camel dung. I took off running.

I passed Mr. Fraser, who had just finished cleaning the men's room and was removing the yellow barrier in front of the door. He looked up and tossed me a friendly wave, but I didn't have time for midmorning niceties, and I ran past him without responding.

The Internal Audits unit was a large obstacle course of a room broken up into a warren of randomly placed mismatched cubicles. A few heads turned when I ran past, but no one seemed to take very much notice. Arvin's private office was all the way in the back. His door was ajar an inch or two when I got there. I knocked and got no answer. I tried to peep through the small opening, but I couldn't see anything. The lights were out, the blinds were drawn, and the room was dark. I thought about last year when my mother had talked me into searching for a missing little boy named Sir and all the doors I'd been afraid to enter then, and for good cause. Nasty surprises awaited me behind each and every one of them. Things I'd been trying to forget, put behind me. The blood, crazy jitterbugging fear, dry heaves. Things I never wanted to have to deal with again. But here I was.

I knocked again and called Clarence's name. Nothing. Finally, I swallowed the bile burning my throat and pushed the door open. A gray metal desk dominated one half of the room. The desk top was neat and absent clutter. Two trays, one marked in and the other marked out, stood side by side at the corner of the desk. Each tray held an equal amount of papers. A brown metal table with a fake wood vinyl top dominated the other half of the room. I didn't see any plants or family pictures. I didn't see Clarence either until he spoke.

"I guess you better come on in." He sounded sad, resigned.

Clarence stepped out of the shadows behind the door, and I saw the shotgun he cradled in his arms. There was an odd look about him, as if he had shut himself away and cried for a long time. The bags under his eyes looked raw. The skein of lank wheat-colored hair that vanity compelled him to comb across his head from one ear to the other in a futile attempt to hide his baldness dangled just over his left shoulder. His bald head was as pink as an udder.

"Just leave it cracked. He always leaves the door cracked a little when he's out."

I did as he asked.

He stood there with the gun. I was an uncomfortable as I had been the time I'd shared an elevator with a naked man. Only this time I was more scared.

"I think you better move over here out of the way. 'Cause when he walks through that door"—he made a loud clicking sound—"I'm gonna blow his head off."

"Listen, Clarence, don't do this. You don't have to do this. You can work it out. I'll help you."

He stared at me impassively, not bothering to respond. I thought of Arvin Gaines, the man he was waiting for. What could he have done to drive Clarence to this? I hoped someone had caught up with Arvin and warned him to stay away from his office. I was worried about Arvin, but the strangest thing, I wasn't worried about dying. Sure, I was scared; Clarence had a gun, and he was distraught enough to use it. But up until the very end I thought I could handle whatever came my way. I thought I could talk him through it, actively listen, whatever. I never even thought death was in the cards.

Using the barrel of the gun, Clarence moved me away from the door. I was fine as long as he didn't point the gun at me, but the thought that he would touch me with it had never entered my mind. The metal against my skin felt dirty, obscene. It was like being fondled by something strange and robotic.

I stopped myself from flinching, calmed myself, called on every resource I had, and started talking. I reminded Clarence how he and I first met more than ten years ago when we both worked in the Department of Water Resources, he as an accounting clerk and I as a personnel analyst. We met at one of those mandatory workshops—"Working Together Effectively" or something like that. He wasn't so much an angry white male then as a confused, beleaguered one. The ground rules had been changed, and nobody'd bothered to tell him. He didn't know what was safe to say and what wasn't. All those young college kids, colored people, women. Affirmative Action this, Equal Employment Opportunity that. Most of them knew next to diddly. They all seemed to be on a fast track. Getting promoted, moving higher than they should. It wasn't so much what you knew now, but who you knew or what color your skin was or whether you were a woman that counted now. And he was left standing in the dust, breathing their exhaust, doing the work they should have been doing. With all that baggage, somehow he and I still managed to become friends. Work friends. Not the kind of friend you'd invite to your kid's graduation, but the kind you're glad to see when you cross paths in the hallway or at a meeting. The kind you take a few minutes to chat with and maybe even have coffee with if you end up in the cafeteria at the same time.

Clarence didn't seem to be listening to me. He stood with his eyes fastened to the door, waiting for Arvin. An old, battered duffle bag lay at his feet. I kept on talking, trying to get some sort of dialogue going, some give and take. Anything.

"Clarence, did you and Arvin argue? Was it your time, the time you've been taking off?"

"No, ma'am."

He answered without looking at me, but I'd made contact. I tried again. "Clarence, how's Linda Carol?"

I saw something flicker across his face. But before

I could get a good read on it, he whirled around, grabbed a handful of my blouse, and slammed me against the wall behind the door. Breathing raggedly, he held me there with my chin cocked awkwardly and my blouse bunching through his fist like a crepe-paper flower for what seemed like hours. My first instinct was to slap him upside his head and tell him to take his hands off me. But I suppressed it. I dampered down—way down—so far down I was barely breathing. Finally, he looked at me as if he were surprised to find us in such intimate proximity, and letting go of my blouse, he turned back to the door.

"Leave my wife out of this," he said.

I nodded, stepping back and stumbling over his duffle bag.

It had taken everything I had not to act a fool when he grabbed me like that. But I wasn't about to give him attitude now. Clarence was clearly a man overboard. He was so far out beyond reason, he was in international waters, swimming toward Bosnia. The best thing I could do was to stay calm or at least pretend to stay calm, and work on quieting that whiny little voice in the back of my head that kept repeating, "You done messed up, girl." I didn't want to admit that I had messed up. Maybe I should have called someone, instead of rushing in here myself. Maybe a professional was needed, someone trained at the U.S. Postal Service or something. But it was too late for that now.

Clarence cocked his head. He seemed to be listening intensely. He'd picked up a sound somewhere. Then I heard it too, and lock-jawed with horror, I stared as Clarence lifted the shotgun and placed it in the firing position.

Chapter Two

I hate waiting. It gives you too much time to think. Too much time to worry, and worry has a way of developing into full-blown panic without your even noticing. Death watches are even worse. Clarence and I waited—he remote and calm except for the sweat that waxed his head and face to a high sheen, and I as agitated as a person with multiple personalities with a tendency to bicker among themselves. The wait was just long enough to make you hyperventilate if you're so inclined. Long enough to get light-headed with desperation if you let yourself. But I wasn't about to let myself. I also wasn't about to let Clarence shoot Arvin either, or anybody else for that matter. Not on my watch. It wasn't that I considered myself a hero or anything. It's just that Clarence was one of the good guys. I knew he didn't really want to shoot anyone. I tried to reach him again.

"Clarence."

He didn't answer. He'd zoned me out. I moved closer. I didn't know what I was going to do if I couldn't talk him out of this, but if worse came to worst, I wanted to be close enough to at least grab the gun.

"He's not coming, Clarence."

Disbelieving, he chuckled deep in his throat.

"He's not coming. I had him warned."

On hearing that, Clarence seemed to sink down within himself like something melting from the inside out. He took a few steps backward, felt for Arvin's desk with his rear, and finding it, sank down on its edge. He looked around the room as if to say, "If Arvin isn't coming, then what am I doing here with this gun?" Then something dawned on him, and he began to tremble and sweat more profusely. I'd never seen anything like it except for a friend of mine who is diabetic. She does that when she's having one of her hypoglycemic reactions. He trembled and sweated as if he were in a hypoglycemic rage.

I moved closer to him. Close enough to smell the despair in his sweat and feel the damp from the aura of mist it created around him. I was all up in the man's space. I could have reached over and grabbed the gun, snatched it out of his hands, but then I probably would have had to shoot him to leave the room with it. Worse yet, he might get into his mind that he had to hurt me to get it back.

I was weighing my options and getting nowhere when the phone rang. It had a loud, raspy ring, the kind old-fashioned phones have. Clarence started wildly, leaping to his feet, but he didn't lose his grip on the gun. The phone rang again, and he spun around to where it sat on the desk and stared at it uncomprehendingly. Then he spun back to the door. He spun to the phone again on the next ring. He seemed caught up in some sort of cosmic wash cycle. I was up on the balls of my feet, rocking in rhythm with his motions. I'd made up my mind to grab the gun the next time he swung away from the door. His balance was a little off then. If I moved quickly and with enough strength and composure and if he remained as disoriented as I thought, I might have a chance of wresting it away from him and getting out the door. Those were two big ifs and an awfully puny little might. But that was all I had, so I decided to go with it. Who knows, I might have pulled it off. I don't like to think about what might have happened if I had tried it and not pulled it off. Fortunately, Mr. Fraser saved me from having to contemplate any of that.

Mr. Fraser came through the door, pushing his cart in front of him like a battering ram on wheels. In the spirit of egalitarianism we use first names at the State; everyone's Bob, Tammy, Ali, or whatever. But Mr. Fraser must be pretty close to Mother's age—I understand he could have retired years ago—and he's a deacon at Mount Pleasant Baptist Church. I've never felt comfortable calling him Benny, which is his first name, so I always called him mister, I guess out of respect.

Mr. Fraser surveyed the room. He didn't seem surprised by what he saw, even when his eyes settled on the shotgun.

"Boy, put that gun down."

Mr. Fraser is a small, wiry, nut-brown man with snow-white hair and the arms of a weight lifter.

"Leave me alone, Fraser. Get the hell out of here."

"Boy, you just about made me curse. I'm not going anywhere. You sitting up here in the dark, got the girl, holding a gun. You lost your mind?"

As he spoke, Mr. Fraser wedged himself and the cart close to Clarence. The room was small to begin with; now it was downright crowded. Clarence was jammed up against the desk so tightly he could barely move. Mr. Fraser squeezed over to the window and opened the blinds.

"Put the gun down and come on out of here."

He gestured toward the window.

"Look here. See these fellows up on that roof? Those are sharpshooters, boy. You think they're going to let you act a fool and then just walk on out of here?"

I peered over Mr. Fraser's shoulder. I didn't see anything on the roof, but that didn't mean they weren't there. If there were police up there, it stood to reason they wouldn't wear fluorescent-colored clothing, or wave banners, or announce their presence in some way.

"They're all over the place. Setting up right outside the door, in the hallway. I knew something was wrong when I saw the girl break and run like that. You come on now. Put the gun down."

"I ain't going nowhere. They'll have to come get me."

Clarence's bravado had the hollow ring of a counterfeit.

"Quit talking all that foolishness." There was a certain gruffness to his response, as though he was getting annoyed, or just a little impatient.

The phone rang again.

"Answer the thing, boy."

Clarence shook his head. He stared at the phone, sweating.

At least Miyako had done what she was supposed to. She'd called the police. This was probably them trying to contact Clarence. Negotiators. Someone to help talk him through this, calm him down, get him to put his gun down and come out.

"I think you should answer that," I said to him.

He shook his head.

"Go on, pick the phone up," demanded Mr. Fraser.

I picked it up and handed it to Clarence. Taking it as if it were hot, he lifted it to his ear. He held it there for almost a minute before he finally said hello. He grimaced when he got a reply.

Clarence nodded a couple of times in response to whatever was being said to him before he caught himself and answered aloud.

"Yes, sir. Yes, sir. No, sir. I'm sorry. I wish I could, but I can't. I just can't."

He swallowed deeply with lots of Adam's apple action. Then he slammed the phone down. I could see the phone negotiation thing wasn't working. It looked like our negotiators hadn't quite found their groove. They're supposed to calm him down, not rile him up more.

"I'm sorry Fraser, old buddy."

"What you talking about?"

Clarence didn't answer. Instead, he lifted the gun. Fraser grabbed it with one hand and forced it down.

"Get out of here," he said to me through clenched teeth, the muscles cording in his neck. "Open the door and leave."

I hesitated, and then I grabbed the doorknob to leave.

"Tell them we're coming out. Me and Clarence here."

Clarence was struggling against Mr. Fraser's strength.

I opened the door cautiously.

"I'm coming out." I made sure I spoke loud and clear.

I stepped past the door and was immediately pulled aside by a couple of officers. They led me around the outer edges of the room to a door and out into the hallway. It looked like they'd set up a command post out there. Mr. Fraser was escorted out shortly after me. We were taken to another floor for interviews, and I didn't see when they took Clarence away.

Chapter Three

After the interviews were over and I was free to go, I went to my car and just sat there. I was beat, drained.

I debated going home, but I couldn't bear the thought of facing the empty house alone. Temp, my husband, had taken the kids, Aisha and Shawn, on a Jack and Jill–sponsored tour of traditionally black colleges in the South. If they were still on schedule, they'd have been at Southern University in Baton Rouge. No, home wasn't where my heart was right then. I needed Mother. There comes a time in every woman's life, no matter how old she is, when she needs the comfort of her mother. After what I'd been through, I needed mine. I thought about calling her. I'd even picked up the cell phone and started dialing, but changed my mind. Since when did I have to call my own mother before stopping by? Mother was always glad to see me—no matter the time, no matter the day. She lives alone in the same house in Oak Park that I grew up in. Although she'd probably be the last to admit it, I knew she was lonely. Mother and I have become especially close since Dad died a few years ago. Not that we weren't always close. Mother has a way of invading your space, sucking out the air, and creating a vacuum that draws you even closer to her. I call it "Mother's Principle of Displacement." The thought made me smile. I started the car, exited the parking lot, and headed for Oak Park.

Up until last year it wouldn't have been unusual for me to stop by Mother's two or three times a week. I was in and out of her house as if I still lived there. But after a while that wore on my marriage, and it began to show the strain, especially after Mother got me involved in the Trey Dog mess that almost got me killed and I ended up getting hauled down to the county jail for questioning. Let me tell you, that was sobering. Right after that I made a promise to Temp and myself to put our family first, him and the kids, to stay out of Mother's messes. And I've been working at it too. But something had to give, and in this case it was my mother time. There's only so many hours in the day. Ten of them are spent at work and getting to and from work. Between soccer games, cheerleading practice, car pool responsibilities, and husband maintenance activities, there's very little time left over for anything else. Which explains why I hadn't been by Mother's in a couple of weeks. The guilt usually doesn't catch up with me until I'm in one of those vulnerable moments just before I drop off to sleep at night. As I thought about it, I realized Mother hadn't called me during the last couple of weeks either. Maybe it was the campaign. Mother was running for president of the Negro Women's Community Guild, and according to her, it promised to be a hard-fought election. Gertha Jackson wanted the office bad, and she wasn't above giving a couple of luaus and slinging a little mud to get it. The campaign was probably taking up a lot of Mother's time.

I parked in front of Mother's and glanced over at

Mrs. Turner's house. I reminded myself to stop calling
it that. Mrs. Turner had been dead almost a year, and
the Bernhiemers, the young couple who bought the
house, had completely remodeled it inside and out.
They'd retained the California cottage look so it still
fit in with the neighborhood, but it had been updated
extensively. There was an expansiveness about it now.
The windows were larger, letting in more light, sky-
lights had been added, even the roof line had been
changed, giving it a tad more pitch. They'd painted it
gray and trimmed it in teal. It was beautiful. The tricy-
cle and other toys scattered about the yard added to
its charm. I never would have thought the house
could've shaken its aura of tragedy, but it had.

I turned my back on the house and entered Mother's gate, closing it carefully behind me. She would
have been pleased. Mother's a passionate gardener.
Her backyard garden has steadily expanded over the
years, and I noticed that it was finally encroaching on
the front yard. Bushy tree collards nearly three feet
tall anchored each end of the flower bed running along
the front of the house, while freshly set out pepper
plants vied for space with the pansies and goldenrod.
The vegetables looked healthier and hardier than
the flowers.

I knocked on the door. I knew Mother was home.
She never goes out after dusk. Besides, the house
emitted a hum, the kind that busy, occupied, happy
houses have, something akin to a cat's purr. I knocked
again. I heard laughter somewhere inside. The girlish,
happy notes sounded like Mother's, but then again
they didn't. There was something different about
them, something lighter. I thought it might even have

been the TV. Standing there, waiting for the door to be opened, I realized I was hungry.

"Mother, open up."

I tried to keep the whine out of my voice.

The door finally opened, and I stood there ready to act ugly. And with good cause. The person who answered the door wasn't Mother.

"Yes?" he said, an eyebrow raised as he studied me. "May I help you?"

May I help you. Now, I consider myself an agreeable person with a certain level of inborn graciousness. I am not lacking in warmth, and my people skills are above average, or I wouldn't have made it very far in state service. In fact, every skills test I've ever taken has rated me high in oral communications. But when that fool stood there in the doorway to my mother's house, looking like something that had been skinned, and asked if he could help me, I nearly lost it. I don't know where it came from, that flash flood of anger and hate and bitterness that I could taste in my mouth. But I was so close to doing something or saying something I would've regretted that it scares me even now just thinking about it. Fortunately, Mother came bustling to the door, and he stepped aside.

"Theresa, come on in baby. I got somebody here I want you to meet."

She grabbed me by the hand, and turning to the man, she said, "Theresa, I want you to meet Raymond Johnson—your brother. Raymond, this is Theresa. You know, the one I've been telling you about."

That's when I started to worry—and choke back my guilt. Because I knew this was all my fault. I'd been so involved in my own affairs that I'd completely neglected Mother. I'd left her alone to her own devices, and she'd tottered off the deep end. I have one brother. His name is Jimmy, and he's in the service, stationed in Germany. He has a German wife and two children. He hasn't been home in years, but I think I'd recognize him. This man was not Jimmy. I knew well enough who he wasn't. It was the question of who he was that had me worried.

Mother stood between Raymond and me, holding one of our hands in each of hers, swinging them gently back and forth. She smiled at him and then me as if she expected us to fall into each other's arms and embrace or something. Raymond smiled just as expectantly. I pried my hand loose from Mother's and faced him head-on. He looked to be in his early twenties, maybe a bit older. It's hard to tell with men. He was slight of frame and not very tall, standing a little taller than me, maybe five seven, five nine at the most. He was dressed neatly in a pair of khaki pants and an oxford cloth shirt. He wore no ring and no earrings. He had no nose piercing as far as I could tell. His only jewelry was a gold chain that hung around his neck, dipping into the vee of his open collar under the weight of a chunky gold ring that swung from it. His predominant personal color scheme seemed to be red—he was red, his hair was red, he had that par-boiled look so many redheads have. But he had cat eyes, green streaked with hazel. I hate cats.

"Excuse me, Raymond, but I'd like to speak to my mother in private, please."

"Theresa, watch your manners," chided Mother.

Raymond held up a hand. "It's all right, Mom. I'll just go see about those rolls in the oven." He smiled at her and left.

"Mother, who is he and what is he doing here?"

Mother looked over her shoulder toward the kitchen. "I hope you didn't hurt his feelings."

"Hurt his feelings?" I exploded. "You have some stranger in your house, purporting to be your son when you know good and well that he's not and you're worried that I hurt his feelings? You should be worried about your safety, about your life. Don't you know how dangerous this is?"

I was more worried than I let on. When Dad died, he didn't know Mother from a shoe, or a chair, or some other inanimate object. It seemed that all the things that made him, his sense of humor, his love of telling tall tales, his funny laugh, dried up and quit working long before he finally stopped breathing. Alzheimer's is a terrible disease. I've never mentioned this to anyone, but deep down, I'm afraid. I don't want to lose Mother like that. I knew Mother had a tendency to get involved in harebrained schemes, plots, and mechanisms. That's just her—she likes that kind of thing. I indulge her when I can and try to steer her clear when I think she's getting in over her head. That's just me—it's my job. But her lapse in judgment had me worried.

"Aw, hush up, girl. You think I'd just let anybody in my house without knowing something about him? I didn't get this old being a fool."

I made a supreme effort to calm myself. It would be next to impossible to talk sense to her if I were ranting and raving myself. Mother sat down in her recliner and used the edge of her hand to trowel her skirt smooth across her lap. I knew the gesture—travel preparations. She was getting ready to take me on a long, circuitous excursion of an explanation. I only hoped that somewhere along the way I would find out what was going on. I sank down on the sofa across from her.

"Okay," I said. "Who is he?"

"He's your daddy's boy.

"I was watering the grass a couple of weeks ago when a cab stopped out front. I said to myself, 'Now, who can this be this time of the evening.' And I saw him climb out and set that suitcase of his on the ground. It was one of those pasteboard ones with that striped band running through the middle. Right then and there something told me this is somebody from down home.

"He looked up at the house number and came over to me and said, 'Excuse me, ma'am, I'm looking for 2225 San Clemente Street.' I said, 'This is 2225 San Clemente Street. Can I help you?' He says, "Yes, ma'am, I'm looking for Walter Lee, Walter Lee Barkley.' I said to myself now, what could he want with Walter Lee. I wasn't about to tell him that Walter Lee had passed on and that I was living in this house by myself. You see, I didn't know who he was or what he might be up to. So, I said, 'Walter Lee's not here right now.' Which wasn't exactly a lie. You should have seen his face fall. So I said, 'Is there anything I can help you with?' And he said, 'Yes, ma'am,' and he reached in his pocket and pulled out a picture and handed it to me. Sure enough, it was a picture of Walter Lee. It must have been taken during the war. He had his shirtsleeves rolled up, and he had on a hard hat, and he was standing next to some kind of machine looked like it was as big as this room. I looked at the picture, then I looked back up at him. The boy was so red he looked right raw, but he was neat and clean and mannerable. You could tell somebody had tried to raise him. My mind started working. I was calculating and figuring. Finally, I asked the boy. I said, 'What do you want with Walter Lee?' He reached for the picture before he answered. Then he said, 'I'm his son. Walter Lee's my daddy.'

"You could've knocked me over with a feather. I studied the boy again, trying to see any Walter Lee in him. I couldn't, but you know that doesn't mean anything. I can recall how people used to tease Mama about me. They'd say, 'Lena, that girl don't look nothing like Chang'—that's what they used to call Papa, Chang. Then I thought to myself, now what is this boy after? You know how it is, somebody dies, and you can pretty well expect kinfolk and folk not so kin to come from the four corners of the earth, trying to get their hands on what little bit he may have left. But Walter Lee's been gone nearly five years, and I would think the grafting period should be over by now. But you never can tell. Walter Lee left me this house and a little bit of a pension, but people down South look at this and think you're rich. I figured if I was going to have to fight for what little bit I had, I might as well know what I was up against. So I invited him in to talk. He was just as polite as he could be, and we talked for a good while."

"Yes, Mother. But who is he? He's been here a couple of weeks? I don't believe this. What is he doing here?"

"That's what I'm trying to tell you if you'll just let me."

She smoothed her skirt again.

"You know how your daddy used to take those trips down South to see his people. Well, I always knew men could be doggish given the chance. It's in the

Bible—'men are one third dog.' Says so right in the Bible. And you daddy was no exception."

"Oh, Mother, why're you so quick to believe something negative about Daddy?"

"I know it's hard for you to accept that your daddy would do something like that. I admit I had a little trouble with it too. And let me tell you, it's a good thing I found out about this after Walter Lee'd passed, 'cause there's no telling what I would've done if I could've gotten my hands on him. But the truth is that boy is your daddy's child. Walter Lee met up with some woman on one of his trips. Of course Raymond can't tell me any more than he knows himself, which isn't much. His mother tried to keep everything from him. Never even told him who his own daddy was. It wasn't until after she died and he was going through some of her papers that he found out."

"Come on, Mother. You believe that?"

"Not at first. I looked for every excuse not to. But he does have the money orders."

"Money orders? What money orders?"

"The ones your daddy sent him. Here, let me show you."

Mother got up from her chair and called to the kitchen.

"Raymond, honey, where'd you put those money orders from your daddy?"

"Raymond, honey"—that hurt to the bone, her calling him that and referring to my daddy as his. Raymond stuck his head out of the kitchen.

"They're in there on the dresser, Mom."

Mother went toward the back of the house. Raymond ambled into the living room, where I waited, and dropped his butt down on an arm of Mother's sofa. He fished the chain out of his shirt and popped the ring into his mouth. I looked over at him.

"Mother doesn't allow anyone to sit on the arms of her furniture."

Without answering, he slid down onto the cushions, leaving one leg dangling over the arm. He sucked on the ring like a lollypop. I got up and moved to the recliner. I leaned forward and stared at him longer than was polite. He didn't seem to mind. In fact, I got the impression he kind of enjoyed it.

"What are you after?"

He looked at me and smiled, showing small, perfectly shaped baby teeth.

"I'm just trying to find out a little bit about my daddy, that's all."

"You're lying. What are you after?"

He swung his leg lazily. "I told you, I just want to find out about my daddy."

I got up from my chair and stood over him with my hands on my hips.

"First of all, he wasn't your father, and secondly, you're getting out of here. Tonight. Thirdly, if you want to discuss your lineage and any dubious connection you may have to our family, you can do so with Armstrong Aloysius Wilson, my mother's attorney."

I knew I sounded pompous and bourgie, but I was mad and—hell, I work for the state.

He opted for his leg swinging rather than responding. I thought I heard him whimper, then I heard a soft hiss, and a split second later I was hit full in the face by a flash fire of stench so noxious I nearly lost my footing, trying to flee its path.

The little bastard.

Mother came back in just then.

"Here they are. They weren't on—"

She stopped midsentence. Her upper lip twitched, just a bit, not enough to notice unless you knew her well. She cast a quick glance at Raymond, but allowed her full and accusing gaze to fall heavily on me. Then she stomped over to the window and jerked it open.

That was it. That did it for me. My very own mother.

"Mother, I want him out of here. Do you hear me? Out of here, right now."

Let Mother tell it, I was completely out of control, ranting and raving and screaming, which is not true. It doesn't really matter though, because things went downhill from there. I guess I said a few things I shouldn't have, and Mother did too, but she won't admit it. Anyway, she made it clear that no one tells her what to do in her own house, including me. I could tell I wasn't wanted around there, so I left.

I was still hungry. I never did get to tell Mother about Clarence and everything. And Daddy's good name was up for grabs.

Chapter Four

I went home and turned on every TV in the house. But it didn't help. The house seemed so empty without Temp and the kids. I checked the answering machine and swore at myself. I'd forgotten to turn it on before I left this morning. I thought about calling Temp, but changed my mind. There's a three-hour time difference between Sacramento and Louisiana, and they would be in bed now. Besides, I didn't want to upset him—he'd only upset Aisha and Shawn in turn. I thought about calling Christine or Tamara—two of my closest friends—but they would have been involved with their families after tough days of their own. Besides, nobody has time for a whiner. The more I thought about it, the more I realized that I really didn't want to talk to anyone anyway. I switched the answering machine on and turned the phone ringer off. I went to the kitchen, dug a Marie Calendar frozen meatloaf dinner out of the freezer, popped it into the microwave, and twelve minutes later, ate it standing over the sink. But there was still an emptiness deep down inside me that Marie Calendar never even touched. Finally, I dialed the Employee Assistance Program hotline number and asked to speak to a counselor. While I was locked in that small office negotiating Clarence's life with him, department management had realized that whatever the outcome they had a crisis at hand. To their credit, they'd acted swiftly and set up a special hotline to the Employee Assistance Program just for department employees. Two hours later, I crawled into bed and slept fitfully, pursued in my dreams by a mechanized Mother wielding a cleaver and a doleful Clarence dragging a duffle bag behind him that was as big as a body bag.

Chased out of bed by my dreams, I was up and had a pot of coffee brewed a couple of hours before the sun rose. By six-thirty I was at work, sitting at my desk, sorting through my in-basket. Allen, my boss, had told me to take some time off, as much as I needed, but I figured it was best for me to get back to work immediately and face down my fears before they got the best of me. Besides, a major department reorganization was in the planning, and I couldn't afford not to be there, if for no other reason than to protect my own interest. Besides that, there was no one to act in my place but Brenda Delacore. No, my best bet was to go to work.

Miyako came in around seven-thirty.

"What are you doing here?"

"I thought I'd come in a little early and catch up on some things."

"That's not what I mean. You shouldn't be here at all. Allen told you to take some time off."

"I'm fine."

"Okay, now, don't take your heroics too far," she cautioned.

I glanced up. Her mouth was curved into that wry little smile of hers. I tried, but couldn't find an edge to what she said. It cut anyway. A hero? That's the last thing I thought of when I thought of myself.

The rest of the staff began to filter in. I went out of my way to greet them individually. They needed reassuring that I was all right, that it was safe to return to normalcy. Some had a glazed, shell-shocked look, others vibrated with curiosity and peppered me with ghoulish questions about what it had been like in there.

TV people were stationed at both the building's main entrances, interviewing employees on their way in. One archorperson dragged her crew and equipment to the personnel office, but I refused to be interviewed. Miyako told them they were causing a disruption and asked them to leave. Miyako is slight of frame with the body of a ballerina and the bone structure of a model. She usually dressed in black, and has multiple piercing in places I never would have even considered suitable for puncturing. She also has the tenacity of a blood-sucking tick and the protective fervor of a mother bear with a cub at stake. They left. I understand Brenda caught up with them in the lobby and tried to sell her story to them even though she wasn't even in the building when everything happened.

At ten-thirty most of the staff went to the first of a series of meetings on personal safety and department security, leaving me alone with my in-basket. I was shuffling through its contents for what seemed like the tenth time that morning when a shadow fell over my desk.

I looked up, and the pear-shaped little man standing between me and the door, blocking the light, thrust a dog-eared business card in my face.

"Lambert, Dale Lambert," he said giving the card a little flutter. "I'd like to interview you about the hostage thing."

The man seemed to take up more air than his size warranted. I stood up to establish authority and to breathe better.

"Excuse me, but how did you get in here? This is a secured area."

"Nobody up front. I wandered around until I found you."

I was a good four inches taller than he was. I could see the bald spot on the top of his head. He had a large head and rather delicate little ears. His hair looked as if it had been buzz-cut with a Cuisinart. He had the pasty coloration of someone who spent his days indoors, or who was nocturnal by nature. His clothes, except for being rumpled, were defiantly non-descript. Proportion-wise he reminded me of a dwarf—a large, rather menacing dwarf.

I took his card and glanced down at it—"Dale Lambert, freelance writer." There was no address. The printed phone number had been crossed out and re-written by hand three different times in three different inks.

"I'm sorry, but I'm not doing interviews, Mr. Lambert. I'm afraid you'll have to leave."

"Ten minutes—that's all it'll take. Ten minutes."

I walked around the desk to the door.

"Five minutes—"

"I'll walk you out, Mr. Lambert. This is a secured area. You really aren't supposed to be back here."

"Impact on the family."

"What?"

"Impact on the family. What if I do the piece on

the impact the whole thing had on your family? That would give us a different perspective, and I wouldn't have to take up too much of your time. I'll talk to your husband, kids, mother, people like that. See how it affected them."

"I'm sorry, but the answer is still no."

"Delayed stress syndrome. You're fine today. Wake up one morning—bam! Hits you in the face. Flashbacks, everything."

We were at the exit now. Lambert stopped and turned to me. He had arranged his face into an expression of solemn sincerity.

"Mrs. Galloway, I really wish I could get you to change your mind."

"Mr. Lambert, I really wish I could get you to understand that the answer is no."

He smiled, hoisted his backpack up on a shoulder, and stepped past the door. "Call me if you change your mind."

I was tired of saying no. I simply nodded.

He shrugged and turned away.

I went back to my in-basket—examination lists, State Personnel Board hearing notices, my file copies of letters that had been mailed, a statistical report on the breakdown of department employees by gender, ethnicity, and disability, and a rather thick, confidential envelope from Aaliyah Truman, the department's Equal Employment Opportunity officer. A missive from Aaliyah in a confidential envelope could mean only one thing—a discrimination complaint. Department procedures require the notification of the personnel officer as well as the immediate supervisor of the person named in the complaint. I slit the envelope and pulled out the document. It looked like eight or ten pages—must be serious. I smoothed the sheets out and read the heading. "Complainant, Gardner A. Reading. Nature of the Complaint, Sexual Harassment"—when will these guys get a clue? Wait a minute. I went back. Complainant is Reading. That means he's the one complaining of being sexually harassed. Then who is the person named? Who's doing the harassing? Dread can do funny things to you. It can dry your mouth out, twist your stomach into knots, and in some cases it can apparently impair your vision. Maybe that's why it took me so long to find the section of the report that named names. Finally, it loomed up at me. The person named in the complaint, the person said to have done the harassing was none other than Brenda Delacore.

I sat back in my chair and closed my eyes. I didn't need this, not now. And neither did Brenda for that matter. She could ill afford the kind of scrutiny that a discrimination complaint brings, especially since she was already treading on thin ice after having been written up less than a year ago. I thought back to when Brenda had came to DEE shortly after the department was established. I'd gone through her personnel file and reviewed the performance appraisal reports done by prior supervisors. They read like a rap sheet. Her supervisors described her as pushy, contentious, overly sensitive about her ethnicity, and lacking in team spirit. One called her militant—a word I hadn't seen used like that since the early seventies— while another wrote that she was downright hostile. But her prior supervisors had all been white males or faux white males, and I tended to discount their evaluations. It had seemed to me they'd had a hard time getting past her Brenda-ness, which I admit can be rather daunting at times. There is an informal network of black managers who work for the state. We keep in touch with each other, share information about job opportunities and technical developments, and back up each other when necessary. I got lobbied heavily by several of them to give Brenda a chance. And, I must admit, I thought she deserved a fresh start in a supportive environment, so I hired her. In many ways, Brenda has lived up to her prior billing as being one of those difficult to supervise employees. It's not that she's not smart. She is. It's not that her work isn't good. It's excellent. Her primary problem seems to be her lack of mother wit. If she just sat at her desk and wrote reports or cranked out classification proposals, she'd be all right. It's when you give her a job that requires even a modicum of common sense that Brenda has problems. Something went wrong during her formative years. Maybe there's an enzyme missing, or her chromosomes got screwed up, I don't know. But I have come to understand that Brenda suffers from a severe mother wit deficiency. Unfortunately, that doesn't qualify her for any kind of disability benefits, and it makes my life a living hell.

I went back to the complaint and quickly read through it. Gardner's a chemist supervisor who works in the Los Angeles field office. For the last two years he and Brenda have served on DEE's health and safety committee that meets quarterly. It seems that each time the committee met Brenda managed to harass him, or so Gardner thought. He cited eight specific incidents. In one Gardner accused Brenda of using a childbirth analogy that he found repulsive and offensive; in another she referred to a certain part of an actor's anatomy as being as flat as pita bread and speculated whether it was due to a war injury. Pita bread? In a third she accused Gardner of not finishing his part of a report because of his excessive dependence on his supervisor and his inordinate need for her approval, speculating that the supervisor probably suffered nipple burn trying to wean him. The list went on.

I should say right now that I consider sexual harassment to be nothing less than a form of assault. I've seen the damage it can cause—the hostile work environment, mangled self-esteem, careers ruined, even nervous breakdowns. I would be the last one to trivialize such a serious matter. But I was having a hard time understanding the harassment issue here. Brenda had made some statements that were at the very least tactless, and others that were undeniably crude. But were they material for a formal complaint—from a grown man? Maybe that's the way they feel when we finally get fed up and complain about them.

I had to brief Allen Warner, my supervisor, on this discrimination complaint, or at least alert him as soon as possible. I owed him that much. Allen hired me to run the personnel office early on when the department was still being put together, and we've been a team since then. We've weathered bomb threats, an employee walkout and work stoppage, and a massive audit conducted by the Department of Finance. We have a good working relationship based on mutual respect and friendship that has developed over the years, which is strange when you consider that we are as different as two people can be. Allen is pale from his sandy hair to his cool, aquamarine eyes. He is also cool of temperament, due I think in part to the fact that he is a vegan. He eats nothing that can plead for its life. Maybe that's why he's so lacking in that blood thirst so many meat eaters seem to have. Considering that, it's a wonder he's lasted so long and moved so high in state service.

Allen had just gotten back from a meeting when I got there. I followed him into his office. He looked tired. His tie was askew, maybe three tenths of an inch. Not much, but a lot for him. His hair was slightly mussed. He took off his rimless glasses and rubbed his eyes. He put the glasses back on and smiled at me. It was a smile tinged with sadness.

"Allen, I just got—"

He held up a hand, stopping me.

"Theresa, before you get started, you need to know there've been some organizational changes. I'm moving to Agency."

I sank down in the side chair next to his desk. "When did all this happen?"

"Agency decided to make some changes. Gabe called one of his meetings yesterday morning, which was, as you know, interrupted by . . ." He paused, searching for the right word. ". . . by more pressing matters."

"Allen, why're they moving you? This doesn't make sense with the department reorganization and everything."

He didn't answer right away. He brought his hands together, fingertips touching to form a steeple, and rested his chin on it. He let his chin bounce a couple of times before he finally spoke. "They've got to place Heather Whitcomb."

Heather Whitcomb is legendary in the department. She'd started off as a junior chemist. By the time she'd been on the job six months, she'd had run-ins with everybody she came in contact with from her co-workers to her immediate supervisor to her division chief. But that didn't matter. Because the chief deputy director just loved her. He thought she was cute. He thought she was smart. And, gosh darn it, she was a pistol, wasn't she? All that and she wasn't even a blonde. Heather was pampered and protected. In a four-year period she'd received six promotions—who says the state is inflexible? At one time she even supervised her prior supervisor with an appalling lack of graciousness. But then again, Heather Whitcomb was never gracious. She didn't know how; besides she didn't need to be. The last I heard she was at the Department of Boating and Waterways, mucking up the waters there.

"What does placing Heather Whitcomb have to do with you?"

Allen sighed. "Gabe won't have her in Agency again."

"So? She doesn't have a job then. Terminate her exempt appointment. Let her go back to being a junior chemist." Fat chance, I knew.

"There's a vacancy in Agency."

"So, there's a vacancy in Parks."

"They've already got administrative problems. They need experienced administrative staff."

"And DEE doesn't?"

"DEE has a cadre of strong middle managers such as yourself. The thought was DEE could better accommodate some adminstrative shuffling—"

"Allen, that's a lot of bull, and you know it."

"I'm just trying to explain the thought process to you, how the decision was made that I would go to Agency and Heather Whitcomb would take my job."

"Wait a minute. You never said she was taking your job. I thought you guys were doing your Rubik's cube dance again. You move, and then someone else moves, and pretty soon sixteen people have changed places so you could get at the one perfect spot for Heather. You didn't tell me Heather was taking your job. You didn't tell me I was going to have to report to her."

I was standing over his desk, yelling, before I caught myself. Allen looked at me with calm, clear eyes, letting me vent. I sat back down.

"Theresa, this is a temporary arrangement. We'll just have to make the best of it."

He wasn't very convincing.

"When do you start?"

Allen looked at his watch. "As of three hours ago."

I didn't ask when Heather would start. I was afraid of what he might say.

By the time I got back to the personnel office, there was an edginess in the air. Everyone seemed to know—Allen was out, Heather Whitcomb was in. Only the fools and office ghouls looked happy. I stopped at Miyako's desk to collect my messages, but she wasn't there. I went back to my office.

Because of the confidential records kept here, the personnel office is a secured area. You need one of those blue computer key cards for access. Since my office is within a secured area, I usually leave my door open when I leave for meetings. That way staff can tell at a glance whether I'm in. Also, I once had an assistant who would wait until I left to search my office, go through my files, read my E-mail, that kind of thing. Those are things you do behind closed doors, which is another reason I leave mine open. When I

got to my office, the door was closed. That was enough
to set me off, but when I saw Heather Whitcomb with
her behind plopped down on top of my desk, reading
through one of my files, I nearly went ballistic. First
of all, I prefer that people keep their butts off my
desk. Sit in chairs—that's what they're made for. I
sometimes eat at my desk, and I find the thought that
someone has smeared her rear end over that same
surface disgusting. Secondly, Heather didn't even
bother to move things out of the way. She was all up
on my blotter. She'd knocked my mug of pencils and
pens into my chair, and they were scattered everywhere. To make matters worse, she was wearing a
pale blue Ellen Tracy knit that I would have killed for.

I said I almost went ballistic when I saw Heather
plopped down on my desk. Well, almost is the opera-
tive word here. I'd seen Heather go off before. She's
damn good at it. There's no way I can compete with
her in the area of histrionics. But I have learned a
few things in those management classes I've taken.
One thing is to pull instead of push. It's next to impossible to push a length of rope, but you can pull it
anywhere.

I stepped into my office, all brightness and sunshine.
"Why, Heather, hello."

Her butt planted firmly, she simply grunted and
kept reading. I edged around her to the back of my
desk.

"Oh, my goodness. Will you look at this. Pens and
pencils all over the place." I scrambled to pick them
up and found the one I was looking for, a large, black,
indelible marker. I slipped the cap off.

"Excuse me, Heather, let me straighten this
blotter."

I took a couple of swipes at her behind with the marker as I tugged on the blotter. Begrudgingly, Heather shifted her rear end an inch or so, just enough for me to wedge the marker between her and the blotter. Then I sat at my desk and watched as the black stain spread.

I stuck it out for the rest of the day, but my heart really wasn't in it, not after Allen's bad news. Even the high from my little tête-à-tête with Heather faded after a while. I thought about calling Mother a couple of times, but fought down the urge. She could call me if she wanted to. But I wasn't about to call her, not after the way she'd treated me. Finally, at five I went home and called Temp and the kids. I talked to Aisha and Shawn first and spent the last twenty minutes engaging in some steamy telephone sex with Temp. It was all one-sided though. He couldn't say much because the kids were in the room, but I had a good time on my end. I don't know why I didn't tell them about Clarence and everything. It just seemed like that happened so long ago it was no longer important.

Chapter Five

I woke up with Mother on my mind and butterflies in my stomach. I was worried, and worry usually affects my stomach first. Who was this Raymond Johnson, and what was he after? Mother was so head over heels enraptured with the little fake, she couldn't see how foolish she was being or how dangerous the whole thing was. Raymond was after something, that was for sure. Was it Mother's pension check, or her modest bank account? Somehow I just didn't think so. He was putting too much time and effort into his little charade. The whole thing—the picture, the money orders, the fanciful story—took some planning, and a lot of nerve. The stakes had to be a lot higher than a few hundred dollars. But what? Mother didn't own anything else of any value except for her home. After everything came out last year about how Mrs. Turner's home had been stolen from her without her knowledge before she was murdered, Mother had gone to her attorney and had him set up a trust for her. Now the house was owned by the Barkley Family Trust with Mother as trustee. My brother, Jimmy, and I were secondary trustees. The house seemed pretty secure to me. My guess was Raymond knew that too. If he'd gone to all this trouble to concoct such an elaborate story, he'd probably done his homework. Unless, of course, he was telling the truth. I forced myself to consider that possibility. What if Raymond is telling the truth? He had documentation, didn't he? One picture and a couple of uncashed money orders. If he were writing a report, they could be attached as exhibits. If he were giving a speech for his Toastmaster's Club, they'd be visual aids. A thousand years from now some anthropologist could base his life's work on them. But they weren't enough to fashion a life on. They weren't enough to make Daddy into something that I knew he wasn't.

There were just too many questions and not enough answers. And the answers that I did have seemed too pat. I made up my mind then and there to find out who Raymond Johnson was and what he really was after. That's another thing I learned in my management classes—be proactive, not reactive. I'd check out a few things, tip over a rock or two. Actually, it shouldn't be too difficult. Then I'd get him out of Mother's house before it was too late.

I packed my briefcase and purse, making sure I had some tampons and Tylenol. Tampons and Tylenol—the working woman's friend. Acting on a brainstorm, I went to Aisha's room and rummaged around in her closet until I found her little Polaroid camera. I came back to my room, popped the camera into my purse, and left for work.

After Mother, Brenda Delacore was number two on my agenda. She knew I'd gotten my copy of Gardner's discrimination complaint, and she'd laid low, managing to avoid me all day yesterday. We weren't going to play that game today. I told Miyako to let me know the minute she came in. But Brenda didn't come in. She called in sick.

Heather Whitcomb didn't show up either. Her secretary informed Miyako, who in turn informed me—the hierarchy thing—that Heather was taking a management course at U.C. Davis. I thought about yesterday's butt/blotter incident and smiled. She'd have to study long and hard to match my management skills.

By lunchtime I'd made a significant dent in my work. I took a break and called Mother. She was speaking to someone else as she picked up the phone.

". . . knew that was her calling and hanging up all hours of the night. And I told her if she didn't stop I'd report her to the law. Yes sir, that's exactly what . . ."

I proffered a tentative hello, but it was too weak-willed, and it didn't stand a chance.

". . . dirty tricks just so she can walk . . ."

"Hello, Mother," I said, raising my voice to give it a little bit of wedge power.

She suddenly became aware of my presence. "Who's that screaming in my ear?"

"Mother, it's me."

"Theresa?"

"Yes. How're you doing?"

"I'm just fine, baby. But I do wish you wouldn't do that."

"Do what?"

"You know, play on the phone like that."

I sighed. I tend to do lots of sighing when talking to Mother, especially when those conversations take place over the phone. She simply hasn't gotten the phone thing down yet. In fact, I suspect that she operates on the principle that the person on the other end of the line doesn't really exist until she actually speaks to the person. It's kind of like Mother's take on the philosophical question about whether a tree falling in the forest makes any noise if no one is there to hear it. Until last year Mother had one of those old, black, rotary phones that weigh a ton. But my husband, Temp, is into technology, and after years of trying, he finally succeeded in convincing her to get a couple of nice, color-coordinated, push-button extension phones and a cordless one to boot. Now whether in her garden, the garage, or even the bathtub, Mother is never without her phone. The only hurdle left is for her to master telephone etiquette.

I took the easy way out and apologized, but it did little in the way of appeasing her.

"And why didn't you tell me about all the mess with that crazy man at your job? Sister Rhodes called me just about hysterical. Lord, you could've gotten killed."

"I assumed you knew, Mother. I understand it was on the news and in the paper. I came by to tell you, but as you will recall, you were preoccupied. You didn't seem to want me around, so I just left."

"I don't have time for all that mess on TV. Half the time I don't even turn it on."

Sure, since Raymond came.

"And that little Bingh kept throwing the paper everywhere but my yard and I canceled . . . What you talking about? What do you mean I was preoccupied? You talking 'bout Raymond? Baby, you don't have to be jealous of Raymond."

"Mother, I am not jealous of Raymond."

"Yes, you are."

"No, I'm not!"

"You come storming in my house, raising sand, telling me what to do. I should have known something was wrong."

"I'm just fine, Mother. The thing with Clarence turned out all right. Everything is okay."

"Everything's not okay. Temp and the kids are still out of town. You went home to that empty house after everything. You didn't have to do that. You know you could've stayed with me. You could sleep with me just like you used to."

"Mother, it's been thirty years since I've slept in your bed."

"Twenty."

"Mother!"

"What? Why you got to yell in my ear?"

I took a deep breath from my diaphragm, held it for a while, and slowly released it. A relation technique I've learned. It gave me time to collect my thoughts and remember why I'd called.

"Theresa, Theresa, you still there?"

"I'm still here, Mother. I was thinking about dropping by for lunch. What've you got cooked?"

They say the way to a man's heart is through his stomach, but the way to Mother's heart is through my stomach. She spends an inordinate amount of time worrying about what I eat and, to my consternation, the status of my digestive system. I'm nearly forty years old, but Mother still hasn't gotten over that spell of constipation I suffered when at two I refused to eat anything but cheddar cheese and Saltine crackers for a three-week period. I think my losing weight over the past year rekindled some latent fear of hers that I would starve to death, or worse—stop myself up. Since my weight loss she's redoubled her efforts to keep me highly fed, as she calls it. I knew asking what

she'd cooked would smooth my path for getting back
into her good graces after the fight we had the other
night over Raymond.

"Oh, let me see. I've got some snap beans and pota-
toes—little red ones, the kind you like—and some
fried chicken from last night, and a peach cobbler I
just made this morning."

I was touched. She'd made all my favorites, probably in the hope that I'd eventually make this very call.

"Sounds good," I said. "I'll be right over."

Mother met me at the door and led me inside, like
an honored guest. She stood beaming as I surveyed
the living room. The Mother smells were there—fried
onions, cinnamon, Esté Lauder Youth Dew—but everything else had changed. It would be a misrepresen-
tation, an understatement, to say the room had simply
been rearranged. A reordering had taken place, something much more basic, more elemental than the mere
shifting of a chair here or a table there. And I didn't
like it, not one bit.

"Mother, what happened?"

"You like it, huh?"

Mother's house usually looks like opening day at a
church rummage sale with boxes stacked everywhere
and every available surface cluttered with piles of
newspapers, old magazines, junk mail, and various
knickknacks. Mother doesn't throw away anything. It's
always been like that for as long as I can remember.
But now the clutter was gone, and somehow it just
didn't seem right.

"Where'd you put everything?"

"Raymond helped me sort it out and put it away.
We have a system, everything's labeled. Did you know

I have collectibles?" She pronounced *collectibles* as if the word itself was easily broken and each syllable had to be handled gingerly. "See this here, your old doll. Chatty Cathy, wasn't that what they called her? Well, this is a collectible now. Raymond tells me it's worth a good piece of change."

Chatty Cathy sat atop Mother's highly polished buffet next to a framed picture of me and Carolyn when I was six and she was ten. The frame was made out of twigs. I looked around. Old photos framed in all kinds of different frames—terra-cotta, wood, brass—were placed in a cluster of organized disorder on top of the piano. Other old photos had been matted and framed and hung on the walls in quirky little groupings. Mother's old dressmaking dummy, Aunt Tillie as Carolyn and I used to call her, stood sentry by the door to the kitchen. She had been painted white, and notes, photos, a variety of trinkets, and even a set of keys were pinned to her bodice. It was all a bit much if you ask me.

I sat down on the sofa, a little overwhelmed. "So, where's Raymond?"

"He's out in the garage, putting some stuff away for me."

"Mother, I want to ask you something about him. Where exactly did you say he's from?"

"You can ask him yourself, baby."

She got up and went through the kitchen to call him.

Raymond came bounding in. He had on an old pair of work pants and a paint-spattered old shirt that I could have sworn were Daddy's. Both were too big, and he'd rolled up the cuffs and sleeves. I forced myself to smile.

"Sistah T, wuz happnin'."

Mother giggled.

"Don't call me that," I said through my stiff-lipped smile.

"You guys go wash your hands, and I'll get the food out."

I reached in my purse and took out the camera.

"Wait a minute," I said, hopping to my feet. "I want to take a picture of you two."

Raymond's face went white. I've never seen a black person do that before.

"Uh-uh, no, that's all right," he muttered, backing away.

Mother snatched him over to her side and clasped him there with one arm. "Aw come on, boy," she said. "Now smile."

She patted her hair with her free hand and tipped her head back and smiled broadly. I pressed the button on the camera, the built-in strobe flashed, and for a split second they were frozen there—Mother her nostrils bared to the world and Raymond looking like something caught in my headlights.

The camera ejected the developing print. I held it by the edges and showed to Mother.

"Don't touch it," I cautioned. "It's still developing."

When it was fully developed, I gave it to Raymond.

"It's all right to touch it now. It's fully developed."

Raymond looked at it and grimaced. "That's why I don't like to take pictures. See here. Look at that. My eyes are red."

I pointed the camera at them again.

"Let me take one more so both you and Mother can have one," I said.

Mother snapped her arm lock around him again, and I pressed the button on the camera. As they were blinking, trying to readjust their vision, I took the first picture from Raymond, being careful to hold it by the edges, and placed it in a small plastic bag I had in my purse. I drew the bag's sealing ridge through my fingers, sealing it tight, aad snapped my purse shut as Raymond pretended not to notice.

We ate in the dining room instead of the kitchen, using Mother's best paper plates. When we finished, I leaned back in my chair and directed my attention to Raymond. "Raymond, where did you say you're from?"

He looked at Mother and winked. I started to get mad. What was that supposed to mean? Did he think he was so clever he could let Mother part of the way in on the joke he was pulling on her?

"Tucker, Arkansas," he said.

"Arkansas. Daddy was from Louisiana—Shreveport, Louisiana."

"I know."

"Tell me something, how'd they meet up, Daddy and your mother—was it nineteen, twenty years ago?"

"Twenty-three."

"Twenty-three years ago. Let's see—that would have made me around sixteen at the time." I looked over at Mother. "That would have been the year Carolyn died."

Mother pressed her lips together at the mention of her lost child. Raymond nodded and pressed his lips together too.

"Well, how did they meet?"

"I don't know. You see, Mama never even told me who my daddy was. One time she said he got killed in Vietnam; another time she said he was an artist and he died of tuberculosis in a cold-water flat in New

York. Mama always lied as a matter of course. She used to make me mad 'cause she wasn't very artful about it. She'd just toss any old raggedy lie off at you and expect you to accept it."

Mother cast him one of her looks. "Now, don't be talking about your mother like that."

"I'm not trying to talk about my own mother, but it's the truth. One time I heard Anty Belva talking to Cut'n Sarah, and she said my father was a married man. That's all I know. How they met, when they met, all that I don't know. I'm afraid it was before my time."

Mother smiled at his last little fillip. He looked satisfied.

I wasn't. "So you found some of your mother's papers, and you put it all together, and that led you to Walter Lee Barkley in Sacramento, California."

"Well, yes, if you want to put it that way."

"And what exactly were the papers?"

"What do you mean?"

"Was there a birth certificate, bill of sale for fifty pounds of seed corn, a motel receipt?"

Mother shifted uneasily in her seat. "Now don't you go getting nasty," she said.

"I just want to know what papers he found."

"The money orders."

"Yes."

"And some letters."

"Oh, letters? Were there letters? How many?"

"Just two or three. They were old, from before I was born."

Mother was very still. If I didn't know her, I would have said that our discussion of Daddy's supposed indiscretions was depressing her. But I knew better.

"What did they say, the letters?"

"Just a lot of stuff. How he loved to juke her, stuff like that."

Mother stood up and started to clear the table. "Well, no need to go into all of that. What's done is done. Let me get you some of this peach cobbler."

"That's all right, I'm stuffed. Besides, I've got to get back to work."

"Here, take some with you. Take some for Temp and the kids, too."

I took some of the cobbler, and Mother walked me through the house, showing me more of the changes she and Raymond had made. I took the opportunity to check her windows to make sure they locked securely. When we got to her room, I inspected the door.

"I sure wish you had a lock on it."

"Why on earth would I need a lock on my bedroom door? All the years you kids were growing up we never had a lock."

"I was thinking in case something got in the house."

"Child, how do you think I got this old? Don't you know I got someone for any fool thinks he can break in on me."

It might have been my imagination, but Raymond looked uneasy.

Chapter Six

Men can sometimes be more trouble than they're worth. That's what Mother used to say, and I was beginning to understand what she meant. I'd waited anxiously for Temp to get home from his trip. The house was clean, dinner was ready, and the lights were low in the bedroom. I met him and the kids at the airport, and he stepped off the plane with an attitude.

"T, you and I need to talk. We have to sit down and go over some things."

Brows furrowed, fists jammed into his pockets, that was his greeting. No hug, no kiss, no how've you been, baby? Nothing.

I took them home and got them fed. I lost my thirty pounds by eating sensibly, drinking plenty of water, and walking the two miles around Capitol Park twice a day. I'd prepared a sensible meal for the family, low in fat but high in flavor, and that's a direct quote from the author of the recipe. However, the author had not taken into account the Aisha and Shawn factor. Aisha was the first to weigh in with delicate subtlety.

"Mom, listen to me. You've got get Rosie out of your kitchen. You hear me, Mom? Send Rosie back to Oprah. Right away. Puh-lease."

"You don't like it?"

Now it was Shawn's turn. "Face it, Mom, we had better stuff on the airplane. It came in neat little plastic boxes too."

Temp intervened.

"You guys finish up and go to bed. Your mom and I have some business to take care of."

"Gosh, Dad, you've only been gone a week. Take a cold shower or something."

"Don't get fast with me." He turned to me accusingly. "She's getting awfully fast."

"Go on up when you finish," I said. "I'll clean up later."

"Honey, you want to talk upstairs?"

"No, T, this is just fine."

I sat across from him, marveling at how fine he was. After eighteen years of marriage the man still turned me on without even trying. And he definitely wasn't trying now. But that was all right, I have a good memory. I could remember the times when he had tried and how hard he'd worked at it. I intended to work him hard tonight.

Temp cleared his throat, and I snapped out of my reverie, wiping the sappy smile off my face.

"We're in trouble."

"What?" Words didn't exactly fail me, but that little thesaurus in my head did snap shut.

"We're in trouble, financial trouble."

Each month Temp and I sit down together and plan out a monthly budget. My entire take-home minus $500 goes into the family account as does Temp's. Temp is self-employed, the owner of Second Generation business and industrial maintenance company. Out of the family account comes family expenses, savings, and investments. We have on-line banking, and

very few checks are written. Temp handles the actual
transactions. Technology is his domain. Theoretically,
we're supposed to get together monthly to reconcile
bank statements and do family bookkeeping. But I'm
pretty casual about that, and Temp usually ends up
doing it himself along with his business accounts. He'd
certainly have a better idea of our financial health
than I would. But I wasn't unduly worried by his announcement. Temp tends to be overly cautious when
it comes to money. He's a fiscal conservative whereas
I'm more of a fiscal libertine.

"Things have been going downhill since I lost out
on that Trilux job last year."

I winced. I didn't want to be reminded of the Trilux
job. Temp had been working on the bid last year when
I got involved in trying to find Mrs. Turner's murderer, and I'd dropped more than a few balls that
Temp had to pick up. He ended up losing that bid;
actually it was rejected because he was almost two
minutes late submitting it. Things have not been the
same with him since then. He works out of the house
in the guest room he's converted into an office. Since
the Trilux thing, he seems to work longer and harder.

"I've lost Zentler Industrial Complex too."

This was his largest job. He employed twenty people
on it alone.

"Honey, no. When did this happen?"

"I found out just before I left to take the kids on
the tour."

"Why didn't you tell me?"

"What difference would it have made? You couldn't
do anything about it. I didn't want to spoil the trip
for the kids. I'd promised, and they'd waited so long.
Now all I have to do is pay for it."

"You act like you're in this all alone."

He sighed.

"No, T, I'm not in it all alone, it just seems like it."

I know this man. He was scared. His fight or flight reflex has only one gear—fight. If I wasn't careful, we'd end up in a full-blown argument, and I still wouldn't know the complete extent of our problems. But that last statement was a cheap shot. I couldn't let it go unchallenged. That's just not me.

"What's that supposed to mean?"

"Nothing, T. Nothing."

He massaged his eyes with the heels of his hands. "I'm going back to the state."

I knew then that things were bad. Before quitting to start Second Generation, Temp had worked for the state for fourteen years as staff counsel in the Legislative Counsel's Office. It had been a good job. Everyone said so—his mother, my mother, the loan officer at the bank, his Omega brothers. But he wasn't happy there. He labored through law school, struggled to pass the bar, and worked for years before finally admitting he hated law, and if he didn't get away, do something else, he would die—have a heart attack, get hit by a car on his lunch break—die. I'd watched as he turned into a nine-to-five zombie, robbed of his will, hating his job, but unable to break out of the gravitational pull exerted by a steady paycheck. But I had a good job. I could carry the family until Temp found something, just as I had when he was in law school. Finally, we'd agreed he had to quit. Temp is smart. He's also hard-working to the point of compulsiveness, and incredibly focused. I was scared, but I knew he would come up with something, although I would rather he had done it before leaving his state job. There is something to be said for security.

Until Temp started Second Generation, a commercial and industrial janitorial service, I'd been unaware that janitorial service could be such a lucrative field. It's also very competitive. Temp had done well though. After his first big contract, he'd bought me a new car—a BMW 525i. And he'd paid cash.

"Look, Temp, maybe we should sit down and go over everything together. There must be something we can do, short of just calling it quits."

"Yeah, like burn that damn Nordstrom's card of yours and Macy's too. And I see you went out and got another Visa card after we agreed it was ridiculous to pay that high interest. We need to pay it off and get rid of it. We should give some thought to Shawn's school, too. Maybe that four hundred a month could be better spent on something else."

He paused a beat. "Also, I'm thinking about selling the Cherokee."

The prized Cherokee? He'd had it less than a year. This was really serious.

"And all this money you and Aisha spend on your hair. We could cut back there, too. Can't you do Aisha's hair the way my mama used to do Wilamena's?"

Wrong question. I didn't want to have to tell him that if I did Aisha's hair the way his mama used to do his sister's, Aisha might very well end up looking like Wilamena used to. And that could be emotionally damaging to a young girl. As much as I love Mother Alma, and I really do, she has all the fashion sense of an armadillo. She knows even less about hair care. Temp was cutting to the bone if he wanted to cut back on hair care—that's the last thing you do to a sister.

I was glad he hadn't mentioned our Sacramento Kings season tickets. That would have been the last straw.

"Wow, you've really given this some thought."

"For the last thousand miles I thought of nothing else."

We went to Temp's office, pulled up the accounting program on his computer, and spent the next couple of hours going over every account, calculating interest and playing out one scenario after another. When we finally dragged ourselves up to bed, we had worked out a shaky plan. But my hopes for romance had faded even before Temp fell into bed, curled himself into a tight little ball, and locked his hands between his knees.

Chapter Seven

"The nipple burn thing, I didn't say that . . . well, not to him anyway. I was talking to Yvonne Pinkham in the women's john. There's no way he could have heard me unless he was hiding in one of the stalls, which incidentally, I don't put past him. What's up with all this bullshit anyway?"

Brenda Delacore and I were finally sitting face-to-face, going over Gardner Reading's discrimination complaint. After avoiding me Wednesday and calling in sick on Thursday, she'd come to work today prepared to do conference room battle in a navy blue power suit with a white silk blouse. Even her pencil-length dreads looked subdued.

"What about the childbirth stuff?"

"What about it? Childbirth is a natural process."

"Come on, Brenda. Did you say whatever it is he's complaining about?"

"Check this out. How many meetings have you been in with the white boys and had to listen to them talk all kind of trash. You know how they talk—'Don't get your shorts twisted in a knot.' How about, 'I've got him by the short hairs,' or 'Don't shoot your wad,' or 'Screw you, it, him,' whatever, 'He has balls,' 'She's ballsy,' 'Don't be a whus'? Then there's all the sports shit—'The balls in your court?' They must be talking about four square or something 'cause those fat, out-of-shape, high-water-pants-wearing motherfuckas have a heart attack you put them on a basketball court. They're what's offensive, but do you see me going around filing some dumb-ass complaint."

Brenda is Mother's peer when it comes to mastering the diversionary non sequitur. But I wasn't letting her get away that easy. "Your sentiments are noted, Brenda. Now, the childbirth stuff?"

"Okay, okay. I said something to the effect that we were going to have to induce labor to get his part of the year-end report. What's wrong with that?"

"Anything else?"

"I might have mentioned a cold speculum a time or two."

"Speculum?"

"You know that thing the gynecologist sticks—"

"Never mind, I know."

"I think proctologists use them, too—"

"I said that's all right, Brenda."

"You see, what we have here is a double standard."

"It doesn't matter. Nobody's complaining about the double standard. Reading's complaining about you."

"Fuck him. Excuse me—screw him."

I had to agree with Brenda on one thing. Reading's complaint seemed frivolous in a malicious sort of way. Here the man was a supervisor, somebody who's supposed to be a part of the management team, complaining about another supervisor. There were a whole lot of ways this could have been worked out without locking it into the formal complaint system, where it would take on a life of its own. Besides, complaints like his have a way of obscuring the real stuff. There are some real problems, but Gardner Reading just didn't seem to be one of them.

Just as I was finishing up with Brenda, Mother called. As usual, she launched right into the talk mode the minute I picked up the phone. No hello, no how are you. Nothing. I used to hate that, but I guess after all these years I'm getting used to it.

"Raymond is missing."

She sounded breathless, as if she had been running.

"You all right?"

"No, I'm not all right. Didn't you hear what I just said? Raymond is missing."

I heard her, but I was busy fighting the urge to say, "Frankly, my dear, I don't give a damn." Mother's sense of humor isn't her strong suit. That's why I was fighting so hard.

"So he's gone, huh?"

"He's missing, and you don't seem very concerned."

Again she insisted on being my straight man. I pinched my lips between my teeth, refusing to take the bait. With a voice quivering with a suppressed giggle I gambled on speaking. "Mother, what makes you think he's missing?"

"Did all that education you got make you lose your mind, girl? Listen closely. Raymond is missing because he's not here."

"I just talked to him yesterday. How could he be missing? He's not under house arrest, is he? He is allowed to come and go?"

"Don't get womanish with me."

"Mother, I am a woman."

"You know what I mean. The boy is missing. He left last night and didn't come back. He doesn't know anybody in this town. Where would he go? Something's wrong."

"Maybe he got tired of lying and just left."

"You still on that? If he was going to leave, he'd take his clothes, wouldn't he? He wouldn't just leave everything here. You wouldn't believe me when I told you Sister Turner was missing either, and she came up dead."

"I think you're getting a bit carried away, Mother. As you will recall, Mrs. Turner wasn't missing, she was ill."

"Same difference. She ended up dead."

"Okay, Mother, so the little raw boy is missing. What do you want me to do?"

"I want you to go see about him."

I should have known better than to have left myself open like that. As far as Mother is concerned, the rhetorical question doesn't exist that can't be answered.

"If he is missing, all I can say is good riddance, and suggest that you check the house to see if anything of value has disappeared along with him."

"Theresa, he could've been in an accident or something. He could be lost. He could've been kidnaped."

"Let me know if you get a ransom note."

"That's all you've got to say?"

"I'm sorry, Mother, but I can't help you. I've got to go now. People are lined up outside my office, beckoning, holding up signs like at the airport."

She didn't even bother to say good-bye before slamming the phone down in my ear.

That was her first call of the day. Her second call came during the noon hour. I was at my desk, going over a classification proposal, trying to stay on top of my ever-expanding workload when the phone rang.

"You'd better come down here right now."

"Mother?"

"You better get down here before I slap the mess out of this boy."

"What's going on? Raymond's back?"

"Raymond? No, honey. This boy, the cook, messed up our orders. Now he's trying to get an attitude."

"Where are you?"

"The Brass Monkey."

"What's going on?"

A little red light flashed on in my mind. Beware. Mother's mess ahead. Avoid at all costs, the flashing light warned.

"I told you. The boy's got an attitude."

I responded carefully.

"Mother, I'm sure you can work it out. You don't need me."

"I'll work it out all right. My right hand's been itching all day. I knew it was itching for a reason."

"Mother, you're not going to slap him. They'll arrest you for assault."

"Call'm up. Get'm here. I'm going back in there, and somebody's going to talk to me. The nerve. Messing up the food and acting a fool in front of the Negro Women's Community Guild. And Gertha sitting there like a Buddha taking it all in."

Now she had me in a bind. Mother has a tendency to go off the deep end, especially when the humiliation factor kicks in. Apparently, she'd had some complaint about the food, and it hadn't been handled with enough deference. She'd lost face in front of the Negro Women's Community Guild, which was bad enough. But for Gertha Jackson, her rival of thirty years and challenger for president of the Guild, to have witnessed it, was nothing short of cataclysmic. There was no telling what Mother would do.

The bottom of my stomach took a slow tumble south. I looked at my watch. It was twelve-thirty.

"Mother, where did you say you are?"

It was a short walk from my office to Old Town, where the Brass Monkey is located. I'd eaten there only once, but I remembered it as being one of those restaurants that tries to be too many things at once. Its decor of used brick, polished wood, old brass, and quirky antiques were fun in a campy sort of way. But the menu was a schizophrenic offering of California cuisine, Thai, and Mexican foods, with a smattering of other regional dishes. California Fats, an icon of the mixed genre restaurant, could have pulled it off. The Brass Monkey couldn't. It did, however, do chutzpa well.

Mother was pacing the floor in front of the maitre d's stand when I walked in. She stopped midstride and surveyed me. "Why you'd have to wear those tennis shoes?"

"You're very welcome, Mother. No, please don't apologize for pulling me away from my work. It's only a job."

A statement like that would have sent Aisha flying from the room, but sarcasm is wasted on Mother.

"And look at you, your hair standing up on your head."

"My hair is not standing up on my head. This is a precision cut. It does not stand, it falls into place."

Mother moistened a finger on the tip of her tongue. "Come here."

"What do you think you're doing?" I demanded, stepping out of her reach.

"You can't go in there looking like that. People talk."

People were also starting to watch us. I struggled to retain my composure.

"Mother, in twenty-five minutes I have to be back at work. It took me ten minutes to walk over here, and it will likely take me just as long to walk back. That leaves five minutes for me to see what I can do to help you straighten this thing out. In exactly five minutes I turn around and walk out that door. You can spend that time critiquing my appearance if you want. It's up to you."

Mother sighed deeply. "We're in the banquet room," she said, turning toward the small bridge that separated the main dining room from the banquet area. A little stream sparkling with brightly colored koi wound underneath. Mother looked down as we crossed the bridge. "Those some sick-looking fish," she said. "I sure hope they don't cook 'em up and serve 'em here."

"They're koi."

"Sick carp if you ask me. Got some kind'a fungus."

We were outside the banquet room. I could hear the buzz of conversation. Then a peal of laughter rang out. Mother stiffened.

"Before we go in, maybe you'd better tell me exactly what happened."

"It wasn't Caucasian chicken, that's what happened. I told the boy. I said, 'This is not Caucasian chicken,' and he said, 'Lady, that's what you ordered.' I said,

'Don't be telling me what I ordered. I know what I ordered and this is not it.' He had the nerve to roll his eyes. And Gertha sitting up there fanning her mouth, saying in a little squeaky voice, 'Ooh, hot, hot,' I have never been so out done.''

"Mother, hold up a moment. You ordered for everyone?'

"That's the way it works. When it's your turn to plan the quarterly luncheon, you pick the restaurant, you choose the entree, everything. I wanted this to be real nice. When it was Martha's turn, she told everybody we were having Mandarin barbecue. We come stepping up there ready for some bar-b-cue. You know what I mean, some meat. They come bringing out some vegetables chopped so fine you didn't even know what they were and meat cut up little too. Fried that mess up at the table and said enjoy. We looked at each other and said okay, but where's the meat?''

"Mother.''

"What?''

"What is Caucasian chicken?''

"You know, some sort of chicken in a white sauce . . . with little pieces of pimentos . . .''

"I've never heard of Caucasian chicken. Have you had it before?''

"Well . . .''

"If you've never had it before, how do you know what you got wasn't it?''

"I don't care what it was. That mess they set before us wasn't fit to slop a hog.''

The buzz in the banquet room had grown to a low roar now. The laughter sounded a bit more raucous. I opened the door and peeked in. There was a riot of cocktail glasses on the table. It looked like they were on their third or fourth round. They couldn't have cared less about Caucasian chicken, Chectian pork, or sick carp for that matter. I turned back to Mother.

"I think the best thing for us to do is go talk to your waiter."

We made our way back to the main dining room.

"Do you see him?"

Mother scanned the room.

"There he is over there," she said, pointing dramatically, leveling her fully extended arm like a gun. She didn't bother to whisper. There was a rustling sound at every head in the place turned toward us.

I looked to where she pointed. A young man with hair an unnatural shade of red glanced at us and darted into the kitchen. Some of the faces in the dining room came into focus. To my chagrin I saw people I recognized. Mother grabbed me by the arm and took off in the direction of the kitchen. As we passed a series of plush, overstuffed booths lining the wall leading to the kitchen, I came face-to-face with Heather Whitcomb. Her lips twitched into a tight little smile. I kept going. We got to the kitchen door, and I dug my heels in.

"Mother, maybe we should just wait for him to come out. I don't think we should go in there."

Ignoring me, she pushed open the swinging doors. Silence engulfed the room. Her waiter was huddled with two other young men at the far side of the room. One of them wore a dirty apron around his waist. He had on a T-shirt with a picture of two dogs mating on the front of it. One of the men, the only other black person there, broke away and came over to us.

"I'm sorry, ma'am, but you can't come in here—public health rules."

"What your name, boy?"

"Rolland, ma'am."

"They send you over here to tell me that?"

"Yes, ma'am."

"Why they send you? You the only one here speak Negro?"

He lowered his head.

"Come on, ma'am," he pleaded. "You really shouldn't be back here."

"I want to see the cook."

He glanced back at the other two.

"That him? The one in that nasty shirt?"

He nodded.

"You go back over there and tell him I want to speak to him. You hear me? I'm not leaving until I do. Tell him I want to talk to him right now."

He left. I glanced around the kitchen. Nobody there seemed to be older than twenty. I wondered what happened to grown people who used to do those kinds of jobs?

The boy cook sauntered over. "Lady, you have to leave."

"Not until somebody takes responsibility for that slop you served us." Mother grabbed me by the arm and thrust me forward. "You tell him, Theresa."

"Uh, my mother's party is dissatisfied with the quality of the meal they were served."

"What was wrong with it?"

Mother stepped in front of me. Now she was standing about three inches from the boy's Adam's apple. "What was wrong with it? I'll tell you what was wrong with it. It was full of pepper, that's what was wrong with it. Somebody must'a poured a whole can of pepper on it. And it was burned black. That's what's wrong with it."

It suddenly dawned on me what she was talking about. I slapped my forehead with the palm of my hand. Why, oh why, hadn't I heeded that little warning light. Here I was standing in these folk's kitchen, breaking countless health and sanitation laws while my mother complained because she ordered *Cajun* chicken and got Cajun chicken—not Caucasian chicken. Sorry, son, just a little mix-up in dialects. I must have moaned out loud. Mother and the boy chef were staring at me as if *I* was the one crazy.

Who knows how long we would have stood there, frozen in our little tableau, if Mother's piercing whistle hadn't ripped through the room, ricocheting off the stainless steel walls and appliances, nearly shattering my eardrums. Angrily, I turned to her just as she darted across the room, her fingers still in her mouth. A stoop-shouldered man with stringy hair pulled back in a skinny little ponytail was a few steps ahead of her.

"Hey, you can't do that. Come back here!" shouted the cook. He was jumping up and down in place.

The stoop-shouldered man hit the door, flung it open, and tore out into the alley. Mother was right behind him. I was behind her.

"Catch him, Theresa! Catch him!"

Ask me twenty years from now, and maybe then I can tell you why I took off after that kid. I didn't know him from Job. He hadn't done anything but exit the restaurant hurriedly. That wasn't a crime. I would have done the same if I could have—Cajun chicken will do that to you. But Mother was screaming, "Catch him, Theresa, catch him." Maybe I thought he'd

snatched her purse or something. I don't know. It was
like a reflex. I just took off running.

One thing I learned last year was how to breathe—
in on one step and out on the next in explosive little
puffs. I was stepping like Jackie Joyner-Kersee, pulling
my knees up high, pumping my arms in rhythm. And
I was gaining on him. He looked back over his shoulder. He was so surpised to see me, he stumbled and
nearly fell. I could hear him wheeze as he sucked in
air. Then he did something I've seen only in movies—
I didn't think anyone ever did that in real life. He
grabbed some crates stacked by a Dumpster and flung
them in my path. I did a stutter step trying to avoid
them, but I was so close up on him, I had to hurdle
one before I could stop. He disappeared down the
alley.

"You let him get away," complained Mother,
breathing as if she had been the one running.

"I don't even know why I was chasing him."

"He's the one came by the house last night."

"Is this about Raymond? 'Cause if it is, I'm gonna
be pissed."

"Watch your mouth. Have you forgotten who
you're talking to?"

I was trying. Boy, was I trying.

"That same boy came by the house last night. Raymond met him in the yard, wouldn't let him in the
house. They had some words. I couldn't make out
what was said, but Raymond was mad. Now he's gone,
disappeared."

"Why did he run?"

"Guilt. He's done something wrong, that's why. He
recognized me."

"Did you know he was here? I sure hope you didn't call me down here for this."

"No, I called about that confounded Caucasian chicken."

I stopped her.

"Mother, before we go back in the restaurant, I better explain something to you about Cajun cuisine."

Chapter Eight

It was nearly two when I got back to the office. Miyako slapped a message in my hand the minute I walked in. It was from Heather.

"She wants to see you, and I quote, 'On the fucking double.'" Heather has a reputation for cursing like a sailor. Some of the guys around here think it's cute. I suspect they even egg her on. No one to my knowledge had ever called her on it. But I intended to. Call it a cultural difference or whatever, I wasn't raised to use profanity, and I didn't appreciate having it directed at me or my staff by anyone, regardless of the position.

I took the elevator up to the twelfth floor, where Allen's office was. Heather occupied it now like some nouveau riche squatter. She didn't belong there, and she knew it.

Heather was busy at her computer. She looked up when I walked in, but turned back to the keyboard without acknowledging me. I sat down. She finished the document she was working on, printed it out, and read through it, nodding to herself. Then she slapped it down on the desk in front of me.

"Read it."

I picked it up and read through it. I finished and

tossed it back at her. She had written me up. I was so mad my ears were ringing, but I knew a contest with Heather was like playing the dozens—the first one to get emotional loses.

"You indulging yourself in a little creative writing?"

"I was expecting some smart-ass comment from you, Galloway. But that doesn't change anything. Your behavior at the Brass Monkey, you and that old lady, brought discredit to the department, and I'm here to tell you it won't be tolerated."

I sat back and looked at her. I ought to call Mother and let her handle this, calling her an old lady. Although I've never known Mother to swear, I'm sure she would've loved to have lit into Heather with a few choice, politically incorrect suggestions. The thought caused me to chuckle. I picked up the memo.

"You really don't know what you're doing, do you? What do you plan to do with this?"

"It'll go in your personnel file, of course."

"Of course. That's real good, Heather. Put it in my personnel file. But let me ask you something. You ever hear of due process. Can you say 'civil suit' as in 'my husband is an attorney'?"

She chuckled nervously. "The eleventh floor is lousy with attorneys. I'll let them handle that."

"I'm not talking about suing the department, Heather. No, I'm more inclined to go after you personally. In fact, I think the first thing we'll do is file a *lis penden*. You know what that is, don't you? It'll tie up all your property. You'll have to resign all your board appointments, especially if you have authority to sign checks because of the liability. It should be fun explaining that to your fellow board members."

That was a particularly low blow because I knew

Heather was a board groupie. She sits on at least twenty of them, everything from the County Schools Finance Board to the Big Tomato Festival. They tell me her father's big in Republican circles and her mother's got the Democrat side covered. One of the dividends is that Heather dear gets appointed to boards. But she had no way of knowing I was talking trash, especially about the legal stuff. My legal expertise is about on par with Mother's. I was rattling off stuff that was as fractured as Mother's at her best. But my personnel knowledge was real.

"Next time, Heather, I suggest you read California State Laws and Rules, Article 2, section 19590 of the Government Code, before you venture off into the mine field of corrective actions. But if you don't have time for reading all those really long words, you may want to consider consulting with your personnel officer."

Heather snatched the memo out of my hand. "This was for, uh, discussion purposes only. But, let it serve as a warning."

"No, Heather, I don't feel like being warned. I don't feel like being threatened, and I don't feel like being harassed. And while we're on the subject, I want to give you notice that I've already had one employee complain about your swearing and use of profanities. You gon' have to clean up your act, girl."

I had the last word, but in the long run, that wouldn't matter. That meeting marked the start of the Heather Whitcomb war of the memos. And nobody knew how to play that game better than Heather.

I'd promised Mother I'd stop by after work and go through Raymond's stuff. I had to admit the incident at the restaurant had me intrigued. Maybe I'd find something that would give me an idea about what was going on and what Raymond's connection to the running man was. But Temp called and said there'd been a break-in at the warehouse where he stores equipment, and he wouldn't be home until late. He reminded me that Shawn had kung fu practice tonight, and it was my turn to give Aisha a driving lesson. That old familiar feeling started to stir in the pit of my stomach, a queasiness as slick as boiled okra. I was being pulled in too many different directions, and my stomach was letting me know.

I called Mother. She answered on the first ring.

"You on your way?"

"No, I don't get off for another couple of hours."

There was a barely audible click on her end.

"Shh!"

We waited in silence.

"You heard that, that little click?" she asked, whispering.

"Yes. You have call waiting or something?"

"No. My line is bugged."

"Mother, come on."

"Noticed it the other day, that little click. somebody's bugging my phone."

"Who would want to do something like that? You aren't trading state secrets or anything, are you?"

"This is not funny, miss. Some strange things have been happening around here lately."

"What besides Raymond?"

"Everything. I get up in the morning, and somebody's been walking through my garden. You know what that means, don't you? Hants walk through freshly turned earth. Don't leave foot prints anywhere else."

"Mother, you can't have it both ways. Either your phone's bugged or you've got ghosts—not both. A ghost wouldn't have to bug your phone. It would use supernatural powers or something."

"That just goes to show what too much education can do to a person. I never would have thought you'd turn out to be so . . . so . . . What's the word?"

"Cynical?"

"That too. Just make sure you get over here first thing after work. There's more I need to tell you, but I don't want to talk about it over the phone."

"Something has come up. I can't come right after work. It'll have to be a little later."

"How much later?"

"I don't know. If I don't make it tonight, I'll see you at lunchtime tomorrow."

There was a resounding silence at Mother's end of the line.

"You used to be such a good child. Now you always too busy. Rippin' and runnin', you don't have time for anybody. Stay away for weeks at a time, then come over acting a fool. Just don't know what's come over you. Where do you think you wouldn've been if I had've taken that attitude when I was raising you, huh? I'll tell you. You'd be lying up in your bed, cold, wet, and hungry. I could have been out partying like the rest of them, living the good life, but I chose to put my family first. And an awful lot of good it did me."

By the time she finished her deadly kryptonite speech, I was silently banging my head on my desk. "Mother, listen. Four days ago I was held hostage by a man intent on killing someone, who had very few qualms about taking me as well. My salary has been cut five percent. My husband tells me his business is failing. I have a new boss who is borderline psychotic. I have a twelve-year-old who is addicted to hardcore electronics. I believe the fact that I have a teenager requires no explanation. I have dinner to make, a house to clean, homework to check. Mother, I feel guilty if I sneak twenty minutes for myself. That is the state of my life."

I had ripped a piece of my insides off and handed it to her, but the only thing she heard was the part that combined "husband" and "failing" in the same sentence.

"Temp is sweet, but you picked the boy, not me. If you had listened to me, you would have married Walter Simmons. They tell me the boy owns three dry-cleaning businesses down there in Hayward."

I was almost overcome by an urge to put my head down on my desk and just cry like a baby. Speaking softly so as not to choke up, I said, "Mother, I've got to go. I'll get by as soon as I can."

Then I hung up the phone and threw up in my wastebasket.

After putting in eight hours at work, I somehow managed to go home and put in seven more. Shawn got to kung fu practice, dinner got made, although it wasn't as wholesome as I would've preferred, and Aisha succeeded in convincing me she shouldn't be allowed to drive until she's at least thirty. Anybody who mistakes the accelerator for the brake and then gets an attitude should be relegated to a life of long-term pedestrianism.

Temp got home around midnight, looking beat—

more emotionally than physically. He waved away dinner and headed for the shower. When he stepped out of the shower, I met him with the comb and brush, and a jar of Indian Sage hair dressing. He smiled and assumed the position. With me on the bed and him on the floor between my knees, I combed his damp hair and oiled his scalp, ritualistically brushing and stroking and soothing away just a few of his troubles. He moaned softly. I leaned down and stuck my tongue in his ear. He moaned again. Then in a movement like some giant cat uncurling, he climbed up my leg, forcing me back on the bed. Like twin pressure valves being released, we both sighed on first contact. Then we lost ourselves in each other. For a moment.

"Is the door locked?"

I couldn't help it, I had to ask. I couldn't relax, knowing that one of the little darlings might wander in on us. Temp mumbled something in my neck like, "Yeah, baby, the door's locked, baby."

We found each other again. He found his rhythm.

"You . . . do . . . have . . . that . . . thing . . . in?" he managed to blurt in little puffs of rhythm.

I answered, "Yes, yes, yes!"

Chapter Nine

The phone rang once. Without even opening his eyes, Temp pounced on it like a predator, wrestled it briefly, and then passed it across the bed to me.

"Your mama," he mumbled and turned back over. In his mouth sticky with sleep, "your mama" sounded almost like that famous playground taunt.

I took the phone. Temp hadn't even put it to his ear—but who else would be calling this time of the night? I sat up enough to see the clock. I opened my eyes wide and squeezed them shut a couple of times, trying to make them focus. It was two-thirty. This all seemed so familiar, like a dream that keeps repeating itself with minor variations each time. I put the phone to my ear. "Mother?"

I heard the breathing—slow, rhythmic, and deliberate. The line cackled with a jolt of static. There was silence. Then the breathing started again.

"Mother? That you?"

"He's breaking in."

"What? Who's this?"

"He's breaking in right now."

"What are you talking about? Who's breaking in? Where?"

The line went dead. There was no click, no hangup. It just went dead. I shook Temp awake.

"I think something's wrong at Mother's."

"T, don't start."

"Temp, something's wrong. Somebody just called. All they'd say was, 'He's breaking in.' "

"T, you ever hear of wrong numbers? You're your mother's child. Go to sleep."

I picked up the phone and started dialing.

"What are you doing?"

"I got to check and see if Mother's all right."

I hung up the phone.

"She didn't answer. I let it ring twenty times, and she didn't answer."

Temp was sitting up, leaning against the headboard now. "That's not like your mother."

"I'm calling the police."

I punched the preset key for the police. "My mother is elderly and lives alone. I just got a call. I think she may be hurt or need help. Can you send someone by there quickly? I think it may be an emergency."

I gave the police the address, hung up, and starting dressing, throwing anything on I could get my hands on.

"Where do you think you're going?"

"Temp, it's my mother."

He sighed and climbed out of bed.

"Where's my pants, woman?"

We woke Aisha and Shawn and told them we had to go see about Mother. They understood. Temp told them he was setting the alarm on instant. If they opened any door to the outside or window, it would go off. We'd ring when we got home, and they'd have to turn the alarm off and let us in. We called the private security patrol that's paid out of our community association dues and requested that they keep an eye on things for us and then we took off.

Déjà vu all over again. I don't know who coined the phrase, but that's what it felt like, rushing to Mother's over deserted streets in the early morning hours—déjà vu. Just like last year. Only then Mother had called at three in the morning, and I'd rushed out to see about Mrs. Turner—actually to see about Mother, who insisted on going herself to see about Mrs. Turner. And Mrs. Turner ended up dead. This trip had to have a better ending. Any other alternative was unthinkable. I'd allow this déjà vu stuff only to go so far.

We were within a half mile of Mother's house when the air in the car seemed to thicken. I found myself struggling to breathe. Streetlights danced under strange halos. I looked up, searching for comfort in the night sky, but all I found was an empty space where the sky should've been. By the time we turned onto Mother's street, my heart had sought refuge in my throat, despite my warnings to it.

"Shit," muttered Temp when he saw the police cars and the confusion of flashing lights. I didn't even try to speak—my throat was too crowded. I stumbled out of the car before Temp had it stopped completely. A few neighbors huddled in their front yards, watching. Déjuà vu. Every light was on in Mother's house. I could see backlit figures as stark as shadow puppets float past the windows. I walked up to the uniformed officer standing guard at the gate to Mother's yard. I would have walked past him, but he blocked my way. I would have walked through him, but Temp grabbed me from behind.

"This is her mother's house," he explained. "We're the one's who called."

Temp tightened his grip on me before asking, "Everything all right? Her mother?"

When the officer responded that Mother was fine, maybe a little shaken, but fine nonetheless, I was glad Temp was holding me. He kept me upright during that split second of emotional release that claimed me. By the time we got to the front door, I could hear Mother instructing the officers on proper evidence collection procedures, and I felt a little sheepish for ever having doubted her ability to take on the devil and survive.

"I told you. Now, don't go putting those blood samples in no plastic bags. Don't you know that'll make them spoil."

Mother was sitting at the dining room table, holding a tea cup in both hands. Her hair was up in curlers, and she had on an old chenille robe I remembered from childhood. An officer was sitting across from her. It looked as if she was trying to take a report. Mother enthusiastically presented us to the officer.

"There she is. She's the one I was telling you about. This is my daughter, Theresa—she works for the government, too—and this is her husband, Temp. He's a businessman. This is Lt. Bivens."

The officer stood up for the introductions. But I was more concerned about Mother. I threw my arms around her. She rocked me like a baby. Temp stood silently, gently rubbing her back.

When I could trust my voice, I asked if she was all right.

"Mother's all right, baby. Mother's just fine," she said in the singsong voice she used to soothe me when I was little.

"What happened?" asked Temp, directing his question to Lt. Bivens.

"I shot him. That's what," declared Mother, pride and awe commingled in her voice.

"You shot who?" I asked. "Not Raymond?"

The officer looked interested.

"No, no, not Raymond for goodness sake. Will you leave Raymond out of this? Somebody broke in." She lowered her voice. "I think he had something on his mind. You know something . . . what do you call it? Something nappy."

Temp and the officer looked confused.

"Kinky, Mother."

"What?"

"I think you mean kinky, not nappy."

"Whatever. He didn't take anything, not the stereo, not the TV, nothing. That's why I say he had something else on his mind."

"Were you sleep?"

"I was in bed, but I couldn't sleep. You see, I was still worried about the boy. I guess I must have dozed off because a funny, scrabbling kind of noise woke me up. I listened. It seemed like it was coming from the back door. I said to myself, 'Girl, didn't you put that alarm on?' I couldn't remember whether or not I did. But it didn't matter 'cause just then the scrabbling stopped. And when I heard the floorboard creak, the one in front of the sink, I knew he'd gotten in. I thought about dialing 911, but he was already in the house, and there was no telling when the police might get here." Mother looked over at Lt. Bivens, "No offense."

Lt. Bivens nodded, and Mother continued. "So, I reached over and grabbed my gun." Mother turned to the officer. "You all will give my gun back, won't you?"

"Yes, ma'am, as soon as we finish running a few tests on it. Make sure you hold on to that receipt we gave you so you can get it back."

"Then what happened, Mother?" I asked, directing her back to her narrative.

"I shot him." She paused to sip her tea. Her hands trembled.

"Did he do anything first? Did you hear him opening drawers, moving stuff around, or anything?"

"No. He walked through my house just as big, like he owned it. Came down the hall. When he pushed my door open, I let him have it. He hightailed it out of here like the devil was after him."

"She apparently hit him," said Lt. Bivens. "He bled on his way out."

"I hope I got him right smack dab in his behind."

"Unfortunately, we have no way of knowing where he was hit. We've alerted local hospitals to be on the watch for gunshot victims matching his description."

"What did he look like?"

The officer cleared her throat. "Well," she said, reading from her notes, "he was male, probably white, kind of tall."

"That's it?" I asked.

Mother looked wounded. "I didn't have my glasses on."

"He wasn't kind of scrawny, could pass for white on a dark night, with red hair, was he?" I asked.

Mother shot me a look.

"Is that someone you know?"

Mother's look developed fangs. I backed down. "No, not really," I said.

"Mom, why didn't you have your alarm on?"

Temp tried to pose that question as casually as possible, but I could read the hurt in his voice. He'd personally installed the alarm for her right after Daddy died. It meant a lot to him that she use it.

"That's just it, I did have it on." She turned to the officer. "You tell them."

"The alarm was disabled. He injected plastic foam into it. It hardened in a matter of seconds, effectively freezing the alarm. We've seen this technique used before. No security system is absolutely foolproof, you know."

Temp shook his head. "I'll be damned. Can I see it?"

"They're finishing up now. You'll be able to take a look in a little bit."

Lt. Bivens handed Mother a card. "This is your file number, and this is my phone number. You can call if you want to know the status of the investigation or if you think of anything else you want to tell me." She patted Mother on the shoulder and turned to leave.

"Wait a minute," I said. "I think I'd better tell you about this strange call we got. Somebody called and told me Mother's house was being broken into. That's why I called the police. But I don't know who it was."

"Uh-huh," said Mother, "I do."

She had all of our attention now.

"A hant," said Mother stating what she felt was the obvious.

Again, Temp and Lt. Bivens looked confused.

"Ghost," I said, acting as the interpreter. "A supernatural being endemic to the colored people of North America and noted for its flamboyant style and ornery disposition."

"Theresa, quit your fooling."

"Anyway, this man called. At first I thought he was a breather, but then he said, 'He's breaking into your mother's house' or something like that."

Temp looked worried. "T, you didn't tell me that."

"I thought I did."

"I better call the kids and see if they're okay." He took out his cellular phone and punched the auto dial button for home.

"Shawn? Oh, Aisha. Well, I'm sorry if you're insulted. I thought it was Shawn. Hey, turn that racket down. What are you guys doing, anyway? You don't need music at three in the morning. Is everything okay? Aisha, I don't want to hear it. I didn't call for all that. I asked you a simple question. Is everything okay? That's all. Okay, fine. We'll be home in a little bit. Just leave the alarm on until we get there."

Temp hung up the phone. He looked punch-drunk.

"About the call," said Lt. Bivens. "Do you think it could have been one of Mrs. Barkley's neighbors?"

"No. It was too weird, almost menacing. It must have been a cell phone call, because it started breaking up."

"What time did you get the call?"

"It was around two-thirty. I remember staring at the clock, trying to make my eyes focus."

"You must have called us immediately. Your call is logged in at two thirty-seven."

"I did. Well, first I tried to call Mother, and when she didn't answer, I called the police. What time did you guys get here?"

"There was a patrol car in the vicinity when the call came in. We responded at two forty-one."

"You didn't see anyone who looked strange and sort of menacing, did you?"

"No, I'm afraid not."

"He had to be here, or at least someplace nearby, watching. Wait a minute. He had my phone number. He knew to call me. He knew how to call me. It has to be someone we both know. Mother, I think you'd better tell her about Raymond."

"Raymond doesn't have anything to do with this."

Lt. Bivens sat back down. "Maybe you'd better tell me about him, Mrs. Barkley," she said.

Mother told her about taking Raymond in after his mother died and how he was a sweet boy who wouldn't do anything like this.

"Just to set the record straight," I said, "Raymond is not the orphan Mother has portrayed him to be. This little foundling child is twenty-three years old."

"You say he's been missing since yesterday. What were the circumstances?"

"He left to go to that downtown market thing they have on Thursday nights, and I haven't seen him since."

"He'd been here two weeks?"

"That's right. He didn't know anybody here, not a soul. That's why I'm so worried."

"Have you tried to contact any of his other relatives?"

"He doesn't have any. Least none that claim him. They disowned him when he told them he was leaving to look for his daddy. They don't ever want to hear his name spoken again."

"That's what he told you?"

"Yes. They're just that hateful."

"There's no one here he could be visiting? No one he could've met since he got here? A girl, perhaps?"

Mother shook her head.

"Mother, what about the running man? Didn't you say he came to the house and had words with Raymond?"

"It was just somebody looking for a handout, that's all. Came in the yard here the other day. Raymond run him off."

"But, Mother—"

Mother held up her hand like a traffic cop halting the flow of traffic. "I said it was nothing."

I let it go for the time.

"Anyway, Raymond doesn't have anything to do with all this. This man who broke in here was tall like Raymond, but he was bigger."

"Mother, Raymond is short, at least for a man."

"He seems tall to me. I have to look up to him."

"That's because you're short. Anybody five-five would seem tall to you."

The technicians were packing up to leave. Lt. Bivens took Temp to show him the frozen alarm. Mother lit into me.

"Who told you to go telling that woman all my business?"

"What do you mean?"

"Don't try to act the fool with me, you know what I mean. I'm talking about Raymond."

"Mother, you're the one said he's missing. Don't you think you ought to report it to the police? They're in the business of finding missing people. Besides, it seems awfully strange to me that Raymond is missing one night and your house is broken into the next."

"The two things have absolutely nothing to do with

each other," Mother insisted with a bit too much conviction.

"Well, one thing I know for sure is you can't stay here alone."

"You're always trying to get me out of my house. Where will I stay if not here in my home?"

"You can come stay with us for a couple of days."

"I don't see how you can even prep your mouth to say that, not after Temp showed out so bad the last time I stayed there."

"Temp was mad at me, not you. As I recall, you took his side, anyway."

"Makes no difference. I promised never ever to sleep under that roof again. Too much confusion. And the language."

"That's okay, Mother. Would you like me to call someone? What about Sister Agnew or Kaylene Simmons?"

"They all went to that Baptist Women's Convention in Memphis."

"Mother Ione, too?"

"Yes. Don't worry about me, child. I'll be just fine. You go on home and take care of your own business, let me take care of mine."

I picked up her phone and started to dial.

"Who you calling this time of the night?"

I ignored the question. On the other end the phone was snatched up on the second ring. "Hello," I said. "Brother Cummings?"

Mother groaned.

"Brother Cummings, this is Theresa Galloway." That's as far as I got before he cut me off. Brother Cummings told me he knew he was needed and he would be on his way as soon as his taxi got there. He said something woke him and told him to get dressed. He'd even called a taxi, although he didn't know where he was going until he got my call. Brother Cummings can be downright spooky sometimes. According to Mother, he's a sometimes seer. A seer is something like a psychic, but without the infrastructure. Brother Cummings is a sometimes seer because his seeing ability isn't always reliable. He's like an adolescent whose voice is changing and you never know when it's going to crack. Sometimes Brother Cummings is right on the target, other times he cracks. This seeing stuff is supposed to run in his family on his mother's side. His maternal aunt, Mother Iola, is renowned in Mother's circle for her ability to tell you things. But Mother Iola lives in a state of grace. Brother Cummings on the other hand, although he's way up in his seventies, squandered his gift on the sporting life until just a few years ago when he finally settled down.

"Why'd you call Cleotis? I don't feel like being bothered by that old man," groused Mother. "He gets on my nerves. I remember when he was a boy. Always trying to look up somebody's dress."

"Well, I doubt if you'll have to worry about that, Mother. I don't think he could get down that low now without help."

Temp and Lt. Bivens came back from checking the alarm. We thanked Lt. Bivens for everything and she left.

"You should see it," said Temp. "The whole box is frozen solid. I'll take it off and see what I can do to get you fixed up tomorrow."

"We can leave as soon as Brother Cummings gets here. He's going to stay with Mother."

Mother sucked her teeth in frustration before stalking off into the kitchen. Temp looked at me with raised brows. "What's the matter with Mom?"

I shrugged and started putting on my jacket.

I could hear Temp muttering under his breath, "These Barkley women. Every last one of them, mother, daughter, granddaughter . . ." but I ignored it. The doorbell rang and Temp opened the door, ushering in Brother Cummings. He wore a rust-colored leisure suit and highly polished, oxblood red, Stacy Adams shoes. He clutched a shopping bag in one hand and a lunch pail in the other. A long object like one of those pom-pom–covered golf clubs stuck up out of the bag. Brother Cummings sat the bag at his feet, and he and Temp shook hands.

"Morning, Brother Galloway, Sister Galloway. True to my word, I'm here. However, I must admit I am a little uneasy about this arrangement."

His uneasiness converted into nervous energy. His left leg was jumping, and his fingers twitched open and closed around the handles of his shopping bag.

"Somebody tried to break in on Mother, but the Police don't feel he'll be back," I said, attempting to reassure him. "It's just that we didn't want to leave Mother here alone."

Brother Cummings shook his head vigorously.

"I fear neither man nor beast. It's just that . . ."

He struggled for words, his leg jumping as if he had electrodes attached to it. He shot a sideways glance at me and then pulled Temp aside and whispered something to him. Temp put his arm around Brother Cummings and patted his shoulder reassuringly. I heard him say, "Believe me, man, I know what you mean," before his voice dropped to a whisper.

I went into the kitchen to say good-bye to Mother.

She'd changed into the emerald green silk robe we
had given her for Christmas. She'd also combed her
hair and put on lipstick. I hugged her and told her
that Brother Cummings was here and we were leaving.

"Tell him to come on back here and I'll fix him
something to eat."

"That's all right, Mother. He's carrying a lunch pail.
I think he brought his own food. He has a shopping
bag too, so I suspect he also brought his own toys."

Mother sniffed. "I hope ain't nothing nappy."

Chapter Ten

"Don't get any ideas now, T. Do you hear me? Don't get any ideas about messing around in police business. Let the police do their job. You and your mother stay out of it. I got enough on my mind right now. I don't need you running the streets like a fool on one of your mother's schemes like last year. You hear me?"

That hurt. Cut me to the quick. This was my man, the father of my children, and he had absolutely no faith in me. I had no intention of getting involved in anything even remotely related to Mother's break-in or anything else. Hadn't I successfully resisted Mother's demands that I look for Raymond? I'm a conscientious mother, a good wife. Didn't that count for something? Didn't I have enough to do, trying to defend myself at work from the Heather Whitcombs and the Brenda Delacores of the world? Didn't he think I had a life other than Mother?

"Honey, you'll just have to trust me," I said. "The last thing I want is to get involved in another of Mother's messes. You remember the promise I made to you last year after everything? Well, that promise still holds. My family comes first—you and the kids."

"Yeah, T, that all sounds good, but I know you and I know your mother."

By the time we got home, it was a little after four. Aisha and Shawn had fallen asleep in the family room with the TV blasting. We rang the bell for what seemed like five minutes before a bleary-eyed Aisha stumbled to the door and started fumbling with the lock. Temp tried to stop her.

"Aisha, no. The alarm, baby. Turn the alarm off first."

Her face was scrunched together with sleep and ill humor. She wasn't in a listening mode. When she finally got the latch disengaged and snatched the door open, the alarm blasted through the still air like an air raid horn. I clamped my hands over my ears. Aisha stood where she was, nailed to the floor by the piercing sound. Temp stepped inside to the keypad next to the door and quickly punched in the disarm code. The air raid sound stopped. He whirled around to Aisha.

"Girl, didn't I—"

But it was a rain-out. Before he could finish, Aisha burst into tears and ran upstairs to her room.

Temp threw up his hands. "Now what? Now what?"

Shawn wandered out of the family room on legs wobbly with sleep. He walked straight into my arms, and I kissed him on the forehead. He's twelve, and give or take an inch he's as tall as I am. "Night, Mom."

"Night, honey."

He wobble-walked over to Temp, gave him five and a hug, and went upstairs.

Temp watched as Shawn climbed the stairs. I threaded my arm through his. "Kinda reminds you of when he was little, huh?"

"Yeah," said Temp. "Aisha, too." He unthreaded my arm, took his jacket off, and headed for his office.

"Where you going?"

He looked at his watch. "T, I've got work to do."

Temp sequestered himself in his office. I went up-stairs and tried to squeeze in a few hours of sleep before it was officially the next day and everything started all over again.

One thing about living in the suburbs—and that's just about all of Sacramento—there's yard work. If you don't get to it, it comes to you. Your neighbors bring it. Let your yard go for a week or two—pretty soon you'll be hearing lawn mowers and leaf blowers in your sleep. Your neighbors will start mowing their lawns earlier and earlier just to get your attention. When it gets to the point where they're mowing at six in the morning, you're just a step away from the community association's board of directors marching on your home with torches lit. I was awakened around seven by the Hidakos' mower. The Hidakos are our neighbors to our immediate south. How did I know it was their mower? Easy, the Hidakos have one of those high-tech machines that sounds like it's powered by a jet engine. Pretty soon Dr. Singh to our east joined them, and the Bartons' dog to the west started to bark. I was surrounded. I climbed out of bed and dragged myself to the shower.

The bathroom is my favorite place in the whole house. It's the one place I've allowed my creativity free rein. It's done in whitewashed oak, imported mar-ble, and a rainforest of green plants. Its centerpiece is the free-standing shower constructed entirely of glass bricks, but I spend a great deal of time, and not all of it alone, in the sunken, jetted tub that seats two. But I didn't linger this morning as I usually do. I show-

ered, did the rest of my grooming, dressed, and was
out of there in fifteen minutes.

I went downstairs to start the coffee and check on
Temp. I didn't bother checking on the kids. I knew
they'd be out, the lazy little bums, until I woke them
up for a meal. Temp had fallen asleep at his desk
with his computer on. Bold letters of his screen saver
scrolled across the monitor—"Power concedes nothing
without a demand."

I shook him awake. "Honey, why don't you go upstairs and lie down?"

He looked up at me through eyes as bleary as Aisha's and stood up on legs as wobbly as Shawn's.
"Wake me up in a couple of hours. Okay?"

I agreed, and he wobbled off to bed.

I went to the garage and found my gardening gloves.
Then I rolled the lawn mower out. I glanced across
the street at the Dixons' architectural whimsy, a half-
timbered, French chateau. Their lawn was every bit as
high as ours, and they weren't even up yet. Somehow
that made me feel a bit more virtuous.

I mowed the lawn and weeded the flower bed,
dumping the grass clippings and weeds in the gutter
in the front of the house. That's a quaint Sacramento
custom. Garden waste is dumped in the gutters to be
picked up by the street cleaners. On weekends after
the nine-to-fivers do their weekly yard work, the city's
gutters are dotted with green mounds like droppings
from some large prehistoric herbivore. The hedges
needed trimming, but I left them for Temp and the
kids. Then I turned my attention to the house. I did
some quick surface cleaning, straightened the family
and living rooms, vacuumed and dusted. Finally, I approached the downstairs bath with good intentions,

but by then my heart just wasn't in it. It takes a lot of heart to clean up a bathroom after a twelve-year-old boy with poor aim and a forty-year-old man with no excuse.

I called it quits around eleven and sat down and had another cup of coffee. I shouldn't have slowed down, because the minute I did, everything crowded in on me. Mother, Raymond, the break-in, gunshots, blood specimens—somehow though everything seemed to come back to Raymond. He seemed to have been a catalyst if nothing else. Look at how he affected my relationship with Mother, the changes in Mother's lifestyle, her house. Mother accused me of being jealous, and maybe I was, but the way I figured it, I had every right to be. After Daddy died, I became the family point person. My brother, Jimmy, lives in Germany with his German wife and children, and my sister, Carolyn, died twenty-three years ago. I was the only one left. And I'd been there for Mother. I was there to help her fight off the depression after Daddy died. I was there when her water pipes burst. I was there for her early-morning and late-evening calls and her harebrained schemes. I was there—not Raymond. So if I was a little jealous, well, I think I have that much coming to me. But jealousy wasn't the problem—Raymond was.

I'd promised Mother that I'd go through his things to see if I could get some idea of his whereabouts. With Temp and the kids out of commission, now seemed to be just as good a time as any to run over there and take a look. Raymond wasn't as smart as he thought. He'd left something that would give him away, and I was going to find it.

* * *

Mother was fully reclined in her Lazyboy. Brother Cummings was on the sofa, his legs supported by a hassock. Their heads were back, their mouths open. Even though I was separated from them by a solid-core door, I could hear the surflike ebb and flow of their snores. I rang the doorbell and stuck my head around the porch enclosure to peer in the front window again. They hadn't stirred. I returned to the door and gave it a good pounding with my fist.

"Mother, Mother. It's me, Theresa!"

I heard some creaking and shuffling, then Mother clearing her throat. Finally, she shuffled to the door. I identified myself again for the record, and she let me in.

I looked over at Brother Cummings. He hadn't stirred. "Doesn't he do that trick anymore where he answers the door before you knock?"

"I'm afraid Brother Cummings's all out of tricks," said Mother. I thought she sounded rather rueful.

"How've things been?"

"Just fine."

"You haven't had any more of those calls or anything, have you?"

"No, it's been just quiet."

"I came to go through Raymond's stuff. But, just out of curiosity, what did Brother Cummings have in that shopping bag?"

Mother pointed to the corner behind the sofa. A shotgun leaned against the wall. I nearly swallowed my tongue I was so surprised. What is it with old people and shotguns? "A shotgun, Mother, a shotgun?"

Mother yawned. "Yes, baby, a shotgun."

"What does he need a shotgun for?"

"What do you think he's doing here? You the one insisted I needed someone to sit with me in case Mr. Man came back. What'd you expect him to bring? Knitting needles? Knit a rope and tie him up? No, baby, a shotgun's just right. You point it and shoot. Don't much have to aim. See here, let me show you."

Mother reached over Brother Cummings' slumbering form and picked up the gun. She hefted it in her hands. "This a nice one too, a Mossberg. Poppa had one similar to this, but it didn't have the pistol grip."

I backed up.

"Aw, girl, it ain't nothing to be afraid of. I've been handling guns for as long as I can remember. Used to hunt with my brothers. Could outshoot everyone of them, too."

"Mother, I spent the longest couple of hours of my life locked in a small room—just me, a crazy man, and his shotgun. So I hope you'll excuse me, but that gun makes me nervous."

"That's what you said last year about that Sig Hauer, but I bet you were glad to have it when ole lady Alston came at you."

"This is different."

"Theresa, you always were picky. You're the same way about food. I remember when you wouldn't eat nothing but Saltine crackers and cheddar cheese and you—"

"That's all right, Mother. I get the point. I'm picky. Please put the gun down."

She placed it back in the corner. Brother Cummings snorted and shifted in his sleep.

"Come on," I said. "Let's get this over with."

We went to the back of the house to Jimmy's old room. It still had the red iron bed, plaid bedspread,

and matching curtains that Jimmy had when he was
there. I started my search with the closet. It contained
two pairs of pants, one casual and one dress, one dress
shirt, and a lightweight jacket. A pair of leather dress
shoes sat on the floor next to an old cardboard suitcase with a stripe running through its middle. I
checked the pants pockets. Nothing. I could see there
was nothing in the shirt pocket, but I checked anyway.
Double nothing. I even turned the cuffs out on the
dress pants and checked there. More nothing. I pulled
the shoes out and examined them. They were well
worn to a point just this side of shabby. I stuck my
finger in the toe, and it jammed up against something
soft. Reaching in, I pulled out the sock and shook it.
I turned it inside out. Nothing. I did the same with
the other sock, then I stuffed them both back where
I'd found them and put the shoes away. I made a
mental note to wash my hands when I finished. I didn't
want to tackle the suitcase yet, but I took it out and
sat it on the bed so I wouldn't forget about it. Next,
I directed my attention to the small chest of drawers.
It was made of particle board and covered with some
sort of vinyl veneer in a wood pattern. One of Big
Al's House of Furniture specials no doubt. I opened
the top drawer. Three pairs of men's boxer shorts
stared up at me. No undershirts. The second drawer
held an old pair of blue striped men's pajamas. I
turned to Mother accusingly.

"These are Daddy's, aren't they?"

"Those *used* to be your daddy's. Baby, Walter Lee's
dead. Your daddy passed on. And you've got to stop
carrying on like he's still here, just stepped out for a
while, and when he gets back he's going to be hopping
mad 'cause somebody's been messing with his stuff.

Those pajamas weren't doing anybody any good sitting up in a box in the garage."

"Mother, I am not carrying on. I asked a simple question, that's all."

Mother sank down on the bed. She looked tired. "Let me ask you something. What would you do if I got married again? Would you carry on like this?"

"Okay, Mother, I get the point."

I wanted to get her off the subject of marriage. There was an old man in the living room, sleeping with his mouth open, making pig-rutting noises. An old man who fancied himself a seerer, who brought his own lunch when he came visiting and carried a shotgun around in a shopping bag. There weren't that many old men around—the y chromosome just doesn't seem to be very durable. I wanted to get off the subject of marriage quickly before she got any ideas.

I turned from Mother and surveyed the room. Focus, I reminded myself, focus. I was getting caught up in too many outside issues. I could miss something, overlook whatever it was I was after. I dropped to my hands and knees and looked under the bed. Nothing there, just a couple of dust bunnies and one of Mother's old slippers. A couple of planks spanned the bed frame, keeping the mattress from falling through. I gave them a couple of whacks with my fist. Nothing. Then I asked Mother to get up for a second and we looked under the mattress. Again nothing. I sat down on the bed next to her. Where, I asked myself, would I hide something if I were a dirty, conniving, lying, little sneak? And just like that the answer came to me—the same place Jimmy used to hide stuff when we were kids and he specialized in being a dirty, conniving, lying, little sneak. I got up and pulled the chest of drawers out from the wall. The back of the chest was nothing more than a sheet of paperboard stapled to its frame. It was warped with old age and buckled in places. I picked the bottom staples out with my fingernail and pulled the backing up. A spiral notebook dropped to the floor. I picked it up. Mother crowded me, looking over my shoulder.

"Now, how did that get there?" she asked.

"Raymond obviously put it there," I answered.

"It could have been in the drawer and got wedged and fell back there."

"No, Mother. This is the same place Jimmy used to hide his stuff."

"Well, if he was hiding it because he didn't want anyone to see it, then he certainly would have taken it with him when he left. He'd have taken his clothes, too, like I been telling you. That just proves something has happened to him."

I thumbed through the pages of what appeared to be a book of pencil sketches. I don't know much about art, but some of the sketches were pretty good, others looked rushed, dashed off, unfinished.

"This is Raymond's, isn't it?" I asked.

"I guess it is. I don't think I ever saw him with it, but he was really crazy about art and stuff. It could be his. It's nothing obscene, is it?"

"Mother, if I didn't know you better, I'd say you were developing an obsession with sex."

She nudged me in the side. "Aw, hush up, girl. What's in there?"

We returned to the bed and sat down. Mother and I went through the notebook slowly, page by page. There were sketches of people doing common, everyday things, kids carrying books on their way to school, women with shopping bags, old men at a table under a tree, playing dominoes. There was also a sketch of a pirate ship, some river scenes, and some sketches that looked as if they had been done by a child. Nothing incriminating. Nothing obscene. Why did he go to the trouble to hide it? Mother and I looked at each other and shrugged. We were thinking the same thing. "What's the big deal?"

I held the notebook by its wire coils and shook it. Nothing tumbled out from between the pages. We examined the insides of the front and back covers. Nothing. A bust. My disappointment was almost palpable. I looked at Mother, extended my hands palm up, and shrugged.

Mother suddenly brightened. "Wait a minute," she said. "What about the suitcase?"

I turned and grabbed it from the bed behind us and sat it on the floor in front of me. I pressed the latches in and tried to slide them open. It was locked. The case was little more than a paper box with a handle. Why'd he even bother to lock it? I could tear the lock off and open it if I wanted to. Mother got up and trotted to her room. She came back with a metal nail file in her hand.

"Here, use this."

I took the file, inserted it between the clasp and the case, jerked upward sharply, and the clasp popped up with barely any resistance at all. I shoved it over to Mother.

"Go ahead," I said. "Open it."

She took the case and flung it open. It opened flat like something that had been fileted. And it was empty. Faded burgundy grosgrain fabric covered the inside. A shirred pouch of the same material stretched across one side. Mother pulled the pouch back and peered inside.

"Looks like there's some papers in there."

She reached in and pulled out a handful of old yellowed papers. We took them and spread them out on the bed. There were machine copies of a couple of magazine articles and what looked like some pages from a textbook and a picture of Daddy. Mother gasped when she saw the picture. I must admit my stomach did a little flip-flop, too. The last thing I wanted to do was find something that actually connected Raymond to Daddy, something that legitimized his claim.

Mother looked befuddled. "How'd he get that? That was in my wallet."

"You sure?"

"Of course I'm sure. Your daddy had that picture taken at the fair in '82 and gave to me. I always kept it in my wallet."

"You mean he stole it out of your wallet?"

I was ready to accuse Raymond of the most heinous crimes known to man. But never in my wildest flights of fantasy did I imagine him having the gall to actually go through Mother's purse.

I took the picture from Mother and examined it closely. It was a black and white, the kind you take in those little booths with the handkerchief-size curtain. Daddy had on his trademark stingy brim hat. It was set back on his head in a relaxed sort of way. He looked directly into the camera and smiled his teasing, I've-got-a-secret smile of his. I turned it over.

"No use looking on the back. Your daddy wasn't much for writing."

"What's this?" I asked. "These numbers?"

Mother snatched the picture from me and studied the two sets of numbers.

"Those nine numbers, that's your daddy's Social Security number. The dashes are missing, but that's his number all right. As many papers as I filled out for him over the years, I know that number."

"You didn't put it on the picture?"

Mother shook her head grimly.

"What about those other numbers? You know what they are?"

Another shake of the head.

"What's going on here? Mother, you know once somebody gets your Social Security number nothing is safe. They might as well have that number you use for the automatic teller machine."

Mother just nodded. Her eyes looked glassy.

"I told you something was funny about Raymond, Mother."

Mother heaved herself up from the bed. "We'd better see if he messed with anything else."

There was something painful about the way she spoke. I'm used to Mother's bluster, her blather, her self-assured assertiveness. This defeated little old lady stuff didn't play well. In fact, it was scaring me.

If the house had been in its usual jumble, we could have told at a glance whether anything was missing. It's a skill you develop. But it was orderly and neat—thanks to Raymond—and we were at a loss.

"Let's check your personal papers first," I suggested.

We went to Mother's room. She opened the closet and took a cash box off the top shelf.

"All my important papers are in here," she said and handed it to me.

A large lock swung from the front of the cash box, but I knew the routine. I flipped the box over and worked the bottom loose. Everything seemed to be in order. Her family trust was there as well as some Social Security and insurance documents. I was surprised, however, to find that she had all three of our high school diplomas, Carolyn's, Jimmy's, and mine. She also had my college diploma. I'd presented it to her and Daddy after I walked across the stage of Sac State some eighteen years ago. "Here," I'd said, "you deserve this as much as much as I do." The funny thing was Daddy was the one who cried, not Mother. I would have expected it to be the other way around.

"What about your accounts? You know, Sears. J. C. Penney, things like that."

"I keep all that stuff in the dining room in the bottom of the buffet. But, let's finish up in here first."

We stood in the middle of the room and surveyed it. It was so tidy it made me nervous. The bed was freshly made. Fresh, crisp curtains hung from the windows. The dresser and matching headboard were polished to a high gloss. Pictures of Aisha and Shawn hung on the wall directly across from the bed. A grouping of old sepia prints of Carolyn, Jimmy, and me hung over the bed. Frilly green plants on wrought iron stands found places to grace.

"Mother, something is missing."

"The sewing machine. I gave it to Georgetta."

"No, it's something else. I just don't know what."

"Maybe you'll think of it. Let's do your room."

After all these years Mother still called it my room. Maybe it was wishful thinking, but I certainly hoped not.

You know how some parents leave your room just

the way it was when you were home? They take reluctant but polite visitors back there and explain wistfully, "This is just the way she left it." Not mother. The Huey Newton poster—the one of him sitting in that big chair, holding a spear—was long since gone. So were the posters of the Funkadelics and Billy Dee Williams. The pink, orange, and purple psychedelic bedspread and curtains were gone. The twin beds had been dismantled and stacked against the wall.

"Looks like a whole lot's missing in here," I said.

"We packed up most of the stuff and put it in the garage."

I didn't say anything more, but I was kind of hurt.

That left the kitchen, which we decided to skip—we would have been there all day otherwise—and the living and dining rooms. I went to the buffet first and pulled out the shoe box Mother kept her bills in. I thought I'd give her accounts a quick going over before tackling the final two rooms. The first thing I noticed was that none of the bills were current.

"Mother, where's this month's bills?"

"Everything's in there. I drop the bills in there until I get ready to do them."

"This is all last month's stuff."

"Come to think of it, mail has been rather sparse this month. I been so busy I hadn't paid much attention. But you know, I don't think I've been getting my mail."

I tried to hide my mounting concern. "I'll check with the post office Monday. Your delivery may have been interrupted for some reason."

We tackled the living room and dining room next, giving them the same going over as the bedrooms. I just couldn't shake that feeling—something was missing. Actually, a whole lot of things were missing if you counted the clutter that had been there, but something was missing that should have been there despite the clutter. I just couldn't put my finger on it. I stood in the middle of the living room and closed my eyes, trying to visualize what was missing. Visualize, I thought, visualize. "She was a vision of loveliness." That was Daddy's courtly description of Mother on their wedding day. Carolyn and I used to crack up every time he said it. I opened my eyes.

"Mother, where's your wedding picture?"

She knew immediately that it wouldn't be there on the piano where it had sat for forty-seven years. She went to the piano anyway and stared at the pictures in the arty frames cluttering its surface. She picked them up one at a time and moved them around like chess pieces. But no matter how she rearranged them, the wedding photo wasn't there. I went to the buffet and took the family album out of the bottom drawer. It was the old-fashioned kind with pages of black paper. The pictures were fastened to the pages with little white paper brackets. I opened the album and turned the pages slowly, gasping each time I came to a dark patch framed by little white brackets where a picture had been.

"He took every picture that had Daddy in it. The one of Daddy and Aunt Laura before she lost her sight, the one you used to keep on your dresser, it's gone, too. That's what was missing in the bedroom."

I wanted Mother to do something, to say something, to rant and rave and storm about. In other words, act normal. Instead, she just looked at me with a curious set to her mouth. Then she reached over, took the album from my hands, closed it, and put it away.

"He's not going to get away with this, Mother. I promise you that."

"Leave it alone, Theresa," said Mother. "What's done is done."

She looked so tired, so beat down, and suddenly so much older than her seventy-two years. It only made me angrier.

"How can you say that? You're the one wanted me to find him. Well, I'm going to find him, and when I do, I'm going to kick his little red butt."

Brother Cummings stirred and chortled in his sleep. Mother leaned over and shook his foot, and he settled back down silently. We lowered our voices and moved to the kitchen.

"Look, Mother, whether you admit it or not, something's very wrong here. Raymond shows up out of the blue claiming to be Daddy's child. Granted, he knows a little bit about Daddy. He has the picture and the money orders, but that's all. Did you notice anything strange about his stuff when we went through it? There was nothing there. Nothing to indicate he had a life. No receipts, no letters from girlfriends, nothing. Everything was so nondescript, as if he went to a secondhand store and just bought stuff. You said he came out here from Arkansas on the bus. He didn't even have a ticket stub. It's like he didn't exist before he came here. And you know what I think? I don't think he did. He's not who he says he is, and that makes me real nervous. You take that and you factor in his sudden disappearance and the break-in last night, and that really scares me. Then there was that strange phone call I got."

That's when she told me about the phone calls she'd been getting for the last couple of days, calls that came at odd hours day and night. Just someone breathing, then the hangup.

"It was Gertha, that's all, trying to scare me, make me drop out of the race for president of the NWCG," Mother insisted.

"Maybe it was a hant," I offered.

Mother actually seemed to be mulling over the possibility, and I knew we had problems. "That's it, Mother. That's it."

"What? What?"

"You have no idea what you've gotten yourself into. You don't need to be here by yourself right now. I have to go to work, I have kids to tend to, a husband. I can't do what I'm supposed to do; I can't concentrate if I'm worrying about you."

"Who asked you to worry about me? I don't need you or anybody else to take care of me. I take care of myself, and I beg you not to forget it either. All I asked you to do is try to find out what happened to the boy, and you didn't want to do that. I asked you to come by and look through his stuff. You said okay, but did you show up? No. Somebody come trying to break in last night. Did I need you to take care of that?"

"Okay, okay. The fact remains that you shouldn't stay here alone, at least not for the next couple of days."

"This is my house. I pay the taxes on it, and I decide who stays here and who doesn't."

"Well, would it be all right if I asked Brother Cummings to stay until tomorrow?"

"I don't care," she snapped. "But I'm not going to wait on him. If he wants something, he's going to have to get up and get it himself."

I went back into the living room and woke up Brother Cummings. "Brother Cummings, could you stay just a couple more days? I don't want to leave Mother alone just yet. We really don't know what's going on. The man who tried to break in may even come back."

Brother Cummings nodded in agreement. I believed him when he told me and Temp that he feared neither man nor beast. He might have been an old man in a rust-colored leisure suit, but he was bad enough to pack a lunch and a piece. However, the prospect of spending the night with Mother clearly distressed him. But Brother Cummings is nothing if not a gentleman, so he choked back his apprehensions and agreed to stay.

I asked Mother if I could take the notebook and the papers we'd found in Raymond's suitcase, and she agreed. I folded them and stuffed them in my purse. I kissed her on the forehead, she patted me on the fanny, and I left to go home to my family.

Chapter Eleven

Most people squander their Sundays dreading Monday, but not me. I like the sense of anticipation, the prep work, selecting the week's wardrobe, reviewing my calendar, packing my briefcase. Mondays are second chances. What went undone last week can be tackled this week; what got screwed up can be fixed. I've learned to respect Mondays, and I always approach them head-on. I did all my Sunday things, but my mind was on Monday, and discovery and debunking. I intended to make this Monday Raymond's D-Day.

Temp and I took the kids to church, and Pastor Miller departed from his prepared sermon to personally greet us from the pulpit. "I want to praise the Lord today for so many blessings. Say amen, church. And chief among them is the presence of the Galloway family in our midst after so long an absence." To that the church said amen without prompting, as if six weeks were a lifetime. "He clowned us," to quote Aisha, but we got through that, and we got through brunch at the Sizzler Restaurant, which won out over the tonier La Salle's, in keeping with our new policy of austerity.

Monday was Aisha and Shawn's first day back to

school after spring break, but they didn't look upon their Mondays with as much respect as I did. Aisha was packing a carton of yogurt for lunch—taking rather than buying lunches is also part of our austerity campaign—and Shawn was wrapping some pizza from a couple of days ago for his.

Aisha tossed Shawn a knowing glance before casually addressing me. "You know Cassandra found a hypodermic needle in her seat on the bus. Now her mom lets her drive the Camry to school so she won't catch AIDS."

"Yeah, Mom. You oughta let Aisha drive your car."

Aisha shot him a look as if to say, "Take it easy, dum-dum. Don't rush it." Shawn shrugged.

I was in a hurry, but I had to stop and marvel at how Aisha had, at such a tender age, managed to master the art of motherisms. "Excuse me, but did I miss something? What's the connection between driving a Camry and AIDS prevention?"

"The needle, Mom," explained Aisha. She was patience personified.

"Yeah, Mom, the needle," vouched Shawn.

"The needle?" I still didn't get it.

"On the bus. It could have been used by someone who had AIDS. It could have been contaminated. It could have pricked her. Now do you get it?"

"I get that part. It's the Camry part—"

"The Camry part isn't important."

"It isn't?"

"No," said Aisha.

Shawn demonstrated his corroboration by shaking his head vigorously.

"Oh, I see."

"She doesn't have to ride the bus anymore. That's

what's important. She drives her mother's Camry. The type of car is not important. It could have been a Prelude, a Cherokee, or"—she paused for emphasis— "a Beamer. The point is she drives."

"Oh, now I get it. At some point within the next ten or twenty years when you finally get your license, I should hand my car over to you to protect you from the danger of misplaced medical instruments on public transportation."

"You make it sound so dumb."

"Yeah, Mom."

"I rest my case."

I poured myself a cup of coffee, passing on the cream and sugar. Ordinarily I'm a cream and sugar person, but lately the cream has been bothering me, and the sugar tastes too sweet, so I've started drinking it black like a real woman. Aisha and Shawn left the kitchen, badgering each other under their breaths.

"I did too back you up," protested Shawn.

"What's up with 'yeah, Mom'? That all you can say? 'Yeah, Mom.' When I do get my license, see if I take you anywhere."

Oh well, I thought, anything that gets them to "play together nicely" even as co-conspirators is a welcome respite from their usual fratricidal battles.

I went in to Temp's office to tell him I was leaving. I didn't know how long he'd slept, but he was already up when the alarm clock went off this morning at six-thirty. He sat hunched over his computer keyboard in the darkened room, still wearing the sweat pants and T-shirt he'd slept in. He was scraggly in some places and matted in others, and when he looked up at me, I could see the very beginnings of desperation in his eyes.

" 'Bye, baby, I'm leaving."

He raised a hand without actually waving and turned back to the computer monitor. I stood there for a couple of seconds, trying to think what I could say to make things better. I'm a mom—I tend to think like that. The other-worldly blue glow of the computer monitor in the darkened room seemed to engulf Temp like some sort of force field. I could see him and hear him, but I couldn't touch him. I stood there for a few more seconds, then I turned and left.

I looked at the day's calendar Miyako had left on my desk. It was a typical day, seven meetings. I put check marks next to the two I planned to attend, the ten-thirty with the Department of Personnel Administration to go over an important classification proposal and the one at three o'clock with the Department of Finance. Then I picked up the phone and told Brenda to come to my office.

Brenda had on another of her power suits. This one was gray with a barely discernible pinstripe. She wore it with the de rigueur white silk blouse.

"Brenda, I'd like you to attend some meetings for me."

Her face brightened. After the last time she'd acted for me, I'd sworn never to let her jeopardize my career again—and she knew it. Without fail, each time I've left Brenda in charge, I've returned to a disaster. So why do I do it? I have no other choice. Brenda's the second highest-ranking employee in the personnel office. Department policy requires that someone be left in charge. Protocol dictates that it be Brenda.

I think Brenda has fantasies that she and I, through some twist of karma, are inhabiting each other's rightful stations in life. In other words, she should be personnel officer, and I should be her scullery maid. I leave her in charge, and the minute I walk out the door she starts making changes, canceling my instructions, issuing proclamations. Once I was gone for two hours to attend a workshop, and she completely rearranged my office furniture and purged my files while I was out. I returned to find her in my office, reclining in my chair with her hands behind her head, and her feet up on my desk, admiring her handiwork. The last time I left her in charge, I was out two days and she redid everyone's assignments, broke up a baby shower in the transactions unit, accused the mail clerk of being a Nazi, and caused a small riot in the cafeteria. Brenda knew I was either desperate, or this simply was her lucky day.

"No problem," she answered with thinly disguised eagerness.

"Okay. I'd like you to start with the staff meeting at nine. Here's the calendar. And Brenda, please treat everyone with courtesty and respect."

That I should demand so much irritated her. She sucked her teeth, making a loud clicking sound, and sighed deeply. But she lived for the times when she could be in charge, and she didn't want to blow it, so she nodded in consent.

"And don't try to handle any disciplinary problems. Okay? I'm going to be gone only a couple of hours. Any disciplinary problems can wait until I get back."

"Come on, Theresa. That last time wasn't my fault. Allen and them blew it all out of proportion, calling the State Police and all that."

"Brenda, Brenda, listen to me. That's over and done with. Okay? It was a learning experience. Just go to my meetings. Treat everyone with courtesy and respect. Don't talk under anyone's clothes. Okay? No childbirth analogies. No references to the anomalies of other people's anatomy. Okay?"

I happen to know for a fact that Brenda is superbright. But sometimes you just have to get real basic with her.

I continued my instructions. "Now, as for Heather Whitcomb, with her just . . . be yourself."

Brenda left happy.

I took off my pumps, exchanging them for my walking shoes, and left. If Allen had still been my boss, I would have called him, and, depending on how thin the ice was that month, either told him I had to be out for a couple of hours or asked for permission to leave for that amount of time. I do my job—I'm damn good at it. Allen knows he can count on me to get the work out. He'd always been pretty flexible with my comings and goings within reason. But Allen wasn't my boss any longer, Heather Whitcomb was. I'd won round one in the Heather skirmishes; round two had been fought to a draw. I didn't want my request for a couple of hours off to become round three, so I didn't ask.

My first stop was the State Library. I said hello to Charles, the security guard, and went to the second floor in the old ornate elevator. I got the phone book for Pine Bluff, Arkansas, and looked up Johnson. There were four pages of Johnsons, several R. Johnsons, but not one Raymond. I really didn't expect to find anything, so I wasn't disappointed. I knew there'd be lots of Johnsons. It's a common name like Smith or Jones. I remember reading somewhere that when people choose phony names for whatever reason, they usually pick one pretty close to their actual name, sometimes even keeping part of their name. I wondered if Raymond Johnson was actually Raymond Johansen or Damon Johnson or Leland Johnston. The varieties were infinite. This train of thought was amusing, but it really wasn't getting me anywhere, so I dropped it.

I turned my thoughts to the running man. What role did he play in all of this? Was he in some way connected to Raymond's disappearance and the break-in at Mother's? If he wasn't, why'd he break and run like that? I put the Pine Bluff book away and got the one for Sacramento. I looked up the number for the Brass Monkey. I could remember a time when restaurants closed on Mondays, but it was a good bet that a downtown restaurant catering to an almost captive audience of government employees would be open. I was on my way downstairs, looking for a public phone, before I remembered my cell phone. Temp bought it for me and insisted I carry it at all times after the thing with Mrs. Turner. I retreated to the farthest corner of the room and dialed the number. It rang so many times I was just about to hang up when someone picked it up.

"Hello," I whispered. "I'd like to speak to . . ."

That cook—what was his name? I'd forgotten his name.

"I'm sorry, I can't hear you. Would you speak up, please?"

I looked around self-consciously. A dapper old man in a herringbone jacket had quit reading and was staring at me pointedly.

"Hel-lo," I whispered again, dragging it out as a

substitute for raising my voice. "I'd like to speak to . . . Rol-land."

But I was too late. I could tell the person on the other end had removed the phone from his ear, because when he spoke he sounded farther away. "Tell Carl we got another one," I heard him say to someone. "Yeah, another crank call." Then he hung up on me. I pressed the end button, folded the phone up, and returned it to my purse. I looked at my watch— nine-fifteen. I figured I had time to take a little stroll over to the Brass Monkey and still make it back to the office in time for my ten-thirty meeting.

I banged on the door. Peering inside the darkened restaurant, I could see chairs stacked on tables and someone in a white T-shirt, mopping the floor. I banged again. The white T-shirt looked up and tried to wave me away. "Closed. Closed. Come back at eleven," he shouted.

I banged again, but this time he ignored me. I was considering my next move when a produce truck drove by and turned the corner. I hitched my purse over my shoulder and took off after the truck. By the time I got to the mouth of the alley, the truck had parked and the driver was unloading wooden crates of vegetables at the Chinese restaurant two doors down from the Brass Monkey. A Latino man in cook's garb squatted just to the side of the Brass Monkey's door, smoking a cigarette that he held in a curious overhanded way as he contemplated the asphalt at his feet. He glanced up as I approached, but by the time I got near enough to speak, he had returned to his cigarette and the asphalt. I stopped just short of where he squatted—I didn't want to loom over him—and waited for him to look up again. He decided to wait me out.

I finally spoke. "Excuse me. Can you tell me if Rolland is in yet?"

The man continued to smoke as if I hadn't spoken. I moved a little closer.

"Excuse me . . ."

He stood up, flicked the cigarette butt into the alley, and turned to look at me.

"I'm looking for Rolland. Would you mind checking to see if he's in?"

He just stared at me, as if he was waiting for something.

"Please?"

That wasn't it.

What am I supposed to do now, I wondered. If this was TV, I'd hand him twenty dollars and he'd smile, toss me a jaunty salute, and leave to do my bidding. But this wasn't TV. I didn't know what else to do, so I tried the money approach anyway. I dug into my purse and found my wallet. I took a five out—this after all was not TV—and showed it to him. "Would you be offended if I offered you this to check in there for Rolland?"

He took the bill, turned, pushed the restaurant door open, and stuck his head in. "Yo, Rolland," he called. "There's a sister out here to see you, man."

Rolland came to the door and saw it was me. "Thanks a lot, Manuel, man," he said.

Manuel tossed him a taunting smile and sauntered past him into the restaurant.

From the doorway Rolland glanced around, as if he was looking for something. Then he walked out into the alley and looked down its length in both directions. He turned back to me. "That old lady with you?"

"No, but I have my cell phone with me. I could get her here in a few minutes."

I could tell by the look on his face he didn't think I was funny.

"Look," I said. "I just want to ask you a few questions. I won't keep you very long, and I would really appreciate your help."

"You a private investigator or something?"

I had to laugh at that. "No, I'm not. I work for the state over at Ninth and O. I'm trying to help my mother, the old lady, find my nephew. We think he used to hang out with the guy who ran out of here the other day."

Okay, so I lied. But I was getting sick and tired of having to claim Raymond as my sibling. If Mother wanted to claim him, it was up to her, but I wasn't going to call him my brother when I knew he wasn't.

"Is he a techno-freak, too?"

"Who?"

"Your nephew?"

"I don't know. I really didn't know him that well."

"If he's a friend of Lyle's, he must be a techno-freak."

"That's his name? Lyle? What's his last name?"

"I don't know. Don't need to know."

"Who's the manager here? Do you think he would give me any information on him?"

"Look lady—"

"Theresa. My name's Theresa Galloway."

He extended his hand.

"Pleased to meet you," he said, as if he had learned

it by rote. Somebody had obviously tried to raise the child.

"Tony," he continued, "he's the manager, but I don't think he'll be able to tell you much of anything. Lyle's a grunt, a casual kitchen helper. They pay in cash. He may work here a week or two at a time, and then he goes somewhere else."

"I don't suppose you know where Lyle lives?"

"Nope."

"Has he been back?"

"No. I think the old . . . your mother spooked him."

I took out the Polaroid picture of Raymond and Mother. "This is my nephew. Have you seen him around here?"

Rolland took the picture from my hand and studied it. "Don't think so," he said. "Even if he had been here, I probably wouldn't have seen him. I mostly work in the back, chopping vegetables and shit . . . Excuse me, vegetables and stuff. I don't see a lot of what goes on out front."

"What's it like to work here?"

"It's all right. I don't eat the fish, though."

I thanked Rolland for his time and asked him to call me if Lyle showed up. I gave him one of my cards.

He took it and said, "You sure you not one of those lady detectives?"

I assured him I wasn't and left.

On the way back to the office, I cut through the Downtown Mall. It's brand new, less than three years old, and for my money, one of the most exciting places downtown. Strains of John Coltrane's "My Favorite Things" wafted through the large open-air rotunda on the west end nearest Old Town. I bought a latte at the cart in front of Macy's, found a seat at one of the wrought iron tables dotting the floor, and for a while watched Sacramento pass by. There were the young people who should have been in school, a couple of teens in baggy clothes, a skateboarder carrying his board tucked under his arm, a grandmotherly woman with a slightly dazed look and two toddlers in tow, and a motley assortment of government employees and businesspeople. I recognized some of the faces, such as those of the elderly couple, a man and a woman in their eighties who sat at one of the sun-dappled tables, sharing a newspaper. I'd seen them having lunch from time to time at the cafeteria in my building. They were always impeccably dressed, he in slacks, sport coat, and tie, and she in a shirt-waist dress with cardigan-draped shoulders, matching purse and shoes, and gloves. It's not until you got close to them, such as when you're standing in line to pay, that you notice how frayed his cuffs were and the numerous places her support hose had been carefully darned.

I was in danger of sinking into a serious people-watching reverie that would have kept me there for the next couple of hours, so I shook myself out of it and looked at my watch. It was ten o'clock. I needed to get back to the office for my ten-thirty meeting, but first I had to call Mother. I took out my phone and punched in her number. When she answered, I recounted my unproductive efforts trying to get information on Raymond and suggested we look on the bright side—at least we knew the running man's first name. Mother responded just as I thought she would. She said that information would do us just about as much good as an ice pack in hell.

I hung up and walked the few blocks back to the Resources Building. By the time I got there, I knew exactly what I was going to do and how I was going to find out everything I needed to know about Mr. Raymond "I'm your son, honest" Johnson. It might cost me, especially if Temp found out, but desperate times ... well, you know.

Chapter Twelve

The Department of Personnel Administration analyst's outrage had grown to the point where it was feeding on itself. Our modest proposal to establish a seven-level classification series that differed from two other current series only in its elevated pay scale had set him off. Now he was advising me, with a certain sadistic glee, that the department's Office Tech allocation was much too rich and what was needed was a formal plan of corrective action. He was getting nasty in a way that I couldn't really call him on, taking little digs, demanding additional justifications for requests he'd been sitting on for weeks. I let him go on unchecked. He'd apparently walked over to the Resources Building for our meeting, and somewhere along the way he'd run into a gust of wind. His solid-color polyester tie had been blown over his left shoulder and rested there now. His charming little Dutch-boy haircut had parted down the middle—all the way to the back of his head, where his soft spot had been when he was a baby. I could see a package of cigarettes and a book of matches in his shirt pocket. His fingertips were nicotine-stained. I kept a steady eye on the clock on the wall behind him, but I protested and explained just enough to keep him going. After a

while he began to gather his papers and make departure noises. I asked a multilevel, open-ended question
that should have taken ten minutes to answer. He gave
it thirty seconds and stood up. I tossed in a "Yeah,
but," and he gave me a sour look and sat back down.
He was fidgeting, his fingers alternately drumming the
table or picking at each other. He took a sloppy slash
at my reasoning, but I felled him with, "Is that in the
Laws and Rules?" We parried back and forth like that
until little beads of sweat began to form on his eye-
brows. When they want a smoke that bad, they can
very easily become violent. So I thanked him for coming and stood up. He left in a hurry, his cigarettes
already in his hand.

I needed to touch base with Brenda and see how
the staff meeting had gone, but she was away from
her desk. Miyako had deposited a fresh batch of mail
in my in-basket after the run at nine. I went through
it, trying hard to focus, but my mind kept jumping to
Raymond. Who was he really? Who was Lyle, for that
matter? What did he have to do with this mess? And
the break-in? Was that connected in some way to Raymond? To Lyle? To Raymond and Lyle?

I opened my bottom desk drawer and pulled out
my purse. I took out the sketchpad and returned the
purse to the drawer. I wanted to go through the
sketches again, this time without Mother breathing
down my back. I studied each drawing. I studied the
details, the line strokes, the scenes. Nothing jumped
up at me, but I kept returning to the river scenes.
Maybe it was because Sacramento is called the River
City. It's bracketed and bisected by two major rivers,
the Sacramento and the American. At one time, when
the rivers were still deep and clear, before high-pres-

sure hydraulic mining washed miles of silt into them, Sacramento had been a major port city. Ships from around the word docked here regularly. Much of Sacramento's heritage flows with those rivers. Modern-day Sacramento is a river recreation paradise. In my neighborhood most houses are built with three-car garages with space for two cars and a boat.

Those are the kind of things you learn talking to Andrew Soderstrom, Handy Andy to his friends. Andrew works in the Department of Water Resource's Water Information Center here in the Resources Building. He's a walking compendium of river lore, plus he must know by heart every mile of the rivers from here to Delta pumping plant in Tracy. The only problem is Andy's a fool. You have to get past his infantile humor and his clunky puns before you can get him to make any kind of sense.

I grabbed the sketch pad and was headed for the door when the phone rang. One thing you learn when you're a working mother is always answer the phone. You never can tell, the aquarium may have spilled on somebody, or somebody may have the cramps. I dutifully picked up the phone and almost immediately regretted it. It was Laura Nicholson, Shawn's teacher at Lawrence Academy. Laura's a gifted teacher with an absolute passion for educating young folk, plus she's just plain, old-fashioned good people. I like Laura, and any other time I would have been pleased to get a call from her, but I could tell this was business and not pleasure.

"Theresa," she said after we'd dispensed with the greeting ritual, "I'm afraid you're going to have to come get Shawn. He's been suspended."

I hung up and tried to call Temp. *His* son had

punched a boy out, bloodied his nose. He's the macho one, let him go get him. I couldn't reach him at home, and I got a message that said the customer was not available when I dialed his cell phone number. I dialed his pager and left Lawrence Academy's number. Then I grabbed the notebook and left before the phone rang again.

I found Andy on the phone in his cubicle. He was decked out in his trademark yuppie duds—navy blazer, tan slacks, and penny loafers.

"That's right, ma'am. The drought was officially declared over during this spring's floods. You're very welcome. Thank you for calling."

He hung up the phone and turned to me. "Theresita."

"What's happening, Andy?"

"The drought's over, mama."

"Andy, how many times do I have to tell you, white is beautiful, too. Will you please stop trying to be black."

"Oh, oh, baby's got her back up."

"You're treading, Andy."

"Was that a pun? Huh, was that a pun?"

"No. I want to talk to you about rivers."

"The Negro Speaks of Rivers." He made his voice sound deep and dramatic. I refused to smile. Just one twitch of my lips, and he'd work his sorry shtick all day.

"Well," I said, "at least you've been doing your reading. Come on now. I really need your help."

"Damn, you ain't no fun at all. Okay, what can I do you for?"

"I want you to take a look at some sketches." I opened the pad and handed it to him.

"Hmm, hmm."

"What?"

"Interesting primitives . . ."

"You can skip that one. I'm interested only in the river scenes."

"Not bad. Nice shading and use of shadows."

"Not the technique, Andy, the places, the sites. Is there anything significant about them? Are they actual places, even? Do you recognize any of them?"

"Damn, mama, I'm good, but not that good. There's more than a thousand miles of waterways in the Sacramento area counting the Delta. There's the Sacramento and the American rivers of course, but there's also the Consumnes, the Tuolomne, and the Stanislaus, plus scores of sloughs. If these sites are real, they could be anywhere."

He laid the sketch pad flat on his desk and took his time on the river scenes, sometimes turning back to compare scenes. He kept coming back to one scene, the one showing the solitary fisherman on the bank in a lawn chair. "This looks like one of the fish groins sites."

He could tell by the look on my face that he had me. Andy takes great pleasure in confounding me with esoteric water facts and terminology. It's a sort of game with him. Ordinarily, I'd deadpan it, let him explain. But I was in a hurry, so I came right out and asked. "What's a fish groin?"

"What do you think?"

"Modesty prevents me from saying what I think."

"See that triangular thing jutting out into the water, looks kinda like an embankment? That's a fish groin. It slows down the flow of the water, creating protective little eddies where fish can lay eggs."

"So where is this thing?"

"They're in the Delta."

"They? Wait a minute, how many are there?"

"About a hundred and fifty."

"A hundred fifty? I'll never be able to find it."

"Come now, do not despair."

He turned to his computer and keyed in a few strokes.

"Here, I'll run the site map off for you. Why's it so important to find this place anyway?"

"It's something I'm doing for my mother."

The map printed out and he handed it to me. "Happy hunting," he said.

"Yeah, thanks."

I returned to my office. There were no messages from Temp. I called Lawrence Academy to see if he had called. He hadn't. Somebody had to pick up Shawn and that left me. I told Miyako I had a family emergency and I was leaving for the day. I asked her to tell Brenda to cover my three o'clock meeting as well as the others she was already scheduled for. Then I left.

Shawn sat with sullen rigidity in the academy's administrative office. He would not meet my eyes. He did not respond to my greeting.

"I'm sure you'll understand, but we just can't tolerate violence of any type for any reason. Shawn has to find other more productive ways of dealing with conflict."

"This is so unlike Shawn," I said. "Can you tell me what happened?"

"He refuses to discuss it with us. He's been like that

since we pulled the two apart. He cried a bit, but that's all."

"Who was the other child?"

"Wally Hansen. He's not talking either."

"Is he still here?"

"No, his parents had the housekeeper come get him."

"How long is Shawn suspended?"

"Just until tomorrow. We want to give both boys a chance to cool down and to think about how they could have handled the situation differently. We want them to understand that violence is never an acceptable alternative."

I agreed. But I didn't see why I should be the one punished. I was the one dragged away from work in the middle of the day when school was just about over anyway.

"Okay, Shawn, what happened?"

We were on our way to the car. Shawn trudged along silently beside me.

"Nothing."

"Nothing? Seems like a little more than nothing. What did that boy do to you to make you go after him like that?"

I stopped walking and turned to him. He kept his head down. I lifted his chin with my hand. We were just about eye to eye then. "Shawn, I know you well enough to know that's not like you."

Something in his eyes telegraphed his pain to me. I knew the teachers and the staff at Lawrence Academy. I'd had a chance to watch them in action, and I liked what I saw. I believed that they would be fair, but I also knew fairness could mean different things, depending on which cultural prism it's viewed through.

"What did he say to you, baby?" I asked with a little more gentleness, and I watched as his eyes filled. Shawn turned away from me so I couldn't see the tears.

"It's all right Shawn, baby. It's all right."

He leaned against me for a couple of seconds, and I hugged him to me. I didn't want to let him go. We went the rest of the way to the car in silence. We were nearly home before he said, "He called me a name."

"What did he call you?"

"You know."

I felt my anger rising, a hot, white flash before I suppressed it.

"What happened then?"

"I just got so mad."

"I know, baby, I know. Did you explain to Laura what happened, what he said?"

"No."

"Why not?"

"I didn't want to."

I left it at that. I didn't press him. I'd wait to get Temp involved in whatever discussion we had.

"I'd'a dropped him, too," declared Temp.

"Somehow, I expected a more reasoned approach to this whole thing from you. I think you're sending the wrong message to Shawn. He can't go around punching people out every time they call him a name. And slapping him five was not the right response, in my very humble opinion."

"Yeah, but I bet homes won't call nobody else a nigger. Probably even scared of the word *Negro* by now."

My husband. God knows I love him, but there's

asphalt in his blood. The street runs close to the surface in him like some swiftly moving subterranean river. It's liable to surface at the most inopportune times.

"Temp, I expected you to explain to Shawn about the historical weight of the word and how painful it is. And how we should never become complacent about hearing it. I also expected you to explain to him that the Hansen kid obviously felt some sort of inferiority, and he wanted to make Shawn feel just as low, so he called him a name. He called him the most heinous thing he could think of because he wanted to get Shawn to react, to act a fool. He pushed his button, jerked his chain. That's the only power he had. Every time Shawn reacts as he did, there's a shift in power. He ends up having his chain jerked left and right, being manipulated. That's what I expected you to say to Shawn, Temp. Not 'gimme five'."

"Yeah, that's what I meant," said Temp. He put his arm around Shawn and drew him aside.

"Come here, man. We got to talk."

Aisha left her TV show to come into the kitchen where we were. She squeezed past Temp and Shawn on her way to the refrigerator.

"Dad teaching Shawn how to be ghetto?" she inquired in an aside worthy of Groucho Marx.

"Did anybody ask you to come butting in here?" demanded Temp, his gorge rising.

"I live here," retorted Aisha, the master dad-baiter.

I put my arm around her shoulder and pulled her aside. Temp and Shawn, and Aisha and I were now in separate corners. "Aisha, we're trying to help Shawn—"

"Mom, you and Dad are making a big deal out of nothing. He'll get over it."

She held up her hand in a peace sign, only it was a horizontal like the scissors symbol in that children's game, thumped her chest once with the hand—the hip-hop way of waving good-bye—and left.

Chapter Thirteen

I got into work at seven. Brenda was already there, sitting at Miyako's desk, waiting for me. She leapt to her feet when I walked in. "Good, you're here."

"What's going on? You sleep here last night?"

She didn't answer. Instead, she grabbed me by the arm and started dragging me toward my office. "Come on," she said. "We got work to do."

My first reaction was to object vigorously. I don't like people putting their hands all over me. But there was something about her intensity that caused me to hold off. I dutifully followed her to my office.

"Turn your PC on and enter your password. I'll take it from there."

I did as I was told.

"What's going on?"

"I'll tell you in a minute. Let me sit down."

I relinquished my chair to her.

She was in the Windows screen. She opened Netscape the Internet browser, clicked her way through a series of windows.

"See this? This is the disk cache? It keeps a record of every site you visit on the Internet. When you finish cruising, click on this and erase all trails. Clean out your E-mail files, too. Discard any messages that are

not business related. If it's set up to save copies of
outgoing messages, go through them and purge all personal messages. Don't send any more personal messages. Go through your WordPerfect files and delete
everything that not absolutely business related."

She was beginning to worry me.

"What is this all about?"

"Listen, let me finish. Go through all of your office
phone bills. Identify any calls that may not be business
related, no matter how insignificant. Write a check
to the accounting office and pay for them, all of
them. Go back over your travel expense claims for
the last year and make sure you can document everything."

"You're serious, aren't you?"

"As serious as a heart attack."

"Then I think you'd better tell me what's going on."

"Girlfriend is out to get you. She called a one-on-
one yesterday around four. Since I was acting, I went
in your place. She got called out just before I got
there, so I waited, and while I waited, I read through
some of her shit. She's written to the Auditor General's Office and asked for an investigation of you. She's
talking fraud, misuse of state property, conflict of interest, you name it."

To say I was dumbfounded would be an understatement. To say I was angry would have been putting it
mildly. "She's trying to ruin my career, destroy me."

"Uh-huh," said Brenda matter-of-factly.

"But why?"

"You fucked with her, Theresa," Brenda explained
patiently. "You know how she is. You got her
started now."

I was still disbelieving. It wasn't that I didn't believe

what Brenda was telling me was true. It was that I couldn't believe a grown woman would stoop to such lethal pettiness.

Brenda was all business again. "Oh, and go over all the time sheets you've signed, and I'm not talking about just yours, I mean any time sheet you've signed over the past couple of years."

"That's next to impossible. I must have signed hundreds."

"Theresa, look at this as war. Not the ordinary type of war with tanks and shit; think gang war, drive-bys. Heather's getting ready to do a motherfuckin' drive-by on you, girl. What you gone do, stand there and say, 'That's impossible?'"

Ordinarily Brenda's language would have bothered me—it's just the way I was raised. But right now I was concentrating on the message more than the delivery. The message was, any way you cut it, I'd underestimated Heather. And I thought she'd stop at a simple barrage of memos. Silly me. I couldn't afford to make many mistakes like that. For that very reason I had to deal with the one unknown in this whole equation—Brenda Delacore.

"What's your role in all of this, Brenda?" I asked unequivocally.

"What do you mean?" she asked, equivocating like mad.

"You know what I mean, Brenda. I'm touched, believe me, but I'm also a little surprised by your newfound loyalty and support. Why just the other day I seemed to have overheard a conversation between you and 'the braided one' that didn't sound too supportive to me."

Brenda looked slightly uncomfortable, but not out-
raged. It was more like I'd been rude enough to bring
up an unpleasant incident that everyone else with any
kind of manners had already forgotten. "Oh that. You
mean Yvonne Pinkham, right? That was her, not me.
I was just talking along with her. I didn't even go
when she went up to talk to Heather. I told her, 'No,
honey. Leave me out of this. I don't want any part
of this.' "

"Yvonne met with Heather about me? Why didn't
you tell me, Brenda?"

Brenda shrugged. Self-analysis is not her strong suit.
"Did anybody else tell you?"

"What do you mean?"

"When Heather was interviewing your staff, did any
of them tell you? Did Miyako?"

"She interviewed my staff?"

"Come on, come on, get with it." She snapped her
fingers in my face. "Heather's out for blood, your
blood. Hey, I could've sat back and let her work her
thing, but that's not me. Don't worry, I had your
back, girlfriend."

I thanked her sincerely, even though I wasn't so
sure about her sincerity. Having Brenda at my back
wasn't as comforting as she seemed to think it was.
I'd rather keep her out front, way out front, where I
could see her. After that, Brenda and I did a perfunc-
tory review of yesterday's meetings. Nothing had tran-
spired of any significance, at least not when compared
to this morning's meeting. I was still dazed by Brenda's disclosures, if the truth be told. I asked Brenda
to keep herself available in case I needed her to attend
a couple of meetings today, and she readily agreed. I
thanked her again.

"No problem, sister girl," she said and raised her clinched fist in a gesture of solidarity.

That's when I really got worried.

For a long time after Brenda left, I sat at my desk, just shaking my head. I nearly succumbed to the impulse to blame myself—I should have seen it coming, I should have done this, I should have done that—but I caught myself. I'd get nowhere doing that, and I'd just burn up valuable energy that could be better used defending myself against whatever forces Heather was marshaling against me. My professional life was at stake. Up until now, I'd lived a rather charmed life for a black person in state service; promotions had come relatively on time, I had a decent boss, I liked my job. I'd never been in the position of having to fight for my survival like this, and I didn't like it worth a damn. Allen was gone, and the allegiances and alliances in the division had shifted. I didn't know whom I could count on anymore. Then there was the Raymond and Mother thing. Maybe if I hadn't been so preoccupied with them the last couple of days, I could have headed some of this off. The old, familiar feeling of being pulled in too many different directions sent surges of anxiety popping and crackling through me. It was as if Brenda had flipped some hidden circuit before leaving, and I couldn't figure out how to switch it off.

Well, you can't sit here all day, I told myself. Get up. Do something. But I couldn't. I couldn't focus. I was emotionally immobilized. It's a funny thing about crises, they can teach you so much about yourself. I learned sitting there at my desk that I simply couldn't handle chaos the way I used to. Temp, the kids, work, Mother—I careened from one impending disaster to the next. I'd lived like that for so long I hardly noticed it. But now it was paralyzing me.

Finding Raymond and Daddy's missing pictures didn't seem nearly so important when I stacked that up against protecting my job. I needed to touch bases with some of the key players in the department, particularly the ones Heather had alienated, which was probably eighty to ninety percent of them. I took a lined pad and worked out my battle plan. I felt pretty good about it, especially since it left lunch and breaks free to search for Raymond. I knew I should have dropped the Raymond mess right then and there and concentrated on what the governor and the people of the state were paying me to do, but I was already in this far and I couldn't drop it now. Besides, I wasn't so sure Mother's intruder the other night had actually been a burglar. I had a feeling, call it intuition or whatever, that there was more to it than that, and it all came back to Raymond. Mother had been lucky this time, but I wasn't so sure this would be the last time. The next time could be deadly.

Miyako was still out, so I made some calls and set up a couple of meetings for later on that day. Then I purged my computer files. After that I retrieved my phone records from the communications office and painstakingly reviewed every call. When I finished, I wrote out a check for fifty-two dollars and turned that in. By the time I finished, it was nine-thirty. Time for a break.

I dragged my purse out of the bottom drawer and took out my cell phone. I'd make no more personal calls on the office phone, no matter how brief. I said the first three digits out loud of the phone number I intended to call. The last four were not as forth coming, and I had to wrest them from my memory one digit at a time—but I got them. I marveled that after all these years I still remembered that number. Temp would be incensed if he knew.

A young man answered the phone. "Howard's Bail Bonds and Investigations," he said. I asked to speak to Bailey, and he put me on hold. I checked my makeup and hair in the small mirror I keep on my desk. I laughed out loud when I realized what I was doing. It was reflex, pure and simple. Bailey and I broke up more than twenty years ago, but I wanted him to eat his heart out for the rest of his life anyway.

He came on the phone brisk and businesslike with a touch of the authoritarian that he has in his voice. "Bailey Howard speaking."

"Hi, Bailey, this is Theresa."

"Lady T. How's life treating you?"

"Just fine, and you?"

"Can't complain. Nobody'll listen anyway. To what do I owe the honor of this call. No, let me guess. Temp got picked up on 314 and you want me to make bail using your lovely person as collateral."

"No."

"Okay. I'll tell you what. I'll arrange for Temp to be picked up on 314 and I won't make bail, but I'll still need collateral."

"Not that either, Bailey, but I do need your help."

"Let's talk about it," he said, smoothly shifting back to the brisk and professional. And we did. I told him about Raymond's appearance and his disappearance, Mother's delusion, and Daddy's pictures. Bailey understood exactly what I wanted. There was no hemming and hawing. He got right down to business and asked me the essentials. Did I have a Social Security number, prior address, license plate number.

"Nothing, Bailey. He's like a newborn baby. No license, no credit cards, no Social Security number. But I do have a big, fat, perfect fingerprint sample."

"I can work with that. You sure it's his and it's a good print?"

"I'm positive. It even comes with a color photo of our subject."

I told Bailey how I got it, and he complimented me on my astuteness.

"You sure you don't want me to have Temp picked up? I still have friends in city P.D., and I think I could arrange something."

I laughed. "No, Bailey. I think I want to keep him."

"Okay," he said. "Just checking. I'll send a courier around to pick up that print."

I thanked him and hung up. Good ole Bailey. I could always count on him—except in matters of the heart.

I had my phone out. I was stressed out. What the heck, I thought, I might as well call Mother.

She came on the phone, hissing and spitting like some poisonous snake. "I got to get this old man out of my house, do you hear me? I'm sick of him. You know what he got up and ate for breakfast this morning? Sardines! Funky sardines! Stinking up my house."

I told her when she'd let me that I might be close to getting some information on Raymond. I couldn't be too specific, especially about how I was getting the information, because Mother wouldn't have approved. Mother believes married women shouldn't have male friends other than their husbands. It just isn't becoming. Besides, she never did like Bailey.

After the call to Mother, I checked with Brenda to see if she'd heard anything new.

"Parking," she barked. "Are you one of those people who lied and said you were in a car pool so you could be given priority for a parking slot? If so, you'd better take care of it."

I assured her I wasn't. But I didn't tell her that what I was doing was even worse. I had found a way to circumvent the system completely and parked free. I was a parking thief, an outlaw. I'd found one of Temp's old parking stickers and affixed it to my car's bumper. Now I parked in what is called "the old state garage" directly across from the Resources Building without paying for the privilege. At one time I'd felt pretty smug about it—I was sticking it to the parking moguls at General Services. I was a dashing parking outlaw. Now I just felt like a thief, a petty thief, but a thief nonetheless—one who may have slipped the noose around her own neck.

Brenda said she'd keep me posted if she heard anything, then she paused delicately, "Uh, Theresa, if you call me, and I'm not at my desk, uh, don't leave a message, okay? Just keep calling until you can reach me."

I said a few choice words to Brenda before slamming the phone down. The phone rang just as I did, and I snatched it up. "Personnel office, Theresa Galloway speaking." Reflex again. No matter what the circumstances, I'll be professional to the end. But instead of a response, I got the breathing. Slow, measured, rhythmic breathing. I hung the phone up gently. I didn't slam it down. There were no histrionics. I was much too frightened for all that.

I picked the phone up again and cautiously held it to my ear. If I heard that breathing again, I'd scream. I got a steady reassuring dial tone. Forgetting about my commitment not to use my office phone for personal calls, I punched in Mother's number and waited as the phone rang a good twenty times.

"Pick up the phone." I willed her. "Pick up the phone."

Mother picked it up midharangue. "I have told you, stop calling here. I'm not going to keep playing with you. You hear me?"

"Mother it's me, Theresa."

"I'm getting sick of these calls. Every time I turn around, the phone's ringing."

"Did you get a call just before this one, someone breathing?"

"Yes, and the time before that, and the time before that too."

"Mother, I want you to call the police. Are you listening? Call the police and tell them about these calls. I just got one here at work, and it sounded like the person from the other night."

"Whoever it is, they don't scare me."

"Mother, listen. You got those calls all week, and then you had the break-in. I got a call warning me of the break-in. You've been getting calls today. I got a call at work. Don't you see the pattern? Just call the police, okay. Call Lt. Bivens, she'll know what to do."

There was resounding silence on the other end of the line.

"Mother, okay?"

"I'll just stop answering the phone. They'll eventually get tired of playing these games and give up."

"Call the police, please."

"Okay, okay."

"Could I speak to Brother Cummings?"

"What do you want with him?" demanded Mother, a proprietary note creeping into her voice.

"I just want to speak to him, that's all."

"Just a minute," she said. Then without turning from the phone, she yelled into the receiver, "Cleotis, phone."

"Good morning, Sister Galloway. How are you today?"

"I'm just fine, Brother Cummings. And you?"

"Can't complain, can't complain. I am a little stiff this morning, a few aches here and there, but they'll work their way out as the day progresses, the good Lord willing."

Brother Cummings and I worked our way through our intergenerational salutations, then I asked him to listen carefully, and I gave him some very specific instructions. He assured me that he'd follow them to the letter, that he'd give his life if necessary. I assured him that wouldn't be necessary—at least I hoped it wouldn't—then I hung up.

The worst thing you can do is mess with somebody's mother. A person will go crazy, do all kinds of outrageous things, act a stone fool you mess with her mother. Somebody was definitely messing with mine, and I was growing steadily more angry, but that anger was tempered by the cold, sharp edge of rising alarm. I could sit here in this office, indulging in a little cat fight with Heather, or I could deal with the real and

see who was messing with my mother. That was a
no-brainer.

I picked up the phone and called Temp, but he was
on his way out to meet with the insurance adjustor
about the other day's break-in at his warehouse. He
hardly even had time to talk, and I knew going with
me on a tour of the Delta would have been out of
the question, so I didn't ask.

Chapter Fourteen

I was on River Road just south of Sacramento before I allowed myself to deal with the fact that I was heading into the Delta with its thousands of miles of waterways, side roads, and hidden places, and I had no idea of where I was going. To say I was going on a wild-goose chase looking for the places matching Raymond's drawings would have been giving me too much credit. I'm not into fishing or water sports, and other than having diner at Holt's Freeport Inn or going to the pumpkin patch in Clarksville, I haven't spent much time in the Delta. Maybe it's the narrow roads and the spiderweb of waterways that make me nervous. Naturally, I've read and archived in my subconscious all the stories about driving mishaps on the Delta, such as the one about the family of four who accidentally drove off the road into slough and their bodies weren't discovered until four days later. I had Handy Andy's map, but it showed fish groin sites, none of which seemed to be near major highways. Love of mother will make you do foolish things sometimes.

I drove around for an hour and a half before finally admitting that I was lost. It took another hour and a half for me to find my way out of there. I'd blown a large hole in my workday and I hadn't seen even a single fish groin. I wasn't particularly anxious to go back to the office and have to deal with Heather. But I was expecting a call from Bailey, and I needed to check my messages, so I went back.

When I got back to the office, I was relieved to see that the staff hadn't completely jumped ship during my absence, and some were actually working. Brenda was nowhere to be found. I checked with the young man filling in for Miyako and found that there were no messages from Bailey, but I had one from a Mr. Cummings and another from a Mrs. Barkley. Brother Cumming's call had come in two hours before Mother's. I went to my office and punched in Mother's number. The phone rang and continued to ring until I finally hung up. Be calm, I cautioned myself. Don't let your imagination run away with you. Just because you got no answer doesn't necessarily mean something has happened. The phone could be out of order or . . . the wires could have been cut. There you go again, I told myself, imagining the worst. I went back and forth like that until I got hold of myself. Then I picked up the phone and dialed the operator. I told her my problem, and she checked the number, confirming that it was not out of order. I hung up and grabbed my purse. I was heading for the door when the phone rang again.

For a moment I thought it was the breather again, And I was getting ready to hang up when the breathy voice registered. "Get over here quick!" Mother whispered in gushes of rushing air, as if she'd been running.

"What's going on?" I found myself whispering too.

"Girl, I don't have time for all of this chitchat, just get your butt over here before he gets away."

"Who gets away? Mother, where are you? Where's

Brother Cummings? Let me speak to Brother Cummings."

"He can't come to the phone. I left him watching the door."

I wasn't getting anywhere, and Mother was getting more agitated by the second. I didn't want her to hang up before I could find out where she was and what was going on, so I forced myself to slow down. "Mother, just tell me where you are. Okay?"

"The Cairo Club on J Street."

"The Cairo Club? What the hell are you doing at the Cairo Club?"

"I think you'd better watch your tongue."

"What are you doing at the Cairo Club?"

"What *you* should have been doing—trying to find out what happened to Raymond. And if you don't get over here soon, I'm going in there without you. Lord knows I haven't set foot in one of those dens of iniquity in fifty years, but I will if I have to. I started to get Cleotis to go in for me, but that would purely have been a waste of time. You coming?"

I sighed deeply. "Yes, Mother, I'm coming."

I didn't see Mother when I drove past the Cairo Club, so I drove around the block and came back cruising slowly. On my second swing around I finally saw her huddled in the doorway of Belle's Sandwich Shop, peering down the street at the Cairo Club. I pulled over, parked, and got out of the car. She came toward me cautiously, keeping her eyes on the club.

"Now, Mother, what makes you think Raymond is in the Cairo Club?"

"Who said anything about Raymond? I'm talking about that other boy, Lyle."

"Lyle?"

"He knows something about Raymond. Why else would he break and run like that the other day?"

"But, how'd you find him? You sure he's in there?"

"Child, I don't have time for all this chitchat," said Mother, starting for the club.

"Wait a minute. Where's Brother Cummings?"

"He's over there, keeping watch on the door." She pointed across the street.

Brother Cummings sat on a bus stop bench directly across from the Cairo Club. He was as upright as a soldier, the well-stocked bag resting on the ground between his feet.

Mother is easily excited, and she has a way of exciting those around her. I hadn't forgotten—and believe me I've tried—the little incident at the Brass Monkey when I'd taken off chasing a complete stranger just because Mother yelled, "Catch him." I shuddered to think what would happen here if she yelled, "Drop him," and Brother Cummings whipped out his shotgun. I could just read the headlines, "Trio of Demented Negroes Blast Neighborhood Landmark: Nine Hundred and Sixteen People Injured." I had to get them unarmed and off the street before anything happened, but it would require using every wile I possessed.

I leaned toward Mother and lowered my voice. "Okay, I'm going in there after him. But let's develop a strategy just in case he tries something funny."

Mother nodded enthusiastically, her eyes as big as saucers. She grabbed my arm and gazed up into my eyes. "Now, Theresa, I know you're mad about your daddy's pictures and things. I am too. But I just want to know that Raymond is all right."

I nodded. "Okay, Mother, I understand."

At that point I really did understand. She just had to know that he was all right. I just wanted Daddy's pictures back. The two weren't incompatible. "Why don't you and Brother Cummings wait in the car in case Lyle runs again and we have to give chase?"

Mother agreed. She walked to the edge of the curb, took a rather large handkerchief out of her pocket, and waved it over her head in a sweeping arch. Brother Cummings stood up immediately, grabbed his shopping bag and came over where we were.

"I tried my best to keep her out of trouble, Sister Galloway, honestly I did. But, you know Sister Barkley."

"That's all right, Brother Cummings, I know you did your best. Let's put your shopping bag in the trunk. I don't think you'll need it."

I got them settled, Mother in the front passenger seat and Brother Cummings in back. I left the keys just in case they wanted to listen to the radio.

"Do not move the car, okay, Mother? I want it to be right here when I come back."

She nodded.

I left to check out Lyle.

The Cairo Club looked as if it had been around for a long time. A harem girl graced the marquee above the door, her torso outlined in neon tubes. A few years ago the Cairo Club would have been just a seedy, old neighborhood bar, but now it had a certain air of campiness. I pushed the saloon-style doors open and stepped into the darkened interior. The smell of eau de bar hit me right away—alcohol, stale smoke, bulk disinfectant, and something else I couldn't quite identify. It was one of those places that provides free peanuts and encourages the customers to discard the shells on the floor. I guess it was supposed to be hip, but I've always found it slightly disgusting. I crunched my way over to the bar and sat down on the end nearest the door. This gave me a view of the six booths lining the opposite wall and the eight to ten tables scattered about the floor. The bartender pulled himself away from the soccer game he was watching on TV long enough to ask me what I wanted. I ordered a diet cola. He drew it quickly, gave me two straws and a cherry, then turned back to the TV without saying a word. And I thought bartenders were supposed to be the personable, gregarious types.

I sipped my cola and surveyed the room. Three of the tables were occupied. A grizzled old man sat at the one nearest me, holding his beer mug with both hands and working his mouth back and forth over his toothless gums. Two women sat at another. They looked like time warp regulars from the bar's early days. One had on a gray wool fitted suit with broad shoulders and a peplum. Her hair was swept up into a jaunty pompadour. The other wore a burgundy-colored suit of a smiliar cut, but her shoulder-length hair was turned under into a pageboy. She also wore platform shoes with little anklet socks. They had perfectly arched brows and cupids bow lips that looked stenciled on. I had to fight hard to keep from staring. The other table was occupied by three yuppie-looking fellows in well-cut suits. The hair of each was trimmed short, and they wore little wire-rimmed glasses. But I was struck by their soft, well mannered, manicured hands. Two of the booths were filled, one by a kid who looked like he couldn't have been more than sixteen, he had books and papers spread out as if he was doing his homework. The other booth was occupied by Lyle, the running man.

Lyle was reading some sort of tabloid paper, leaning in close as if he were having a hard time seeing in the half light. A few lank strands of hair had worked themselves loose from the rubber band that held his ponytail and hung down in his face. He didn't bother to brush them back. I got up and went over to his booth. He was so engrossed in what he was reading, I stood there for several beats before he looked up. For a moment his face was blank, then the shock registered. He looked as if he might bolt again or break down and weep.

"Excuse me," I said. "My name is Theresa Galloway. I'd like to talk to you for just a moment."

I handed him one of my personnel office cards. His eyes darted up to my face and then down to the card. He had a tic in one eye. One of his shoulders was jumping. He seemed to be trying to control body parts individually, and each time he got one part under control another part would start to twitch.

"I really don't want to bother you, but I'm trying to find my brother, Raymond Johnson, and I understand you're a friend of his."

He'd started shaking his head even before I'd finished.

"But my mother says you came to visit him just before he disappeared."

"I don't know where he is."

His voice was higher and tighter than I would have expected. Maybe it was stress. It was obvious that he was uncomfortable talking to me. It must have seemed that I was looming over him.

"May I sit down?" I asked with the most disarming smile I could muster.

He was at the head shaking again. "No. I . . . I mean I was just leaving . . ."

I sat down anyway. Under different circumstances that might have been a bold move—just walk up to the man's booth and take a seat. But I could see there was little risk in it for me. Lyle had all the markings of those people who are perpetually frightened. They're born that way, and they seem to accept it as a matter of birthright. People who are that scared are usually cowards, too. I figured I had nothing to worry about with Lyle as long as other people were around. I wouldn't take any bets on a dark alley though.

His distress was changing hues now. He'd gone white as a sheet when I first walked up; now he was a flaming red. I slid into the booth across from him, and just as I'd feared, he jumped up. He wore one of those zippered purses strapped around his waist, the kind bikers and joggers use. His was outsized and black and hung obscenely low under his belt line.

"Please don't leave. I really need your help."

He was gone before I could get the words out. He left his paper behind. I turned it over—*News and Review*. Just under its edge was a little black device similar to the electronic key to my car. I picked it up and went to the bar.

"Excuse me," I said to the bartender. When he ripped his vision away from the screen, I said, "Lyle left this," holding the little remote thing up and making sure to use Lyle's name as if we were friends or something. "I'll take it to him, but I'm not sure exactly where he lives."

The bartender extended his hand. "Give it to me. I'll make sure he gets in the next time he comes in."

I moved mine back out of his reach. "I really think I ought to make sure he gets it today. I think he needs it."

The bartender had already dismissed me and gone back to the TV.

"Try the Claridan Arms, honey. Twenty-two, twenty-five L Street. I think that's where he's crashing these days."

I turned around. It was the woman in the burgundy suit. Her voice was low and raspy, probably from too-much liquor and too many cigarettes. She smiled rakishly. The other, the one with the pompadour, threw her head back and laughed a big haw, haw, haw. I wasn't in on the joke, but I was grateful for the information anyway.

"It's either apartment four or five, way in the back."

I thanked her.

"That's all right, honey," she rasped. "We girls have got to stick together."

I was getting ready to ask her if she knew Lyle's last name when a car horn started to blast right outside the door. Then I heard Mother's voice.

"Theresa! Get out here!"

Mother had pulled up outside the Cairo Club—in my car. I was pissed, royally pissed. If I wanted my car wrecked, I would have turned it over to Aisha. I marched around to the driver's side. I wanted to snatch the door open and haul her out.

"Mother," I said with admirable restraint, "I asked you not to move the car."

"Get in," she demanded. "He's getting away."

"You are not driving anywhere. If I have to throw myself down in front of this car, I will."

That got her attention. I was serious and she knew it. Brother Cummings was in the front seat next to her. They both had to get out so he could climb in back and she could take his place. Somehow during these complicated maneuvers they managed to lock the keys in the car. I held up my hand the way Moses must have when he was calming the worried Israelites. Then I fished in my purse and found my electronic key. I dramatically pointed it at the car, the alarm made a chirping sound, and the locks popped open.

Old people and children—I like to impress them whenever I can.

We all got loaded into the car with me in my rightful place behind the wheel. When seat belts were fastened securely, I drove to the corner and turned right.

"Hey, where you going? He didn't go this way."

"Mother, I am right here, not down the block. You do not have to yell. I am taking you and Quick Draw McGraw here home where you belong. And before you remind me again that Lyle's getting away, I should tell you that I have his address."

"Well, why didn't you say so in the first place?"

"Because I had other things on my mind such as protecting the other drivers, innocent pedestrians, and various and sundry household pets."

"Are you trying to say something about my driving? 'Cause if you are, I'll have you know I drive just as good as the next person, don't I, Cleotis?"

Brother Cummings wisely kept quiet.

As we drove to Mother's house, I explained what I had learned from Lyle.

"Nothing, absolutely nothing," said Mother, paraphrasing what I'd just said.

"Mother, I have just one question for you. How in the world did you find Lyle?"

"Well, after you told me what that boy at the restaurant told you about Lyle working at all those places under the table, I got an idea. I got dressed, put on my walking shoes, and caught the bus downtown. Then I walked over to Old Sacramento and worked my way through those restaurants until I found out where this Lyle hung out."

"You just walked in, asking questions, and they told you?"

"No, girl. I had to use a little bit more sense than that. First off, I went to the back doors. They're always standing open, and the people I wanted to talk to would be the ones who work back there. I told them I was Lyle's fourth-grade teacher and I was just in town for a few days and I wanted to see him and see how he turned out. They all thought it was funny. I take it he hasn't turned out too well. But by the third restaurant I had learned his last name is Chromsky, and by the fifth one I knew he liked to go to the Cairo Club. So I caught the bus and went there."

"I was with her every step of the way," added Brother Cummings.

"You mean you didn't know for sure that he was even in there when you called me?" I asked incredulously.

"Well, I had a feeling," said Mother.

I wanted to respond to Mother's feeling, but it wouldn't have done any good, so I clamped my jaws shut so tight my ears started to ring. Coming fresh off my humiliation in the Delta, I didn't need any of this. I sure hoped Bailey had something for me soon. My protective fervor for Mother was fading fast. It was almost five, and I had something important to do at home, but for the life of me I couldn't think what it was.

We finally pulled up in front of Mother's house.

"Did you lock up good and tight?" I asked, more in the way of making conversation than anything else.

"Of course I did, miss. And I would have put the alarm on too except your husband hasn't fixed it yet."

She was sniping. Brother Cummings looked uncomfortable. I let it pass. All I wanted was to get her unloaded and into her own house and then I was out of there.

I parked and opened the door for both of them. While they were coaxing balking joints to cooperate so they could haul themselves out of the car, I went to the trunk and removed Brother Cummings's shopping bag. I came back and gave Mother a hand as Brother Cummings succeeded in extricating himself from the backseat.

"You are coming in, aren't you?" asked Mother.

"No, I've really got to get home."

"Suit yourself. But I wanted to show you the keys I found."

"Mother I'm tired, I've had a difficult day thanks in part to you, I have something to do that I can't remember, and I have the feeling that Temp, Aisha, or somebody is going to be pissed off at me when I get home. Please, Mother, don't play with me."

Mother turned and marched through her yard and up the stairs to her front door. Brother Cummings followed, lugging his shopping bag, and I, hating myself every step of the way, brought up the rear.

Mother went straight to the buffet. She scooped up the keys, handed them to me, and watched with satisfaction as I examined them.

They were three relatively nondescript keys. One, the bronze-colored Schlage, obviously was a door key. It was the right size and shape. It was harder to tell with the other two. They were smaller, silver-colored, with no markings.

"Where did you find them?"

"In the suitcase."

"But we checked the suitcase."

"I know, but after you couldn't get any information about Lyle, I went back over that room with a fine-tooth comb. I made up my mind if there was anything else there, I was going to find it. I was searching the suitcase, and I stuck my hand in that pocket where we found Walter Lee's picture. I was rubbing it around in there, and I felt something like a lump on the suitcase wall. I peeled back the lining, and there they were, taped to the wall of the suitcase under the lining. Now, if you had a key you didn't want to lose, you might pin it to your underwear—I've done that myself—but tape it to the wall of a suitcase under the lining?"

"Did you try them on the doors around here?"

"Of course."

Mother was smiling smugly.

"And?"

"They don't fit anything."

"So where does that leave us?"

"It's simple," replied Mother. "We find out what these keys belong to, and we've got our answer."

I took the keys from Mother, not because I thought I could do anything with them, but because I didn't want her running around all over town checking people's locks for a fit. I said good-by and left quickly before she came up with anything else.

Chapter Fifteen

I headed home, still struggling with the nagging feeling that I was forgetting something. Whatever it was vanished completely when I drove up to the house and found Aisha camped outside on one of the landscape boulders, waiting for me. I stopped in the driveway and got out. "What are you doing out here, honey?"

"I was just waiting to say good-by," she said with a touch of melodrama. "I'm leaving. I can't stay in this house."

"Now, what happened?"

She looked up at me accusingly. I was supposed to be on her side.

"Daddy's always on Shawn's side. Come yelling at me calling me names. He called me a spoiled brat. He called me impertinent."

She was wailing now, her head resting on my stomach.

"Come on in the house, honey."

"No, I'm not going in there. I'm leaving."

"Where're you going?"

"Anywhere but here. I'll spend the night with Grandmother and then I'll decide."

"I don't think it would be a good time to stay over at Mother's. She's been having some troubles at her house, and Brother Cummings is staying there right now."

I finally convinced Aisha to go inside and consider other options. Temp was stomping around angry and refused to talk to me, except to say it was my fault that Aisha was so mouthy and it was also my fault that Shawn was having problems at school. He stopped short of saying it was my fault that his business was suffering and he was scared. He slept downstairs that night with the TV remote his only comfort. And I never did figure out what I'd forgotten.

The auditors showed up at eight-thirty. I showed them where the files were and retired to my office. Bailey's call came a short time later.

"Well, Lady T, I've got the information you wanted. Give me your number and I'll fax it to you. It is confidential, to make sure nobody else intercepts it."

"I've got auditors here and everything. Can you just give me the information over the phone?"

"Sure, here goes. Name: Raymond Johnson."

"Really?" I interrupted. "That's his real name?"

"According to the records. Date of birth: March 6, 1971. Place of birth: Manila, Philippines. California driver's license number EO 765223. Last known address—"

"Wait a minute. Did you say place of birth the Philippines? You mean he was born in the Philippines?"

"Generally speaking, place of birth is where you were born."

"You're not playing with me are you, Bailey?"

"Afraid not. According to the state's data base the prints you gave me belong to one Raymond Johnson who was born in Manila on March 6, 1971. My guess is his old man was in the service."

"He wasn't born in Pinebluff? What's going on?"

"Bad guys don't always tell the truth, T."

"Tell me about it. He even has a California driver's license. What's his address?"

Bailey gave me the address and warned me not to do anything foolish. I assured him I wouldn't, thanked him politely, and hung up. I was like that proverbial duck—calm and polite on the surface but paddling like hell underneath. My heart was pummeling the inside of my chest so hard it was as if I had a tiny kickboxer locked in there. I counted to fifteen to calm myself down. If I wasn't careful, I'd end up with another of my migraines, and this was no time for that now. Not when everything was finally falling into place. I had Raymond's address, and that proved he was a liar, a cheat, and a phony. The little raw boy's goose was cooked. I should have been estactic. Now I could expose Raymond for the liar that he was. And expose Mother for what? A lonely old woman who wanted to believe that a young man who just showed up one day really did carry her husband's genes. A lonely old woman who may have secretly begun to believe in reincarnation. Suddenly, I didn't have the stomach for all the exposing I'd have to do.

Raymond was already gone, and that saved me the problem of getting him out of Mother's house. The only thing that remained was getting back Daddy's pictures. I imagined myself bogarting my way into Raymond's place, demanding Daddy's pictures, and then pulling him out of there by the scuff of his scrawny neck, marching him back to Mother's and letting her tongue lash him to within an inch of his life.

If only life had imitated daydreams, things would have been so easy. And there wouldn't have been any blood.

I pulled myself together and called the River City Buffet, the eighth-floor cafeteria, and ordered two large carafes of coffee, one decaf and the other regular, and an assortment of pastries and fresh fruit. When the order was delivered, I set up a continental breakfast for the auditors in one of the vacant interview rooms and invited them to help themselves. They looked surprised and pleased. I reminded them that my staff would get them whatever they needed, but I had a meeting out of the building and I wouldn't be available until that afternoon. I called Brenda and told her she was in charge.

Then I left for Raymond's house.

The Claridan Arms was a fancy name someone had given an old, rambling, clapboard house that was now divided up into a series of apartments of odd dimensions. Number five was way in the back, just as the woman in the bar had said. From the looks of it, the apartment had once been the carriage house but was now connected to the main house by a breezeway. It had the most peculiar door. It was an old, faded, sturdy door. It was nicked and scared and discolored. But the shiny door handle that replaced the doorknob obviously was new. So was the small electronic keypad with the blinking red light that had been carefully fitted into the doorjamb at shoulder height. It didn't look like any home security system I'd ever seen. First of all, it was on the outside of the house instead of the inside, and second it looked like something that belonged on a car. Strange folk.

I pulled myself away from my musings about why people do strange things and knocked on the door. No answer. I knocked again. Still no answer.

"Lyle, Lyle Chromsky," I called.

I didn't bother calling Raymond. If he was hiding out, he wouldn't answer anyway, but Lyle might. I pounded on the door this time, no genteel little tap, tap, tap. No answer. Nothing stirred either.

I squeezed between the house and the fence to see if any windows were open. Not that I was planning to crawl through any. It was just that when you live this close to downtown I'd expect you to close your windows when you go out. So if windows were open, that would indicate to me that someone was home. None of the three windows on that side were open. In fact, they were boarded up, each one of them. Old scrap wood with bright swaths of paint still on them were nailed across them. I came back around to the front and walked through the breezeway to the street side of the house. None of the windows on this side were boarded. Strange. Who would squeeze between the house and fence to break windows out and leave the perfectly accessible ones whole? Even if it had been a burglar, he wouldn't need to break three windows, one would do.

I went back to the door. It didn't seem that anyone was in there, and I was tired of knocking. "Now what?" I said out loud. Try the key. It was uncanny how the thought popped into my head. I had forgotten all about the key. It had to fit something. It was just as likely to fit this lock as another somewhere else. I took the keys out of the side pocket on my purse, where I'd stuck them. I stood there holding them in

my hand just staring at them, and my conscience
kicked in.

"What the hell do you think you're doing? I hope
you know this is breaking and entering." I don't think
it's actually breaking, not if you have a key.

"A technicality. You're trespassing at the very
least."

Okay, okay, I'll just try the key and see if it fits,
that's all.

The key glided in just as smooth. And quickly, before I could have second thoughts, before the more
rational part of me could talk me out of it, I grabbed
the handle with my other hand and quickly turned it
until I heard it click. And set off an explosion of sound
so piercing I felt the plates in my skull grinding against
each other. I dropped my purse, scattering its contents
on the ground and clasped my hands over my ears.
My eyes were watering, and I felt nauseated, the
sound was so intense and engulfing. I remember thinking fleetingly that it was enough to wake the dead. If
only it had been.

Somehow between the pulses of expanding sound
crowding my skull and threatening to crack it, a
thought lodged itself there. I dropped to my knees,
and with hands that seemed shorn of fingers—maybe
the sound had blasted them off—I patted through the
contents of my purse until I found the little device
Lyle had left at the Cairo Club. Clutching it awkwardly, I aimed it at the door and pressed everything
on it that even remotely resembled a button. At some
point I realized the sound had stopped. And it hadn't
destroyed me. What do you call death by sound
anyway?

Surely the neighbors would be piling out of their

apartments by now, summoned by that fiendish blast
of sound. The police would be on their way here, having been called hours ago when the alarm first went
off. I swung around to face the accusing eyes and
pointing fingers, but no one was there.

All right, I told myself, so far so good. If anybody
was in there, by now I'd know it. I got this far, I'm
going in. And I did.

The first thing that hit me was the smell. It was
stronger than just plain old funk. Stronger and
stranger too. I felt my pores tighten against that smell.
My nostrils shut down all operations, closed off communications, and I was breathing through my mouth.
It was dark in there. The boarded-up windows shut
off most of the natural light. I felt around the door
for the light switch, and when I found it and clicked
it on, the second thing that hit me was that something
terrible had happend here. It was as if the demonic
sound had taken on a physical being and had flung
furniture around until it was nothing more than jag-
gered sticks, put its foot through the TV screen,
dashed electronic equipment against some walls,
punched holes in others, and ripped clothes into
threads.

I knew I should have gotten out of there right then
and there, but somehow I just couldn't. It was like
being trapped in one of those sleepwalking dreams
where you have to face all kinds of horrors even as
you're fighting and struggling with all your might to
wake up. The front door opened into the living room,
and I could see the entire living quarters from where
I stood. Directly ahead was the bedroom, to its right
was a small bathroom, and to the right of that was an
efficiency kitchen. Every room seemed to have suf-

fered similar abuse. In the kitchen the small refrigerator was lying on its side in a puddle of water and spoiled food. But the greatest abuse was to be found in the bedroom. There, stripped naked and beaten almost beyond recognition, was where I found Raymond. As a final indignity and an act of unspeakable brutality, the murderer had propped his body up and nailed his outstretched hands to the wall.

Chapter Sixteen

A patrol officer got there first. He asked me to show him where the victim was. But I refused. I stood rooted to the ground, weeping like a child and shaking my head. A crowd hadn't gathered yet, but a few people were taking note. A couple stopped to watch. The officer left me sitting on the steps in front of the Claridan Arms like some outsized latch key kid and went back to make his own grisly discoveries.

By the time the homicide detectives and their entourage of technicians and lights and camera folks got there, I had pulled myself together. The little makeup I hadn't cried off I wiped off with the lone tissue I found in my purse. I'd run a comb through my hair and straightened my clothes. And I was ready for their questions. Lt. A. Rivera and Det. G. Lant took my statement as a team of officers worked their way through the Claridan Arms, interviewing the residents, and another team canvassed the neighborhood.

"You said Mr. Johnson was your brother?" asked Lt. Rivera.

"No," I explained, "not exactly. Raymond claimed to be my brother. He showed up at my mother's one day out of the blue, said he was from Arkansas and he was looking for his father. He said he was my father's child by another woman. My mother believed him and took him in."

"But you did not?"

"No, I didn't. I knew he was lying, trying to take advantage of her."

"How was he trying to take advantage of her?"

"I'm not exactly sure, but I felt he was after something. Why else would he have lied his way into her house? He wasn't homeless or anything; he had his own place. He was after something."

"What do you think he was after?"

"I've racked my brain on that one, and I just don't know. Nothing's missing as far as I can tell except for some family pictures."

"Okay, go on."

"A couple of days ago Raymond disappeared, and my Mother and I had been trying to find him."

"Why?" asked Lt. Rivera.

"Why?" I parroted.

"If you didn't believe he was your brother and you thought he meant to take advantage of your mother. When he finally left, why did you try to find him?"

I started to tell him that if he knew Mother he wouldn't have to ask that question, but I didn't think an answer like that would be prudent. Instead, I explained, "Mother thought he'd gotten lost or something. You see he'd told us he was from out of state and he'd never been here before. Besides, I wanted to get those family pictures back from him."

"Okay, now would you explain again how you found out where Mr. Johnson lived."

"Mother had seen this man, Lyle Chromsky, come by the house. We happened to see Lyle last week at the Brass Monkey, where he worked as a kitchen helper. Lyle left before we had a chance to talk to him. But some people told us where he lived, and that's how I ended up here."

"Was the apartment locked when you got here?"

"Uh, yes."

"How did you get in?"

"I used a key Mother found in Raymond's luggage."

"You knew Raymond lived here too?"

"That's what one of the people we talked to told us. Look, I really wanted those pictures back. When I got here, I banged on the door and nobody answered. In fact, I banged several times. As a sort of lark I tried the key Mother'd found, and unfortunately it worked."

"Why do you say unfortunately?"

"I didn't want to find him in there like that. Not in a million years."

They asked me to tell them exactly what I did after I unlocked the door, what I touched, how long I was in there, what I observed. I answered as best I could. Then Det. Lant asked me about Mother.

"Do you think she'd be willing to talk to us?"

"Oh my God, I forgot about Mother. Somebody will have to tell her."

I looked at Lt. Rivera and then Det. Lant. "It might be better if it came from someone she knew," said Det. Lant.

I knew she was right, I just didn't want the someone to be me. I gave them Mother's address and asked them to give me a half hour before they came. Det. Lant hesitated.

"If you don't mind, we'll have someone drive you there and bring you back later to get your car."

"There'd be a police car outside of her house. She'd

know something was wrong the minute we drove up, and that would only make it more difficult for me. Believe me, once she gets over the shock, she'll want to talk to you. She'll probably look you up herself if you don't get to her soon enough."

"We won't send a marked car."

There was something in the way she said that. Were they considering me a potential suspect? Mother too?

To say I dreaded walking in Mother's door, carrying this burden, would have been the understatement of the year. I thought back to last year when I had to be the one to break the news to an old man that his sister had been killed and he really acted a fool on me. Started cussing, breaking up furniture and things. Threw me out of his house. You never can tell how a person will take bad news. I wasn't worried so much about Mother acting a fool—I deal with that every day—it's the quiet tears that get me. Like when Carolyn died and Daddy.

I broke the news to Mother with Brother Cummings hovering in the background. When he thought things were getting too intense, he fled to the kitchen, where he busied himself alternatingly boiling water and cracking ice. If Mother had been having a baby, he would have been well prepared. I don't know what the ice was for—maybe cocktails.

"I knew it, I knew it. Didn't I tell you, didn't I? I said, 'Something has happened to that boy.' Somebody kidnaped him and did away with him. Theresa . . ."

I held her hand. "Don't even say it, Mother."

She started sputtering "buts."

I held firm. "We're going to let the police handle this one."

"But . . ."

"I know you accepted Raymond as Daddy's child . . ."

"No, I didn't."

"What?" I asked with disbelief.

"I said, 'No, I didn't.' I knew he was lying when he said Walter Lee wrote those letters."

"I knew he was lying way before that, but what did the letters have to do with it? To me, they and the picture were the most credible parts of his story."

"That's all well and good, but I know for a fact Walter Lee didn't write those letters."

"But you believed him up until then. You were calling him 'Raymond, honey,' and he was calling you 'Mom.' And you were so concerned about his feelings, you got mad at me when I told you he was lying."

"The boy's dead, and here you are still acting jealous."

"I am not jealous."

"Yes, you are."

"I am not."

"Ladies, ladies," interrupted Brother Cummings. "I believe someone's at the door."

"Cleotis, don't you be starting with your parlor games," admonished Mother. But before she could go any further, we heard the knock on the door. And I remembered the detective waiting in the car to take us downtown for our interviews.

"Mother, I forgot to tell you the police would like to ask us some questions."

"Well, open the door, baby, and let them in."

Mother readily granted the detective permission to go through Raymond's things. When he finished, he drove us to the police department where Mother answered all their questions and then some. They thanked us when they finished, and an officer drove us back to my car, which I'd left at the Claridan Arms.

We drove a couple of blocks before Mother turned to me. "I tried to tell them Lyle did it."

"Yes, Mother, you did your best. But you never can tell about the police. They seem to be a lot better at asking questions than answering them. For all I know, they could suspect me."

Mother pooh-poohed that idea.

"You have a good job working for the state. Why on earth would you go around killing people? You could lose your job for that."

"Mother, I did find the body."

"Yes, but you don't know how long it had been there. He could have been killed anytime within the last five days. Did he look like he had been dead a long time?"

"How was I to know? He was dead, that's all I know."

"I'm just trying to get an idea when he was killed. Did he look all stiff?"

"Mother, I tried not to look at him at all, it was so pitiful. But it did look like he had been dead for a while, maybe a couple of days. I really don't want to talk about how he looked."

Mother put her hand on my shoulder. "I know, baby. It must have been horrible for you, finding him like that."

I nodded.

"You can imagine how I feel. He was almost my son."

She was serious, so out of respect I didn't say anything. Besides, I was busy trying to run a few dates through my head. I met Raymond on a Tuesday, I had lunch with him and Mother on a Thursday, that same night he left home and didn't return, Mother had the break-in early Saturday morning, and I discovered Raymond's body on Monday. Something had been set in motion five days, two weeks, maybe as long as two decades ago, and it was inexorably working its way to a close with Mother standing smack dab in its path. Many lies and one death down—I hated to think what the final toll might be.

"Explain that to me again," said Mother. "Raymond was from Sacramento, not Tucker, Arkansas?"

"He's even listed in the phone book. I never considered looking there. He was born in the Philippines, apparently to a military family. I probably could get more information on his background, but it hardly matters now. I guess Lyle was his roommate. He was probably in on whatever Raymond was trying to pull. I guess that's why he ran when he saw you."

"To think I trusted that boy."

"Mother, we've got to face the fact that the person who broke into your house and the person who killed Raymond may be one and the same."

"You think so?"

"It's a possibility. If he didn't find what he was looking for here the first time, which I doubt, and if he didn't get it from Raymond either before or after he killed him, then he may be back."

"That's good. That's just what we want."

"No, Mother, that is not what we want. You want to win the lottery and settle in Aruba, I want to run the Bay to Breakers and finish. Neither of us wants a murderer making impulse visits in the middle of the night."

"You seem to have forgotten that I shot my burglar.

If he does come back, I don't think he'll be moving that fast."

"Yes, but he'll probably make up for his lack of speed in attitude. He'll probably be very pissed—that is, if he comes back himself."

"I'll tell you one thing, I'll be ready for him this time. I sure wish the police hadn't taken my gun, though."

"Mother, what are you planning?"

Mother sat back in her seat, smiling smugly. She didn't bother answering my question.

Chapter Seventeen

The auditors were still at work going through personnel office records. They were courteous and polite, but they were doing a thorough job looking for evidence of my maleficence. And they ate more donuts than anybody I'd ever seen. Personnel office staff seemed overly subdued. It was almost as if they were listening for some alarm that might go off any minute, and they wanted to be ready when it did. Heather was lying low, letting the machinations she'd set into play work their way through. Brenda had on yet another power suit, and every now and then I'd catch a glimpse of shiny vinyl orange braids as Yvonne Pinkham flittered by.

I was caught in a web of family obligations, work intrigues, and murder. And here I was sitting in my little office with walls that didn't even go all the way up to the ceiling, trying to defend myself from Heather, mediate Brenda's messes, attend my meetings, and do all of the other things that make a bureaucrat's life so full and rewarding.

I opened a desk drawer, took out a vacation request form, and filled it out before I had second thoughts. I needed to keep everything clean and aboveboard. I'd take the rest of the week off on vacation and leave Brenda in charge. Let Heather deal with her. I was going over my calendar, trying to decide what meetings could be rescheduled, when I got a call that a Mr. Lambert was here to see me at the front counter.

"Mrs. Galloway, I'm back. I hope you won't throw me out on my ear again."

He was back all right. He looked a little more pasty than before, if that's possible, and there were dark circles around his eyes that I hadn't noticed on our first meeting. But he emanated a curious sort of energy, a buzz almost. He was still GQ-ed down in his ragbag pickings, but now he'd topped everything off with a down skijacket. He must have gotten a deal on the jacket and meant to get plenty of wear out of it, even on unseasonably warm days like today.

"I haven't changed my—"

He interrupted me. "I'm working on something different now."

He leaned toward me across the counter and lowered his voice. "I'm doing something on gay bashing."

"I don't see how I can help you. Maybe you should talk to Aaliyah Truman. She's the department's Equal Employment Opportunity Officer."

He looked perplexed. "You are the one who found the body, aren't you, that Johnson kid? I didn't think there were two of you, two Theresa Galloways."

Now it was my turn to look perplexed. "Well, yes I am. But I fail to make the connection."

"The police didn't tell you, did they?" He paused as if considering the possibility of the police withholding information and smiled. "No, I don't suppose they did. The kid was another bashing victim. The seventh this year."

"Bashing victim?"

"He was gay. That's what got him killed."

The police hadn't told me anything. Nobody had told me anything. So Raymond was gay. I toyed momentarilly with feeling a bit smug—not only was Raymond a liar . . . But I remembered how I'd found him, and my heart rebelled. I'd been mad enough to hurt him myself, but he didn't deserve what happened to him. Nobody deserved that.

Lambert studied me as I tried to process the little nugget he'd dropped on me. There was something about his expression. It wasn't pity or compassion or even ghoulish curiosity that I read there. It reminded me of that look you have when you're waiting for one of those instant photographs to develop and you're wondering if it took.

"Mr. Lambert, tell me something. How did you get my name in connection with this?"

"It was in the paper."

"I don't recall talking to any reporters."

He held up the Metro section of the *Bee*.

"It's right here. They probably picked it up from the police report. Look, I won't take much of your time. I know this must be a difficult time for you."

"And you're on this story, too?"

"Like I told you, I freelance. I see a story, I get on it. Already got this one sold. Sacramento *News and Review*. Holding the presses."

"I wish I could help you, Mr. Lambert. But I found the body, that's all. I really didn't know him all that well."

"What about your mother? You think she might be able to give me some background information?"

"No, absolutely not. My mother knows even less than I do. I don't want her disturbed. I hope you understand, but she's just not well."

He looked skeptical.

I was almost tempted to talk to him, answer a few questions, and send him on his way. Anything to keep him from snooping around Mother's house. Things were already bad enough with the hant, the burglar, and now the murder. But I didn't know this man. He said he was a freelance writer, but anyone could call themselves that. It wasn't like he worked for the *Bee* or something. And even if he was a writer, I didn't want my family's business spread all out before the reading public. In fact, a writer was the last thing I needed right now. I wanted Daddy's pictures back, but I didn't see how a freelance writer could help me with that. Maybe if he had said he was a psychic, I would have been more interested.

"Mr. Lambert, I know you're probably tired of hearing this, but I just don't think I can help you."

He nodded. "I'd like to try to change your mind. Let me take you to lunch—my treat?"

"No, I'm sorry. I really don't have the time."

"You change your mind, give me a call."

I agreed, and he turned to go. I watched as he walked to the door, his body held a little too rigidly, as if he had slept bad the night before and woke up stiff. I wondered if he was homeless, sleeping where he could, trying to make a buck selling stories. I'd heard of stranger things. I understand the guy who stands in front of Woolworth's on the K-Street mall, playing a kazoo, has a Ph.D.

I got his call a couple of hours later.

"I got something I think you might be interested in."

"What is it, Mr. Lambert?"

"Some pictures. Bought 'em off a kid. He's still

here. If you hurry, you can take a look at him, see if you know him."

The Tom Tom Club where I agreed to meet him was another of those fine neighborhood establishments on the order of the Cairo Club, only this one offered recreation in the form of one pool table and three arcade games. I could hear country music, the kind with lots of yodeling, playing inside. I was getting tired of touring these funky little joints, and I made up my mind that my next meeting with a freelance journalist, murder suspect, or whatever would be at the Café Bernardo.

An old man sat to the side of the Tom Tom Club's door on an overturned crate, selling homemade crepe paper flowers. It didn't look like he'd sold many.

"How much?" I asked him.

"Anything you want to give, ma'am."

I dropped in a dollar as I passed.

"Ma'am, don't forget your flower."

I came back and took one.

"For that much you should get two, ma'am."

But I didn't know what I was going to do with this one, so I waved him off and kept going.

Lambert must have been watching for me. He stood and waved me over to his table as soon as I walked in. He still had on that damn down jacket.

"Glad you could make it," he said. "Can I get you anything?"

I declined.

"You have a hard time finding the place?"

"No. Mr. Lambert, about—"

"Lambert is fine. You can drop the mister part. I keep turning round to see if my old man's here." He laughed a couple of snorts. "How you like this place? Kinda homey, huh?"

It depends on the kind of home you come from, I thought. But I was much too police to say so.

I got down to business. "You said you had some pictures."

He pulled Daddy's picture from inside his jacket and handed it to me. My breath got caught in my throat. "How'd you get this?"

"Some kid mentioned that this other kid had a bunch of Johnson's stuff. I tracked him here. Bought it off him. He swears he didn't steal it. Says it was with some stuff Johnson gave to him."

"He still here?"

"Naw. Left right after I called."

"That's my father," I explained. "Some other pictures are missing too."

"This was the only one he had."

"May I have it back?"

"Yeah, sure."

"What else have you found out about Raymond?" I asked.

"He was well known on the local gay scene. And well liked, I might add. Could have been elected mayor of Lavender Flats if he wanted to. Liked to party. Got busted a few times, nothing serious. Numerous partners. Supposedly true love left him a year ago and set up housekeeping with someone else. But I understand they keep in touch."

"How do you know all this?"

"I'm a professional. I got busy after talking to you this morning. Actually, I was already working on this one indirectly. Remember that Gonzales kid who was on his way to work and got shot standing at the bus stop? And that other kid, Pinter? Gay bashing. And that's only the tip of the iceberg. I got some figures will put you off your feed for a month. Gay bashing is at an epidemic high right here in River City."

"How can you be so sure that's what happened to Raymond?"

"It has all the earmarks. Look at the way he was beaten. What are the reasons for beating a person? To humiliate, to control, to inflict pain, to disable, to kill. I'll bet you dollars to donuts what was done to Raymond went way beyond that. You know what it makes me think of, huh? Performance art."

The image of Raymond, his hands nailed to the wall, flashed through my mind. "Why would anyone do something like that?"

"To teach a lesson, instill fear, leave a message."

"What kind of message?"

"A message of hate."

I sat there shaking my head. I seemed to have been doing that a lot lately. I was about ready to cry in my beer, except I didn't have one. Lambert watched me.

"I'm trying to reconstruct Raymond's last forty-eight hours for my story. Pathos. Walk a mile in his shoes. That kind of thing."

"Who did you say you're writing this story for?"

"Freelance. I freelance. I've written for all the major rags, and some not so major, the *Times*, the *Observer, The New Yorker, Mother Jones*. I even had a piece in *Rolling Stone* once."

I found his résumé a little hard to beleive considering his scruffy attire and his lone, recycled business card.

"This seems to be more of a local issue. Aren't you

putting a lot of time and effort into a story that those publications might not even be interested in?"

"That's the nature of the beast. I'm not too worried. I'll sell it somewhere. The story's the same anywhere you go. Change a name here, a place there, it's still the same story. I did a cock fight down in the Delta, sold the story to a rag in Phoenix. Now there's a story where the real story went untold. Made myself eight hundred dollars that night."

"Raymond's friend, you called him his true love, what did you say his name was?"

"Mettler. Gil Mettler. Owns Pronto Prints on Marconi."

He seemed to be sizing me up.

"Look here, I've been open with you. I even found that picture for you. You think you can answer just a few questions? I want this story. And I know you want to find out what happened to your brother."

"Wait a minute. I think we'd better straighten this out right now. Raymond wasn't my brother."

He held up his hand. "I did a little homework before I even went to your office today. I talked to a few people. Raymond told folks that he had a new-found family here in town. I thought that might be you and your mother."

"Raymond made a lot of claims that were untrue. He claimed to have been from Arkansas, which you and I both know was untrue. He also claimed to be my father's child, which was untrue. However, my mother believed him, and she allowed him to move in with her."

Lambert was nodding his head as if it all added up.

"He was there for a couple of weeks, and then he disappeared. That's it. You know the rest."

"He wasn't your brother. That does give things a different slant. Could he have been blackmailing your mother?"

I laughed out loud. "Come on now."

"Okay, I'd say he was trying to run some kind of scam on her. What was he after, her pension check?"

"I don't know. We've racked our brains over that, but we haven't been able to come up with anything."

"Was anything missing after he left?"

"Just some family pictures."

"Paintings?"

"No, snapshots of my father. That's it. We've searched the house, and that's the only thing we can find that's missing. He even left some of his own stuff there."

"What?"

"Just an empty suitcase, a couple of pieces of clothing, that's all. Oh, and a notebook with some sketches."

"I'd sure like to see that. You got it on you?"

I pulled it out of my purse and handed it to him. He flipped through the pages.

"Nice pictures. Do you think they mean anything?"

I shrugged. I didn't want to have to go into my escapade on the Delta.

He closed the notebook and sat drumming his fingers on the table. "Say, I'd really like to talk to your mother."

"I'm sorry, but that's out of the question."

He seemed to accept my response.

"Raymond apparently was really into art. There was the sketchpad and everything. Did he run with the art crowd? It may be a long shot, but that's an angle to check out."

"Haven't run across anything. You're right though. I should check out that angle."

"What about his roommate?" I asked. "His name is Lyle Chromsky. He seemed to be a kind of wimp, but you never can tell."

"He didn't have a roommate."

It was my turn to study him. He sounded snappish. Maybe he thought I was finding fault with his research.

"None of the people I talked to mentioned a roommate."

"I don't think he was exactly a roommate. He was more like someone Raymond let crash there from time to time."

"How could I have missed that?"

"I think I read somewhere that most murders are committed by someone close to the victim."

"Yeah, that was before drive-bys and random mayhem became such a popular way of saying you care."

"Even though you say this was a hate crime, I just can't shake the feeling that Raymond got killed because of something he was involved in. And he got my mother all tangled up in the whole thing without her knowledge or consent, and now he's dead and I don't know where that leaves her."

"I can see why you're worried. That's why you really should let me talk to her." He held up his hand. "I know, I know. It's out of the question. But I get along real well with older women. They tell me things they don't tell their own children. I was doing a story once in Conway on school desegregation. *Brown v Board of Education* twenty years later. Went to interview this old lady, Miss Phenia. She'd been a cook at the high school back in '55 when it was desegregated. Was talking to the old gal and discovered she had a whole attic full of antiques. She sold them all to me, five hundred dollars. Made me a killing. Old ladies like me."

I looked at him. I bet they do. They probably want to wash you, pat powder in all those little folds, and comb your hair. I looked at my watch. It was after four. "I'm sorry, but I've got to go. I hope this helped with your story."

"It has, more than you know."

"You know how to reach me. I'd appreciate it if you'd let me know if you find out any more about what happened."

He agreed, and I got up to leave. Lambert walked me to the door with his peculiar gait. The flower vendor was still there. I'd been his biggest sale all day, and he wanted to show his gratitude. He hopped to his feet when we walked out.

"Flower for the gentleman with the lovely lady? It's on the house." Lambert waved him off brusquely. The flower man shuffled around in front of him and tried to pin a flower to his lapel.

"My compliments, sir."

At first I thought the old man had stuck Lambert with the pin or something. Lambert made a strange sound in the back of his throat. I would have thought he was in pain if there hadn't been so much anger in it. When I realized what was happening, I yelled, "Hey, don't!" But my admonition was too late. Lambert struck the flower man with a solid blow to the face. The flower man instinctively brought his arms up in a futile attempt to shield himself. He staggered backward. There was blood on his hands. Lambert swung at him again and connected. The man dropped heavily to his knees. He was just an old man who'd tried to give Lambert a paper flower. I couldn't believe what was happening. It was like watching a runaway car plow through a crowded sidewalk. But I wasn't going to stand there and let Lambert kill the man. I grabbed Lambert's raised arm from behind. He whirled around to me. There was so much hate in his eyes I didn't even recognize him. He was strong. This pudgy little man had the strength of a bull. But I didn't let go. I threw myself at him, stuck my face right up into his and screamed, "Leave him alone!" spraying his face with spittle.

By then people were pouring out of the Tom Tom Club. A man went to the old man moaning on the ground.

"Lennie, you all right? Come on, Lennie, get up," he pleaded.

Lambert looked confused. He turned to the gathering crowd, his hands extended apologetically. "He oughta keep his hands to himself. He shouldn't have touched me."

"You better git," warned the man from the bar. "Git on outta here. Leave him alone."

I was already at my car. Lambert ran up after me.

"Hey look, I'm really sorry—"

I slammed the door and locked it. As I drove away, I noticed I had blood on my shoes.

I drove around for a while, trying to calm down and shake the feeling that things were getting out of hand. The incident at the Tom Tom Club left a bad taste in my mouth. Lambert was such a repulsive little worm, beating up on an old man like that. But he also seemed to have access to a lot of information, and I had to admit that was very enticing. That was also the problem. It was a little too enticing, perhaps by design.

It might, I thought, be a good idea for me to back off a little. After all, Raymond was no longer a threat, and Brother Cummings was with Mother. That's what I'd do, I decided, I'd back off.

Finally, I returned to the office. I was going to be off for a few days so I wanted to get my calendar and make sure I hadn't left anything lying around for Heather to use against me. I looked at my in-basket. I considering tackling it before I left or even doing some filing. Anything to keep me here, to delay my having to face Mother and tell her what I knew. But I knew I couldn't delay it indefinitely, and the longer I lingered at the office, the longer it would be before I got home and had to contend with Temp. It was after five when I finally left. I jaywalked across Ninth Street and darted through the alley between N and O streets to get to the side door of the old state garage. The entire first floor of the four-story building is taken up by an auto maintenance shop that services the state's pool of vehicles. It's an old building, and there are no elevators. I was parked on the third floor, which wouldn't have been a difficult climb except that the briefcase and tote bag I was carrying made it kind of awkward. I hefted my load and started up the stairs, the hollow sound of my lonely footsteps bouncing off the walls. The garage clears out quickly at the end of the day, and it was just about empty except for a sparse scattering of cars on each floor. Generally, I park in the same place each day. That way I don't have to worry about trying to find my car at the end of the day. I went straight to it. A old van was parked next to it on the passenger side. I unlocked the trunk and tossed in my briefcase and purse. I slammed the lid, and then screamed before I could catch myself.

Like an apparition, a soft-stepping hant, across from me on the other side of the car stood Lyle Chromsky.

I glanced down at his hands to see if he had a weapon. They were empty. I looked at his eyes to judge intent, and they darted away from mine. I would have been worried, except he was wringing his hands and dancing around as if he had to use the bathroom, and I felt that put me at an advantage. He didn't have a gun, and I didn't see a knife. I figured I could handle him if he got crazy. I didn't expect him to start crying.

I waited on my side of the car, he on his, and watched as his Adam's apple did a reckless little jig.

"I loved him," he gulped. "I didn't kill him."

"The boy's body ain't even cold yet, and you round here trying to drag his name down."

"Mother, that's not it at all. I'm just telling you what I was told. But, if you think about it, it does make sense. It explains Lyle's involvement. Why he came here that time, and why he ran when he saw us at the restaurant. If you could've seen him tonight, you'd know his feelings were real."

"I don't care what you say. That boy wouldn't be messing with no man."

"Mother, you have to get past that part."

"I just can't. It's an abomination, its unnatural, and . . . it's disgusting."

"As far as I'm concerned, anything somebody else does unless they're doing it with me is disgusting."

"But, two men—"

"Mother, let it go."

"I don't believe it anyway."

"That's fine. Denial works for some people."

"That Lyle did it, and now he's trying to cry his way out of it."

The TV was on with the volume turned down low. Brother Cummings sat caught in its rays, his legs up on a hassock, his head back, asleep. He made a gurgling sound. Mother reached over and shook his foot. He shifted position. The gurgling resumed in a different key.

Mother looked at him and shook her head. "I'm going to have to get him out of my house."

"Not yet, Mother."

"Pretty soon people will begin to talk."

"Remember what you taught us. Sticks and stones."

"Aw, girl."

Chapter Eighteen

"Temp, don't play with me. I'm tired. I had a rough day. I am not in the mood."

"I want you to tell him not to be calling my house."

"You the one talked to him. Why didn't you tell him when you had him on the phone? You know, brother to brother, Q-dog to Q-dog. Why didn't you just say, 'Look man, don't call my house.'"

"He's your *friend*. And it's Omega Phi Psi, not Q-dog. He's not an Omega and you know it. He's a jive, sorry ass, Alpha."

"Temp, I'm going to say this one more time, and then I'm going to bed. I asked Bailey to get some information on Raymond for me. We talked by phone. I did not see him in person, so technically I'm still pure. When Bailey read in the paper that Raymond had been found dead, I guess he got worried. Apparently, he tried to reach me at work, but I wasn't in, so he called here. That's it. End of story."

"No, T, that's not it. I'll tell you what's it. This is my house, not Bailey's. You are my lady, not Bailey's."

I had to stop and take a good look at him. "Honey, how long have we been together?"

Temp refused to answer.

"Going on twenty years, and you're still tripping on

Bailey. Has the thought ever occurred to you that if I wanted Bailey I'd be with Bailey?"

Temp morphed through several different expressions as he sorted through possible responses, discarding each in turn. Poor baby.

I tried to slip my arm through his, but he jerked away.

"You just tell the Negro not to be calling my house," he said and stomped out of the room.

That's the way it is with us every time we have one of those heart-to-heart rap sessions. One of us usually ends up getting mad and stomping out of the room, and it usually isn't me. Temp was already angry about my increasing involvement in the Raymond and Mother thing. It didn't help that I'd inadvertently, sort of accidentally, discovered Raymond's body while I was supposed to have been at work. But to have Bailey call inquiring about me—Bailey who used to be my man some twenty odd years ago; Bailey whose hair hadn't even started to thin; Bailey who drove a Porsche and got his picture on the front page of the Sacramento *Observer* seemed like every other week— that was just too much for Temp's emotional circuitry. He'd been coiled pretty tight lately with his business problems and everything. I thought it best not to tell him about my encounter at the Tom Tom Club—information overload can be ugly.

One thing I've learned about myself over the years is there's certain things that I've got to do no matter what the consequences. I had to find out what happened to Daddy's pictures and get them back. And in order to do that, I had to talk to Gil Mettler and find out what he knew about Raymond. Another thing I've learned is if I discussed everything I intended to do with Temp, I wouldn't do anything at all except go to work and come home and go to church and come home. That would make me the good colored wife, but my life would be dull as dishwater, and it'd probably make me mean as hell, too. Call it a cop-out, but I didn't tell Temp that I'd taken vacation and that I was planning to spend some time looking for Daddy's pictures and possibly Raymond's murderer. As I said, I wouldn't do anything if I had to get my husband's approval first—and I am, after all, grown.

Pronto Prints was a ma-and-pa operation located in a bustling little strip mall on Marconi just east of Fulton. The usual assortment of price lists, paper company ads, calendars, and examples of the shop's work were tacked to the walls. Large binders of sample invitations and letterheads littered the counter. A couple of life-sized photographs of oil paintings were mounted side by side on the wall to the right of the counter. One was a voluptuous brown nude by Frieda Kahlo. The other was of Whistler's famous, corset-restrained mother. The photographic image was so sharp I could almost see the painting's brush strokes. The placement of the two side by side created a curious juxtaposition with more than a hint of irony. Toward the back of the shop an ink-smeared operator labored over a noisy offset machine. Although a shop apron covered his shortsleeve sports shirt and slacks I could see that he was pleasingly buffed. The muscles in his arm jumped and danced as he made adjustments on the machine. Up front a flustered young man in a shirt and tie worked the counter. There were only three people ahead of me, but the young man behind the counter stopped and insisted that everyone take a number. I plucked one out of the dispenser. It was number 6009. The sign on the wall said they were serving number five. I figured I was in for a long wait.

When it was my turn, I hesitated for a moment. I didn't know exactly how to begin.

"Yes, can I help you?"

He had a curious accent—sort of a cross between a midwestern twang and something else I couldn't put my finger on. There was a hint of urgency to his request. But I felt it had little to do with me or his desire to be of assistance.

"I'd like to speak to Gil Mettler, please," I said, plunging right in.

"Yes," he responded.

"Mr. Mettler, I'd like to ask you a few questions about Raymond Johnson."

He jumped as if I had scalded him. His reaction was so unexpected I flinched a bit myself. He cast a quick look over his shoulder. The operator adjusted a setting. The machine's steady hum went on uninterrupted.

Mettler pulled one of the sample binders to him and opened it in front of me. He pointed to a particularly garish wedding announcement. "Who sent you here?" he demanded, almost under his breath.

"No one—"

He stabbed his finger at the wedding announcement. I looked down. He stabbed again.

I decided to humor him. I looked down at the invitation and directed my response to it. "No one sent me."

Mettler's mouth clamped shut. His lips went as straight as a dead man's cardiograph. Somehow I got the feeling he didn't believe me.

I fumbled in my purse and got out one of my cards.

I handed it to him. "Look, my name is Theresa Gallo-way. I'm here on behalf of my mother. She asked me to talk to Raymond's friends and find out as much as I could about him. We really didn't have a chance to get to know him before he got killed—"

"What!"

He'd forgotten his charade of talking to the book of samples and was staring at me wild-eyed. The shop seemed to have gone quiet. I didn't hear the offset machine.

"I'm sorry. You didn't know, did you? It was in the paper. I'm awfully sorry."

Mettler slammed the sample book shut. "Ma'am, I have customers to attend to."

I looked over my shoulder. Like the chopped-off tail of a worm, the line behind me had regenerated itself. Mettler leaned around me and gestured to the woman behind me, indicating he was ready to serve her.

"Mr. Mettler, just a couple of questions. I could come back a little later if that would help."

He shook his head and waited for me to leave. But I wasn't ready to leave, not just yet. I looked around the shop. My eyes settled again on the two photographs.

"How much are those?" I asked, pointing to them.

His eyes climbed to where I pointed. "They're not for sale."

"I really like them. Can you tell me who the pho-tographer is?"

"Look, I don't know. They're promotional stuff some company sent. I don't even remember which company."

"Okay," I said, "I know you're busy."

He lips tightened into a smile as he nodded me to a finish.

"If you find some time to talk, I'd appreciate it if you'd give me a call."

"Yes, sure," he said.

But, I could tell he didn't mean it.

I left Pronto Prints, got in my car, and drove down Fulton to the Town and Country Village. I parked in front of Starbucks and went in. I ordered a half-calf, blended, hazelnut, no-whip mocha—the nectar of the gods—and retired to a sunny corner to go over my encounter with Gil Mettler. It had either been a bust or richly rewarding, depending on how you looked at it. Mettler hadn't denied knowing Raymond, but he'd refused to talk to me, refused to answer any questions. That alone spoke volumes, but in a language I wasn't quite literate in. His shock when I told him Raymond was dead was genuine though. But shock is one thing—I was shocked when I heard that George Wallace had died—grief is another thing altogether. I'm pretty good at reading people, and grief wasn't written on his face anywhere. I thought about that. How would I react if someone told me one of my old boy-friends had died—Bailey for instance. I'd be shocked and saddened. But how would I react? That depended on how I was told and by whom. If a total stranger walked in off the streets and announced that Bailey was dead, I'd be shocked for sure, but I wouldn't fall down wailing and rend my garments or anything like that, at least not in Temp's presence. I slapped my forehead with the palm of my hand. The man working the offset machine—how could I have been so stupid? No wonder Mettler wouldn't talk to me. Oh well, I thought, what's done is done. Mettler'd have to learn how to manage his man, just as I had to learn how to manage mine. And somehow I had to manage to talk to Mettler again, this time alone.

I got that chance sooner than I expected.

Mettler's call came as I was merging onto Business Eighty off El Camino. I snatched up the phone and barked hello into the receiver. I know I sounded curt, but I was risking my life just answering it. A big-rig with the desiccated remains of a Christmas wreath stuck in the teeth of its grille was bearing down on me with the unerring accuracy of a heat-seeking missile, while a battered Metro in front of me struggled to reach the speed limit.

"What did you mean coming here like that?"

"What?"

"This is a business, a family-run business. You had no right to come barging in here. I will not be pressured. Everything is off. You got that? The whole fucking thing is off."

The big-rig was riding my bumper.

"Hold on a second. I've got to pull over."

I flipped on the turn signal. He slammed the phone down in my ear. I pulled over anyway. I sat on the shoulder of the freeway and watched the seagulls circling over the city dump and tried to figure out what the call was about. What was off? Could he have mistaken me for someone else when I walked into his shop? A creditor perhaps? An old girlfriend trying to get her lava lamp and Al Green albums back? Or maybe a co-conspirator? I thought about calling him back, but I didn't have the number—I'd have to get it from information—and the shoulder of the freeway is not my favorite place to conduct business. I considering getting off at the next exit and going back. But

I didn't think a face-to-face confrontation would work—it hadn't earlier. Besides, Mr. Mettler seemed to be into playing games. It was best to hold off a little until I could figure out the rules before I got too deep into this little game, whatever it was.

I pulled back onto the freeway and got over into one of the left lanes. When the time came, I transitioned over to Ninety-nine south, took the Fourteenth Street exit, and headed to Mother's house.

Mother and Brother Cummings were watching a talk show when I got there. Moving like a sleepwalker, Mother opened the door and let me in without taking her eyes off the TV screen. Her ears were red, and Brother Cummings's leg was jumping. Mother silenced me with a wave when I attempted to speak. Finally, a commercial came on, releasing her from her trance, but leaving Brother Cummings still enthralled in TV's flickering glow.

"That woman's husband ran off 'cause she's a nympho-man-i-ac," explained Mother in a voice hushed with awe. "He changed his name and everything, but she tracked him down. Used his Social Security number. Now he wants to have a sex change, but she's suing to stop it. Lord, some people."

"Mother, I got one of Daddy's—"

"Lorraine, they back on," interrupted Brother Cummings, his leg pumping like a piston. "You better come on, girl."

Mother flopped back down on the sofa next to him.

"Oh, you'd better call Temp," she said over her shoulder. "He called here looking for you."

"Temp?"

"Yes, baby, Temp, the boy you married to."

I let myself out. I could hear the expressive thump,

thump, thump of Brother Cummings's leg and Mother's nervous giggle as I closed the door.

Temp called me at Mother's. That was not good. It could only mean he'd called me at work first and found out I wasn't there. I'd had enough game playing for one day. I got in my car and drove home.

The Cherokee was parked in the driveway. I parked beside it and went in. Temp was in the family room, wrestling with the patio door. He'd taken it off the track and was looking for some place to put it. He settled for the sofa—Italian leather. I interceded.

"Uh, honey, why don't you put it on the floor? Just lay it flat on the carpet."

He turned to stare at me, giving me one of his looks. I swear, steam came from his nostrils.

"Where the fuck have you been?"

Temp knows how I hate to be cursed at. My own daddy never cursed. Until the day he died, I never heard him swear. He was more into the whimsical invective. Except for an occasional "shit," "bearhugger" had been his most scathing. Mother doesn't curse either. Carolyn, on the other hand, took great pride in being able to out curse anybody. Jimmy was sneaky about his. And I had to marry a man who thought cursing was part of his ethnic heritage. It wouldn't have done me any good to say anything, so I ignored him.

"What're you doing to the door?" I asked instead of answering.

"T, I know you heard me. You didn't go to work today. Where have you been?"

"I've been out. I had some . . . business to take care of."

"What kind of business? No, don't tell me—it was something for your mother."

"No, it wasn't for Mother."

"It had something to do with your mother. Tell me it didn't, and you're lying."

I didn't want to get into this kind of contest, so I didn't say anything. Besides, he was right. It did have to do with Mother—indirectly. I shrugged, and that really made him mad.

"Oh, so it's like that, huh. You can come and go as you please without so much as a word. You can run the streets, have your men calling—"

He was getting way out into left field, and now my gorge was starting to rise. "You know what," I said. "If I were you, I wouldn't even go there."

"If I were you, I'd get my shit together. You sisters running around here reading *Waiting to Exhale* . . . If I were you, I sure would get my shit together. That's all I got to say."

He took a screwdriver out of his pocket and started taking apart the door's latching mechanism. "And another thing, T—"

"I thought that was all you had to say."

He raised his voice and repeated himself. "Another thing, T,"—according to Temp's rules of engagement, the one who talks the loudest wins—"I'm getting sick of people calling and hanging up in my face. Tell your friends," he said, rolling the word *friends* in a heavy coating of sarcasm, "I don't appreciate that. I also don't appreciate your friends,"—again the sarcasm—"sending little love notes and shit to my house."

"What are you talking about now?"

He stood up, stomped over to the fireplace, and snatched a small red velvet box down from the mantel.

It was the kind that fancy jewelry, cuff links maybe, would come in. He shoved the box at me. "I'm talking about this."

I took the "this" and turned it over in my hands. "Who is it from?"

"You tell me."

"Was there a card or anything?"

He reached in his back pocket and pulled out a small envelope about the size of a thank-you note or a party invitation and handed it to me. I put the box down on the sofa and took the envelope. It had apparently been opened without the aid of a letter opener; in fact, it looked as if something had been chewed open.

"You opened it?"

"It didn't have a name on it."

"Then how'd you know it was for me? It could've been for Aisha or Shawn or you even."

"Just read the card."

I opened the card. Someone had scrawled "Merry Christmas and Happy New Year" across it with a red felt-tip marker. "Merry Christmas and Happy New Year," that's all. Nothing else—no signature or anything.

"What is this supposed to mean?"

Temp stood with his arms folded across his chest and his lower lip sucked in against his teeth, nodding his head. "Uh-huh," he said, dragging it out for emphasis.

"Uh-huh, what?" I demanded.

"Don't pretend you don't know."

He was starting to get on my last nerve. "Temp, don't be playing games with me. Where's the box? What's in the damn box?"

I picked it up and opened it, folding back the tissue to get a look at its contents. Nestled on a cotton cushion was a strip of film, a photograph negative with three pictures on it. I took the strip and held it up to the light. Temp looked deflated. I don't know what he expected, but I could tell by his sheepish look it wasn't a strip of film.

"What the hell is that?"

"You opened the card and read my mail. Why didn't you just open the box too and find out?"

"I wanted you to have the pleasure—"

"How'd this get here?" I asked, cutting him off. "Did it come in the mail?"

"Somebody dropped it off. Left it on the porch."

"When?"

"This afternoon less than an hour ago. I went to OfficeMax to get some supplies. It was by the front door when I got back. If I'd have gone in through the garage, I would have missed it."

I held the negatives up to the light again. I looked at the first picture. Lights and darks were reversed, but I knew the picture anyway. I'd seen that brown, voluptuous nude before. I looked at the second one, old lady Whistler. I didn't recognize the third picture. The most I could say about it was it looked like something done by a child.

"Let me see those."

Temp took them from my hand before I had a chance to respond. He held the negatives up to the light and stared for several seconds. "Just as I suspected . . . uh . . . negatives."

I sank down on the sofa, feeling a little disoriented. It was like my sense of what was real and what wasn't was just a hair off. It must have been how Alice felt when she fell through that looking glass. I started talking, trying to find my way back.

"Temp, I went to see this man today about getting Daddy's pictures back."

Temp started to sputter.

"Wait. Listen. He was supposed to have been one of Raymond's friends, a very good friend. But he wouldn't even talk to me. He didn't know Raymond was dead, and he was shocked when I told him. Funny thing though, two of those pictures on the negative were hanging in his shop. I even asked him about them; I was curious about who took them. He said he didn't know. Now, I get home a few hours later and here they are all gift wrapped and everything."

"This friend of Raymond you talking about. This one the fruit?"

"Temp, I really wish you wouldn't say stuff like that. It's just not right."

"What do you want me to say—fag, fairy, homo? It all means the same. It means he does men."

"You sound like a bigot. I don't want to raise the children like that. I wouldn't want them to hear you right."

"The children aren't here."

"It doesn't matter. You get in the habit of talking like that, and pretty soon it won't make a difference who's here and who isn't."

"So, now you my mama?"

I found myself sucking my teeth like Mother. "Where was I?"

"You were explaining how you left the house this morning like you were going to work, but decided to go kick it with some of your homies down at Faces instead."

I threw up my hands. "I can't talk to you."

"T, answer just one question. Raymond, how did he die? Do you remember what you told me?"

"I remember."

"Was it pretty? That the way you want to die?"

I didn't answer.

"Next question, do you know who killed him? Was it Lyle? Or how about Raymond's love-buddy you met today? For all you know, it could have been Brother Cummings. It could have been any-motherfucking-body. Do you know why he was killed? You don't have to answer. All you know is you want your daddy's pictures back. Right? Check this out. You don't know the who, the what, or the why this brother got offed. But you gonna go messing around in folk's business, and you don't even know what the business is. If something went down, you wouldn't even know which way to fall. To say nothing of the promise you made to me and your kids to stay out of shit like this."

I hate it when Temp makes sense. "I see your point . . ."

"No, I want you to do more than just see my point. You have to let this go. You don't have your daddy's pictures; maybe you weren't meant to have them. Let it go. Let the police handle it. Stay out of it. Okay?"

Temp massaged his temples with his fingertips as if that had taken a lot out of him. He looked weary. He stopped and looked at his watch. "I have to go," he said absently. "Got to see an attorney."

"Taxes?"

"No, the business."

He leaned over and kissed me just as absently and turned to leave.

"Hey, what about the door?"

"Oh, yeah."

He snapped the latch back in place, tightened the screws, and worked the door back onto the track. "That ought to hold it until I get back."

"What's wrong with it?"

"I don't know. It's not locking right. Keeps tripping the alarm."

Temp left. It was a weekday. I was home alone. If I had been thinking clearly, I would have taken advantage of the few hours before the kids got home and climbed into the tub for a long soaking. But I wasn't thinking clearly, so I locked up the house, put the alarm on, and went to Mother's instead.

Brother Cummings was out front digging in the garden. He wore an old pair of overalls over his leisure suit and a battered felt hat I thought I recognized.

"You getting some exercise, Brother Cummings?"

He answered without looking up. "I thought I'd give Sister Barkley a little privacy, seeing as how she has company."

"Company? Who?"

"Far be it for me to meddle in her affairs. But you go right on in. I'm sure the gentleman will introduce himself to you at least."

I heard a burst of laughter, a duet of high girlish giggles and raspy chortling. I did as Brother Cummings suggested. I pushed the front door open and went in. "Mother, it's me—"

I stopped short and choked back whatever else I was going to say when I saw Mother sitting at the dining-room table with her guest. She turned toward the door when I called her name. So did Dale Lambert.

"What the hell are you doing here?"

"Theresa, watch your manners."

"Excuse me Mother, but I told this man not to bother you."

"Oh it's all right, baby. Me and Mr. Lambert are old friends now. Aren't we, Mr. Lambert?"

On seeing me, Lambert had sunk down in his chair. Like some yogi with incredible powers he seemed to have actually made himself smaller. And meeker. His oversize head seemed to almost totter on his frail little neck. His lips twitched as if his smile had developed a short circuit. And he had on that cursed down jacket.

"Didn't I tell you to call me Dale?" he croaked.

Mother patted his hand. "That's right. Dale."

Turning back to me, she said, "Dale here's from Shreveport. Can you believe that? He was born right down the road from where I was. I think I even know his people. He's traveled all over the country. But, for the last few years he lived in Pine Bluff. Now don't that beat all?"

"Mr. Lambert, I think you'd better go."

Mother sat at the table, smiling sweetly. She didn't protest that I was taking over her house as I expected her to. Lambert stood up abruptly, disturbing the table. He reached down, grabbed the paper bag at his feet, and hugged it to his chest.

"Well, Mrs. Barkley—"

Mother shook her finger at him. "Uh, uh, uh," she chided. "It's Lorraine. I don't know how you come up with this Mrs. Barkley stuff."

"I guess I'll be going . . . Lorraine."

"Remember," said Mother, "Dupree. Make sure you look up the Dupress the next time you're in Shreveport. They my people on my mother's side."

Lambert shuffled his way to the door without looking at me and left. Brother Cummings came in so
quickly after Lambert's departure he must have been
standing outside the door, waiting for Lambert to
leave. He went straight to the sofa, reached behind
it, and pulled out his shopping bag and shotgun. He
rearranged the bag's contents, placed the shotgun in
it, and fitted the golf club cover over the barrel. Then
he went to the kitchen. When he came back, he had
shed his overalls and the hat and had gotten his lunch
pail and jacket. He stood facing us, his back to the
door.

"Ladies, I'm sorry, but I too must leave."

I started to protest, "But Brother Cummings—"

Mother stopped me. "Let Cleotis go on."

Brother Cummings clamped his jaws shut so tightly
I thought his dentures might shatter.

"Can't I give you a ride or something?"

He stood his head vigorously. Then he fumbled with
the door for a few seconds before flinging it open and
leaving without another word.

I turned to Mother. "What's going on? What was
that man doing here?"

"Now, don't start that again. I told you when Raymond was here, and I'll tell you again. This is my
house. I do what-so-ever I please in it."

"Do you know who he is?"

" 'Course I do. His name's Dale Lambert. Writes
for some paper."

"Did you know he's been hounding me ever since
that incident at work, trying to get an interview. Want-
ing to talk to other people in the family. Now he's
been coming at me about Raymond's death. There's

something about him. He's just too much in my business."

"For your information, he didn't even mention that crazy man at your job."

"That's not all. I saw him beat an old man for no reason at all. Beat him badly."

"He didn't mention that either."

"No, I don't think he would. What exactly did you and he talk about then?"

"Oh, just stuff. Mostly I was trying to figure out why he wore so much liniment and why he kept that jacket on. But when he found out I was from Shreveport, we kinda got sidetracked."

"How'd he know you're from Shreveport?"

"He looked so familiar. I told him that, and he started naming off his people. When he got to the Joshuas, I said, 'Wait a minute, Taffry Joshua?' And sure enough, he's kin to the Joshusas back in Shreveport."

"But, Mother, what was he doing here? Okay, you both were born in Shreveport. You didn't know that when you let him in your house. I can't believe this. He was a stranger off the street, and you let him in your house. That was so incredibly . . ."

I wanted to say "incredibly stupid," but you don't win friends and influence people by pointing out their failings. Especially not Mother. She looked at me from beneath lids lowered to half-mast.

"I'm glad you had sense enough not to go all the way with that."

I took a deep breath, closed my eyes, and did my frog swallow. "Mother, all I'm trying to say is it was dangerous letting that man in your house. You don't know anything about him. You've already had a break-in. There's the phone calls. Now this. Who knows what could have happened. It's just dangerous, that's all."

"Child, you really do think I'm a fool, don't you? I don't get myself into any situation without first having a way out. You don't think I'd sit up here talking to anybody I don't know without some protection, do you?"

I looked around the room. "What protection? Brother Cummings's shotgun? It was behind the sofa. Things happen fast. A lot of good that shotgun would have done behind the sofa."

She fixed me with a rueful smile and shook her head. "I'm talking about this."

Reaching into her bosom, she extracted a small aerosol canister about the size of one of those spray-in-the mouth breath fresheners. It was black with white lettering. "This is all the protection I need," she said, waving it in my face.

"And what is this?"

"Power Punch," she said, handing it to me.

"Power Punch, caution flammable, severe irritant, contents under pressure," I read the front panel out loud. "What's this, Mace?"

"Something better."

I turned the canister over in my hand. "Mother, this stuff looks dangerous."

"Of course it is, honey."

"Where'd you get it?"

"Out of one of those catalogues."

She got up and went to the buffet and retrieved a catalogue from the top drawer and handed it to me. The cover was a colorful collage of law enforcement patches. Shomer-Tec, Law Enforcement, and Military

Equipment was printed across the front in bold white lettering. She'd marked several pages with little strips of paper. I turned to the first one.

"That's it right there," Mother said proudly. "Power Punch."

I read the description out loud. " 'An instantly effective less-than-lethal aerosol subject restraint weapon. A one-second spray into the face dilates the capillaries of the eyes, causing temporary blindness. It induces choking, coughing, and nausea, and mucous membranes swell to prevent all but life-supporting breathing, giving rapid 'knockdown' and preventing further aggressive activity.' "

"Mother, this stuff is dangerous. It's probably illegal too."

"If it was illegal, I'd have to go down on Stockton to buy it. I ordered it right out of this catalogue just like I do with Finger Hut or JC Penney."

"But, Mother, you can't fool around with this stuff. You don't even know how to use it."

Mother sucked her teeth in frustration and snatched the canister out of my hand. "You always was such a scary child. Besides, I wouldn't need it if the police would give me my gun back."

I continued thumbing through the catalogue. "And what's this vomit fluid? Un-natural gas?"

Mother snatched the catalogue from me. "Give me that. I don't want to hear any more of your mouth."

"You wouldn't need any of this if you hadn't dogged poor Brother Cummings."

"That old man gets on my nerves."

"I don't care if he does. That wasn't the way to treat him after all he's done to help you."

"I don't need him here if he's going to get an attitude."

"An attitude? An attitude about what? Mother, I really don't think we're on the same page here."

"Now, don't you start. Too much confusion and I can't think straight. I almost forget to tell you about the fifty dollars."

She waited for me to ask, "What fifty dollars?" But I refused. Sometimes, I can be just as perverse as she can.

"Lambert gave it to me."

She had me hooked now. "Why in the world would Lambert give you fifty dollars?"

" 'Cause he ain't as smart as he thinks he is. Bought one of my knickknacks, the one of the little girl milking a cow. Fancies himself some kind of collector. Said it was rare, an antique. I let him have it for fifty dollars. I bought it last year at Target."

"You sure about that, Mother?"

"Sure about where I bought it?"

"No, the fifty dollars."

Instead of answering, she reached down in her bosom again, this time extracting a couple of twenties and a ten. "Anybody who'd pay fifty dollars for a two-dollar knickknack is more a danger to his own bank account than he is to me."

Mother laughed until her eyes watered. But I just couldn't find anything funny in it. I couldn't find any rhyme or reason to Lambert showing up like that, buying Mother's junk. In fact, there was very little over the past few days that I could find rhyme or reason to. Mettler, Lyle, and now Lambert. One thing for sure, I had to get those biological weapons away from Mother and hope she didn't find a catalogue sell-

ing surplus nuclear weapons. But how was I to get
them? I can be just as bold as the next sister, but
there was no way I was going to stick my hand down
Mother's bosom. I was likely to draw back a nub. I'd
just have to bide my time.

Mother was still rumbling with laughter when I left
with a promise to come back later on that night. In
spite of her protestations to the contrary, she needed
someone to stay with her. Keep an eye on her for a
few days. Things were just too weird. She'd run
Brother Cummings off. Unless I could find one of the
sisters to stay with her, I just might have to do it
myself, and that was all I needed.

Since I was out, I decided to pick up Shawn and
Aisha from school rather than have them ride the bus.
I swung west on Fourteenth Avenue and stayed on it
until it merged into Sutterville. Temp sometimes picks
them up depending on his schedule. Other times they
ride the bus. I got out my cell phone and called Temp
to let him know that I had the kids, just in case he
was planning on getting them. I got no answer. I tried
his office phone, and the answering service picked up.
On being informed he was in a meeting, I asked the
service to tell him that I called and that I was picking
up the children.

"Oh, Mrs. Galloway, there's a message for you from
Mr. Galloway. He says he'll be in meetings until late.
Don't hold dinner for him. He'll grab something."

Chevy's, here I come, I thought as I turned onto
Fruitridge from Freeport and headed for Lawrence
Academy to get Shawn. From there it was a short
jaunt to Kennedy High for Aisha.

It was dark by the time the kids and I got home. I
pulled into the garage as the overhead door slid shut

behind me. Temp's car wasn't there, which meant he still wasn't home. The kids, after having gorged themselves on chicken fajitas and virgin Margaritas climbed out of the car as docile as kittens and stumbled toward the door leading into the laundry room. Shawn had opened the door about an inch or so when I realized something was wrong. I didn't know what it was. Something just wasn't right.

I grabbed Shawn by the shoulder maybe a little rougher than I should have and he screamed. I slapped my hand over his mouth. "Get back in the car," I said, trying to keep them from reading the fear in my voice. "You too, Aisha. Get back in the car."

Aisha started to protest. I grabbed her by the collar and slung her toward the car. Shawn sneaked a look at me as he scrambled to the car. There was pure terror in his eyes. I hit the driver's-side door just as the garage lights went out. They stay on only a minute or two after the garage is opened, just long enough for you to get out of the car and go inside. I had the car in reverse before I even opened the garage door, and I would have busted right through it if Aisha hadn't reached up to the dashboard and pressed the remote button.

I was on the freeway heading north doing eighty before I could regulate my breathing. I looked in the rearview mirror. All I could see was a sea of wavering headlights staring back at me. I eased my foot off the gas and slowed down. I glanced over at Aisha. She sat huddled against the door as far from me as possible. I found Shawn in the rearview mirror. He was sitting unnaturally erect, staring at me with kewpie-doll eyes. Poor babies, I thought with a twist of pain, they're scared of me. They think I've lost my mind.

"Hey, you guys, I'm sorry for acting crazy back there, but I thought someone was in the house. I just didn't want to take any chances."

I didn't want to scare them any more than I already had, but I thought for sure I'd put the alarm on before I left. I was the last one to leave, and I'd put the alarm on before I left. I couldn't tell what had alerted me at first, and then I realized that it was the high-pitched whistle the alarm makes when you open the door if it's set on delay. After that you have sixty seconds to key in the code and disarm it. If you don't, the alarm blasts for five minutes before shutting itself off. The whistle didn't sound when Shawn opened the door. Somebody had been in there, or maybe was still in there.

Aisha sighed, and I thought I heard Shawn sob. I felt even worse.

"Everything's all right I'm sure, but I just wanted to be safe."

There was silence. After a while Aisha said, "Mom, you had your cell phone."

"It weighs all of six ounces. What did you want me to do with it?"

"You could have called for help. You could have dialed 911."

"And what was I supposed to do while we waited for the police to get there?"

"You could have shot him," said Shawn, "like Grandmother did."

"No," I said, "I didn't need to shoot anybody. We just needed to get out of there the way we did."

But I thought to myself, a little fire power probably wouldn't have hurt. I sure wish I'd had a canister of Mother's Power Punch back there. Unfortunately, that wasn't the last time that night I'd entertain that thought.

Now I found myself in a quandary. I didn't know what time Temp was coming home, and I didn't want him to walk in on something dangerous or return to find us missing and the house in shambles after having been ransacked or something. But I couldn't go back. Even if nobody had gotten in, I had spooked myself and the kids much too badly for us to go back home and go about our routines without looking over our shoulders every few seconds and jumping at the slightest noise.

"Aisha, get my phone and call Greenhaven Security."

Aisha did so and handed the phone to me. I told the security officer I thought someone had tried to break in and asked them to check for me and alert the police if necessary. I gave them my cell phone number and Mother's number and asked them to call me if they found anything. Then I had Aisha call and leave a message for Temp. Finally, I asked her to call our neighbors, the Hidakos and the Dixons. I explained to them that I thought I'd had a prowler and asked them to keep their eyes on things until Temp got in. They agreed, and I gave them the phone numbers and hung up.

That taken care of, the next thing was to get back to Mother's now that Brother Cummings was gone. Whatever I proposed, I had to proceed carefully. I knew my kids. If I didn't sell it right, they'd dig their little heels in and I'd be sunk. I finally settled on aversion as a tactic.

"Hey guys, I almost forgot. I promised to press Mother's hair tonight."

"Oh no," groaned Aisha. "We don't have to go, do we? The last time Grandmother made me trim her corns."

"Ooh, gross!" squealed Shawn.

"How about if I take you guys over to Rob and Anita's?"

"Alrightie then!" shouted Shawn. Aisha shrugged. I could tell she was pleased too.

Anita is one of the Jack and Jill mothers. She's diminutive, wears her hair in a shoulder-length bob, and dresses with an understated elegance that I've long admired. Also, she carries a handgun in her Fendi bag. I don't know what kind of gun it is, but it's powerful and she knows how to use it. She had to learn. It's part of her job as a probation officer.

I asked Aisha to get the phone back out of my bag and call Anita's number. She did and handed it to me. I made the arrangements for Shawn and Aisha to spend the night and hung up.

"Hey, what about nightclothes and things like that?" said Aisha. Shawn couldn't have cared less.

"Don't worry, Anita will fix you up. And Shawn, this time don't O.D. on ice cream, okay? You know what it does to your digestive system."

"Oh, Mom," complained Aisha, coming to her brother's defense, "now you're starting to sound like Grandmother."

Chapter Nineteen

"Now tell me about this boy. You say he wouldn't talk to you when you went to his shop, but he called you up after you left and just about cursed you out?"

"And hung up on me, too," I added.

Mother and I were going over the events of the past few days. She was on the sofa with her feet propped up, and I was on the floor, trying to organize what was left of her picture album. I went on with my recitation, counting off the incidents on my fingers.

"The negatives. Don't forget the negatives. And the house. Someone was in my house."

"Uh-huh," said Mother. "Now, I know a thing or two about people walking through places they don't belong. Anybody ever died in your house? You hear footsteps late at night?"

"Mother, it wasn't a ghost. Lambert. Let's not forget Lambert."

"Might as well add Lyle to the list, too. Now what do we have? All these people had something to do with Raymond."

"And one of them could have killed him. Then again, he could have been killed by someone we don't even know about. Someone he had just met—"

"Don't start that again."

"Or someone who broke into his house. A burglar or something."

Mother and I looked at each other. We were both thinking the same thing.

"I think I'd better try to reach Temp again."

I picked up the phone and called Temp's cell phone number. To my surprise he answered.

"Honey, where are you?" I asked.

"I'm here celebrating."

"Celebrating what?"

"My bankruptcy. Bankrupture. Tore the bank. Ripped."

"Bankruptcy? What backruptcy? Honey, you been drinking?"

"You can't celebrate without drinking a little something, now can you, T?"

"You need a ride? Want me to come get you?"

Mother's eyes were burning a hole in the side of my head. I found myself sweating trying to talk to Temp without disclosing too much to her. "Temp, I think somebody broke into the house .."

"I'll take care of it in the morning . . ."

"Temp, listen to me. I think somebody got in the house. I took the kids over to Rob and Anita's and I'm at Mother's. You shouldn't . . ."

"Tell Mom I said hello."

"Mother, Temp says hello."

"Just leave me out of it before I have to give the boy a piece of my mind."

"Temp, Mother said hello."

I turned away slightly and cupped the phone to my mouth. "Where are you? What's going on?"

"Nothing now. Not Second Generation. Nothing. Gotta go, T. Ta ta."

He hung up.

"Don't say it, Mother."

"I didn't even open my mouth."

I went back to my task.

Mother kept silent for about ten seconds.

"Don't you think you better go get him?"

"I don't know where he is," I admitted.

"Well, let's just hope he's at a bar somewhere and not somebody's house."

I fumbled with the pictures in silence.

"You know, you need to pray more—"

"I do pray."

"—and go to church."

I sighed. "I go to church, Mother."

"Since when? I haven't seen you there in I don't know how long."

"You go to the eight o'clock service. You wouldn't see me anyway."

"You know what I'm talking about."

"No, Mother, I don't know what you're talking about, and I'd appreciate it if you'd just drop the subject altogether. Okay?"

"Miss Testy, huh? Well, let me take myself up from here and go to bed before I say something in my own house that Miss Testy doesn't want to hear."

Mother got up with a great deal of rustling and went to bed. I gave up on the picture album. My heart just wasn't in it now. I was worried about Temp, worried about the house, and just worried in general. I thought about turning on the TV, but stultification wasn't what I really needed. Finally, I got my purse and dug out the sketchpad and articles we'd found in Raymond's room and sat down at the dining-room table to go over them.

I thumbed through the sketches. I guess I'd done that so often, they all looked familiar now. When I got to the one of the fish groins, I kept going. No need to re-live the humiliation. I came to the one that didn't seem to fit with the rest of them. A large animal, some kind of cat, a cross between a tiger and a leopard, with both stripes and spots, was pouncing on a mouse that seemed to have the face of a man. It was rendered in a very simplistic style as if a child had done it. But, for all its simplicity there was something powerful, something very compelling about it. In a flight of fancy I wondered if there could be any connection between this drawing and the one on the negative. It was hard to compare a negative with an actual sketch of something different and find similarities— I'm not that good. There sure was a lot of art stuff— missing pictures, mysteriously appearing negatives, a book of sketches. I closed the sketchbook, set it aside, and took out the articles. They weren't in the best condition to start with, and the time they'd spent crammed down in my purse hadn't helped them any. I smoothed them out on the table. They'd been marked with a yellow highlighting pen, but the markings had faded to a fuzzy stain. I skimmed through the first one. It was on outsider art. "Who are outsider artists?" it asked. "Are they folk artists? Primitives? Self-taught artists? Naifs? Hermits? People have argued for years what to call them. 'Outsiders,' with its romantic overtones, is the most popular term—it certainly works as a marketing catchphrase—Collectors and dealers are now beginning to see outsider art as big business . . . Outsiders are now in, and the price of their art from the heart is on the way up." I checked to see who had written the article. Eleanor

E. Gaver, *Art and Antiques* magazine. I'd never heard of it, but that didn't mean anything. Until a few days ago I hadn't heard of fish groins either. I read on. It seemed outsider artists were usually older black folk from the rural South who turned to art late in life, often to exorcise private demons or convey a visionary message. The article discussed some of the most famous outsiders, Delta bluesman and sculptor of skulls James Son Thomas, mud artist Jimmie Lee Suduth, Mose Tolliver, and Blind Lula. Blind Lula was the only woman of the group, and the only one without a surname. I read on wondering why.

According to the article Blind Lula was born in Tucker, Arkansas, in 1906 or thereabout. Unlike most outsiders, she started to paint as a young woman. She lost her sight in a battle with diabetes, but continued to paint. The paintings she made before her illness are prized by collectors for their fanciful figures and her wry take on somber subjects. However, her work done while blind is the most prized and sought after. Lula is said to have painted from memory with paints made from barks and herbs to her specifications. She is quoted by a Swedish interviewer as saying that she could hear the colors, feel them, even taste them, and she used all of her senses except for sight to produce paintings that praised the Lord. Her work can be found in some of the great collections. However, the most prized of all her paintings is the *Devil Gonna Get You* triptych. Only two of the three panels are accounted for. The third has been lost for more than forty years. The writer speculated that if it were found today, its value would run well into six figures.

Blind Lula. I wondered what her real name was. And whether it was too late for me to learn how to paint. Oh well, I thought, that was fun, but it really didn't get me anywhere. I looked at the next article, "Sharecropping in the Art World." It was even more ratty than the first one. It was a copy that had started off crooked and had gotten worse with each reproduction. Someone had folded the edges back to neaten it up. This article dealt with the exploitative nature of collecting, how artists are paid pennies for their work that is sold, in turn, for thousands of dollars. The article went on to recount how some artists have actually had work stolen by collectors, while others, ignorant of the works' value, had given them away for a few dollars or a bottle of whiskey—the old blanket and string of beads syndrome. It listed some examples, and the author recounted how he discovered a brilliant outsider artist toiling in obscurity and offered him fifty dollars for three paintings. The artist agreed, but the writer's conscience wouldn't let him take advantage of the artist. Instead, he explained the value of the paintings and gave the artist some names of collectors who would pay a fair price. That had taken place in Conner, Arkansas.

Connor. That rang a bell with me. Dad used to talk about a place called Conner. I wondered who wrote this one. There was no byline. I unfolded the edges and smoothed them out to see if there was any more text. I found the name at the end of the article. It said "by Dale Lambert." Now, that was too much of a coincidence. "What is going on?" I asked out loud. Raymond appears out of nowhere with these articles hidden away. Raymond disappears, and Lambert appears. Well, not quite. Lambert had already made his appearance before Raymond disappeared. It wasn't too hard to see that there was a connection.

I sat at the table, trying to connect the dots in my mind, trying to figure out what it was they were after. I couldn't come up with anything that was recognizable. I looked at my watch. It was only ten o'clock, but my mind was beginning to feel like a sieve. Information overload. I'd have to go to bed and let my subconscious work on this one.

Mother and Raymond had taken down my old bed, and there was no way I was going to sleep behind Raymond, so I went to the linen closet in the hall and took out a couple of blankets and a pillow and prepared to bunk down in the living room on the sofa. I was already dressed for bed in a pair of pink, silky pajamas belonging to Mother. She'd gotten them for one of the pajama holidays—Christmas, Mother's Day, something like that—but had never worn them because, and these are her words, they made her "feel too slippery." I turned off the light and settled in on the sofa. But I was thirsty—Mexican food always does that to me. Hauling myself up from the sofa, I padded into the kitchen without turning the lights back on. I stood at the sink, idly staring out of the window over it into the backyard as I finished up my glass of water. Mother's backyard is brightly lit. It is so bright, in fact, that neighbors at one time complained about it. They said they had a hard time sleeping with the light shining in through their windows like that. Mother has since reduced her wattage, but it's still bright enough to land a plane back there. Actually, I could hardly blame her. One of the houses abutting hers from the back, the Tyler place, is vacant and occupied from time to time by a series of glazed-eyed squatters; another, the Simmons place, is the scene of loud parties and lots of drive-up and walk-in traffic. In Mother's case bright lights served the same purpose as the crucifix in vampire movies.

I finished my water and left the glass on the sink. I yawned, extending my arms over my head and then pulling them behind my back as far as they would go. I was in that position—arms back, chest thrust forward, mouth wide open—when I saw something move in the shadows on the periphery of Mother's yard near the Tyler place. I froze—arms back, chest thrust forward, mouth wide open. I must have stood there like that for a good two minutes without seeing anything else. I ran my eyes along the fence. It leaned crazily. In some places slats were missing, giving it a snaggle-toothed look. But thirty years of overgrown foliage had formed a second fence behind it that was probably a better barrier than the original had ever been. Near the corner by the Tyler place a telephone pole rose up and disappeared into the night. There was nothing else out there. Nothing. But I'd seen something. I knew I had, and I've learned to trust my judgment on things like that. I stood there for a few more minutes, wondering what it had been. A squirrel scampering up the telephone pole? A cat picking its way along the top of the fence? A hant pointing out the house to the other hants? Something else? Something far worse? I went back to the living room and sat down on the sofa. I knew I wouldn't get to sleep tonight until I found out what was out there.

Chapter Twenty

I'd seen too many movies where there's a noise outside and a woman with creamed spinach for a brain
opens the door to see what it is and wanders out
empty-handed into the hands/tentacles of the slasher/
monster. I wasn't going to put myself in that position
now. I, quite simply, am not the ingenue type. I do
not have long-flowing hair. I do not wear see-through
negligees out of doors. I don't have congenital ankle
malformation that causes them to twist and pitch me
to the ground when I should be kick-boxing for my
life. And I am not a fool. I went outside to check
things out. I had to. My mother was inside sleeping
like a baby, and I couldn't let anything happen to her.
I'm a middle child—we have responsibilities. But I
went prepared. As quickly and quietly as possible, I
rummaged around and found the overalls Brother
Cummings had worn and slipped them on over my
pajamas. I grabbed one of Mother's sweaters and put
it on over that. Then creeping along the edge of the
hall so the planks wouldn't creak, I went into Mother's
room and stole her Power Punch off the dresser. I
went to the front door, then stopped and thought
about it. I turned around, went back, and got my
purse. I took my cell phone out and shoved it into

one of the pockets on the overalls. Then I went back to the door, turned the porch light off, and slipped out into the night.

I stood in the porch enclosure for a while, just listening to the sounds around me as my eyes adjusted to the dark. I ventured to the edge of the porch and looked down the street in both directions. The street was quiet with that kind of insular feel you sometimes get in the suburbs. Mrs. Fellows's house was dark. And so was Mr. Aragon's. I could just make out a faint glow in the Bernheimers' living room window and imagined Alex asleep in front of the set while Cathy worked on one of her quilts in the kitchen.

I slipped off the porch and crept around to the side of the house, trying not to trample too much of Mother's garden in the process. I ducked down, just in case, when I passed her window. As I turned the corner of the house leading to the backyard, I hit a low spot and stepped in something wet with my left foot. I shuddered, but went on. Occasionally, when I stepped on a snail, there was a cracking noise that seemed to my ears to be as loud as a shot. I finally made it to the back, where I settled in the darkness to watch rather than stepping out into the light where I could be watched.

I leaned against the house, but straightened up immediately when I felt something crawling on my neck. I thought about Rolland at the Brass Monkey asking me if I was one of those lady detectives and chuckled softly to myself. Nothing could have been further from the truth. Even if I had aspirations to be one, if it meant hanging around in the dark, stepping in wet stuff, and fending off spiders, I'd have to disqualify myself.

The chill night air began to seep through my ill-chosen attire, and I became aware that I had to use the bathroom. There was nothing to lean on, nothing to sit on, and I was beginning to think this wasn't such a good idea when Mother's phone started to ring. It rang about ten times, and I was thinking about going back inside to answer it when I heard it stop. I thought Mother had picked it up, but I couldn't be sure. Not long after it stopped ringing, I heard the clatter of the receiver being slammed down.

This is stupid, I thought. I really should just go on back inside the house. I would have gone back then, but I waited a while just to give Mother time to get settled back in bed so I wouldn't have to deal with her. It's a good thing that I did, too. Because if I hadn't, I wouldn't have caught Lyle as he slithered down that telephone pole, like a huge python with a stringy ponytail.

I crept around from the side of the house just as Lyle was about to step down on the fence. I made a little more noise than I intended, and he froze the way a cat does when it's listening with all its senses. I lunged for him, grabbing his leg and trying to pull him down into the yard. He resisted and tried to fight me off, but I'd taken him by surprise and he was off balance. I grabbed a good handful of his pants and jerked hard. He started to fall.

"Stop! Stop! I'm falling!" he pleaded.

Then he fell.

I still had a grip on him, but we were rolling around on the ground like two mud wrestlers. I struggled to reach into my pocket to retrieve the Power Punch without letting him go. Finally, I got it and I climbed over on his chest and held him pinned to the ground with my left forearm. I stuck the Power Punch in his face with my spraying finger cocked.

"It's worse than Mace," I warned him.

He stopped struggling.

"Let's talk, Lyle. Okay?"

He made a noise deep in his throat and nodded, rubbing his head back and forth in the dirt.

"Before I let you go, it would only be fair to warn you that the old woman—the police gave her her gun back. You woke her up with your crank call, and now she's pissed. You know how old people like to get their sleep."

Lyle was rigid now. I let him up, keeping the Power Punch trained on his face.

"Let's just chat for a little while."

Lyle gulped and nodded.

"What were you doing up there?"

He gulped again before he spoke. "I was just checking," he whispered.

"Checking on what?"

"Her," he said, nodding his head toward the house.

"So you could see if she was asleep and break in again?"

"No-o-o." He shook his head vigorously. "It wasn't me."

"Who was it then?"

Lyle averted his eyes. I shook the Power Punch canister so the little ball in the bottom of it rattled against the sides. That got his attention.

"It wasn't me, honest. I just check, that's all. I always check."

"You used to check on Raymond?"

He nodded.

"But why do you keep bothering my mother, making all those crank calls?"

"I check on her, that's all. I like to check," he insisted.

"You're the one who called me when someone tried to break in, aren't you?"

He nodded.

"Why?"

"I don't know."

"Who did you see?"

He tried to scoot away from me.

I tightened my grip.

"Who did you see?"

"Nobody. I didn't see nobody."

"Raymond? Did you see Raymond? Come on, answer me. Did you see Raymond?"

"He was dead."

It came out as a wail.

"What?"

Either it was my question, or maybe it was his answer, I don't know, but it seemed to affect him in a very physical way. He got the roving jitters. One part of his body would quiver and jerk and then another. I could see he wanted to tell me something else, but he was fighting physically to keep from doing so. A few seconds more and I'm pretty sure he would have almost literally spit it out. But I didn't have a few seconds. While Lyle was rocking and rolling and I was holding on to him the best I could, Mother flung open the back door.

"Child, what're you doing out here?" she demanded.

Lyle lurched away from me, leapt to his feet, and bolted around the side of the house to the street. I didn't bother to chase him. Mother raised her hand as he ran past and kept it raised until we were sure he was gone.

"I'm glad he had sense enough not to come up on this porch."

As I got closer, I saw she was holding something that looked like a makeup compact.

"What was that all about?" she asked.

"I think I caught your hant."

"I doubt if you could unless you got yourself some red pepper and some—"

"Lyle, Mother, I think it's been Lyle all the time. The footprints, the phone calls. Rolland called him a techno freak. I think Lyle knows how to tap into people's lines, do all kinds of things."

"Then why'd you let him get away?"

"He got away, Mother. I didn't let him get away."

"Well, come on in the house."

I turned around and surveyed the yard one final time and then followed Mother inside.

"What're you doing up anyway?" I asked her.

"How could anyone sleep with you going back and forth through the house, making all kinds of racket, phones ringing and stuff. I might as well have teenagers in the house. By the way, give me back my Power Punch."

"I only borrowed it. I would have asked, but I thought you were asleep."

"That's what you and Jimmy and Carolyn used to think back then too, but I always caught you." She stood waiting with her hand outstretched. "Give it here."

I dug in my pocket, took the little canister out, and dropped it in her hand.

"Since you're up, can I ask you a couple of things?"

"Might as well," said Mother, settling in on the sofa where I had been headed. "I doubt if I'll get back to sleep tonight."

I looked around the room. Since Raymond's departure, the clutter had started to creep back. I spoke without thinking. "Where's all that junk you used to have around here? You know all those boxes and stuff?"

Mother drew herself to her full seated height. "I beg your pardon, miss. That was not junk, and please don't call it that. I don't see the need to wear something once and just throw it away. Nor do I see the need to toss out a saucer just because it has a little nick on it. I can remember the times when we didn't have anything to drink out of but jelly jars and—"

"That's all right, Mother. I apologize. Forget it."

I didn't want to argue. There was too much to do and too much at stake.

"Mother, the picture that's missing, the one with Daddy and Aunt Laura—is there anything significant about it?"

"Laura had on some stockings two shades too light. Made her legs look right ashy."

"Something other that, Mother. Something that might give us an idea why Raymond stole it."

"Child, I don't know." Now she was the one sounding a little testy.

"Mother, describe the picture to me."

"You saw it. You know what it looks like."

"I want you to describe it. Tell me what *you* saw."

"Well, like I said, there's Laura with her ashy legs and standing next to her is Walter Lee."

I nodded, encouraging her to go on.

"Walter Lee is only eleven, but he's almost as tall as Laura. He has on his Sunday clothes, a pair of pants with real sharp creases and a white shirt buttoned all the way up. Laura has on one of those drop-waisted dresses and she's holding her Bible."

"Okay. Go ahead. What else? What's around them? Where are they?"

"They're outside standing in front of that old barn with all those geegaws hanging off it."

"What kind of geegaws?"

"Those things they say Laura made and hung up all over the barn after just about all her kinfolk died in that influenza epidemic. Folks said they would whirl and spin in the wind and make a terrible racket. Laura said they kept the devil away. She painted that barn up like a billboard for a circus too. It was just awful."

Mother leaned forward and lowered her voice. "Folks used to say she didn't have good sense."

I nodded solemnly lest Mother regret having squandered a family secret on me.

"But none of those Barkleys ever had a lick of sense anyway except, of course, your daddy."

"So Aunt Laura was the artist in the family—the outsider."

"Girl, I wouldn't call that mess art. Any five-year-old could do that."

"Did you ever actually see any of it?"

"Uh-huh. One year Laura sent a bunch of that mess up here. Walter Lee got all excited. I said, 'Humph, last year she sent a smoked ham.' "

I was getting excited. "She sent some of her work here?"

"That's what I said."

"Where is it?"

"Child, I don't know. It's around here somewhere."

"What do you mean you don't know? How could you lose something like that?"

"How could you lose your gym clothes three times in one year when you were in the ninth grade? How could you lose Jimmy when you were supposed to be watching him that time at Fairytale Town? How could you 'lose' your way home the time I let you go to that Lindsey girl's party?"

"Okay, Mother, I get your point. Now, moving on up into this decade, do you have any idea where the stuff might be? Could it be in the garage?"

"I doubt it."

"Why? That seems like the logical place for something like that."

"Because," she said, hesitating a bit, "because Raymond cleaned out the garage for me."

"Oh," I said. That's all I could think of to say. "Oh."

Again, all roads led to Raymond. I decided to try a different tack. "What happened to Aunt Laura's things? You know, who disposed of everything?"

"Lord, please don't bring all that up again. That was the biggest disgrace I ever saw. I thought Walter Lee was going to have a heart attack or kill somebody over that."

"How come?"

"Laura's other nieces and nephews—you know, the ones who never did anything for her when she was alive—they took everything. They were supposed to divide it up equal, but Tyree and all of them got a'hold of it before your daddy got down there and they sold everything."

"Everything?"

"Everything. The house, her clothes, that old car she hadn't driven in years, even the little bit of land she owned in Conner."

"Conner—you said Conner?"

Mother nodded.

"You know, I think I should have had this conversation with you a long time ago."

Mother nodded again and smiled the smile of the newly redeemed.

"Do you have Tyree's number?"

"I have it around here somewhere. What you want to call that ole big-headed boy for?"

I told her why.

Mother found the number. It was written on a shoe box with shoes in it—a pair she had never worn—that was neatly stacked on a shelf in her closet with other shoe boxes. I've trained myself not to even wonder about things like that.

"Go ahead and call him," urged Mother.

"Maybe I'll wait. Isn't there a three-hour time difference? It's probably two in the morning there."

"There is no rest for the wicked. Call the boy."

I called his number and a woman answered. Mother was right; Tyree was not resting. I could hear some low-down, dirty blues playing in the background and almost smell the barbecue over the line. I told the woman I wanted to speak to Tyree, making sure I added please at the end of my request. She called out to him that some heifer was on the line and then dropped the phone on some sort of hard surface from what seemed like four or five feet.

Tyree was speaking to someone as he picked up the phone. I was surprised at his deep, rumbling voice.

"Uh, Tyree, this is Theresa Galloway . . . your second cousin . . . Walter Lee's daughter . . ."

I was running out of credentials, and he still hadn't indicated he knew who I was.

"Yeah," he said. It was more a question than a statement.

"I'd like to talk to you about Aunt Laura . . ."

"You gotta to be crazy calling here with this shit at three in the morning."

"I apologize for calling so late. I just need to ask you a question . . ."

Mother snatched the phone from me.

"Tyree? This Lorraine. You stop acting a fool and talk to this girl. You hear me? Good."

She handed the phone back to me.

"Look," he said, "I just don't want to be stirring up old shit. Okay?"

Tyree sounded petulant.

"Tyree, I promise you I don't either."

"You the one the lawyer?"

"No, that's my husband."

"Okay, what do you want?"

"I just need to know what happened to Aunt Laura's stuff—her pictures and things. That's all."

"We got rid of it."

"I know that. Look, I'm not after anything. Okay? I'm writing the family history, trying to tie up some loose ends."

So I lied, but I got him to talk to me.

"We sold it at the flea market."

"All of it? Everything?"

"Uh-huh."

"You must have worked your tail off going back and forth to that flea market every weekend?"

"Nope. Only took one day. Soon as we got it set up, some fella' comes up and buys all that junk. Took it right off my hands."

"Tyree, tell me something. Do you remember who bought it?"

"Naw, some white boy. That's all I remember."

"Just one more thing. Was Aunt Laura ever called Lula?"

"Not that I know of. One of those women she worked for before she lost her sight could have called her that. You know how they be messing with folks' names."

I thanked Tyree and hung up.

Mother was already up when I finally crawled off the couch around nine and headed for the bathroom. She was in Jimmy's old room, moving around furniture and cleaning, trying to exorcise Raymond's presence. Jimmy's old chest of drawers sat out in the hall where she had pulled it, and the mattress from his bed leaned against the wall next to the open window.

I did my toiletries and reviewed my agenda. The first thing on my list was to contact Mettler one more time and try to get him to talk to me. I tried calling this time.

"Pronto Prints."

I didn't recognize the voice.

"May I speak to Gil Mettler, please."

"Of course you may. This is Gil speaking."

"Mr. Mettler? I didn't catch your voice. This is Theresa Galloway."

I waited for him to explode or hang up in my face. When he did neither, I continued. "I know you didn't have time yesterday, but I'd really like to talk to you.

It'll take only a few minutes. This is so important to our family. I'm sure you can understand that . . ."

"Okay."

"What?"

"It's okay, Mrs. Galloway. I'll be here all day. Come on by."

I was confused now. I wondered if this man had a split personality or something. He was just as sweet as he wanted to be now, while he'd acted like a fool yesterday.

"Thank you. I'll be there in about fifteen minutes."

I told Mother where I was going. She nodded absently and walked me to the door.

"You know," she said, "I read those articles this morning while you were sleeping. And those paintings, the ones painted by this Lula, the ones missing—'bout how big you think they are?"

"I understand some are pretty large—big planks of wood. She painted on barn sidings, things like that."

Mother seemed to be deep in thought. "I think I'll call Cleotis and beg his pardon. Get him to come on back over here."

"That would be nice. I'll call you when I get back."

"Did you say that place where you found Raymond was real dark?"

"Mother, you're not dwelling on that, are you?"

"No, I was just wondering why anybody would keep their house so dark."

"Some of the windows were boarded up."

"Yes, that's what you told me."

"Mother, is there anything I should know?"

"Why you ask that, baby?"

"I don't know. It's just something about your expression."

"You worry too much."

I shrugged. Maybe I do.

"Don't forget to call Brother Cummings."

"Oh, I won't," she answered. "I won't."

Gil wasn't there when I got to Pronto Prints, at least that's what I thought when I first walked in. But the buffed guy was there, and he was working the counter this time. This didn't seem to be their busiest time of the day. There was only one woman ahead of me. She made a single copy of some official-looking document, paid for it, and left. Then it was my turn.

"Gil Mettler, please."

The man smiled and extended his hand.

"Pleased to meet you."

"Wait a minute . . ."

"I saw you yesterday talking to my partner, Darryl."

"That was Darryl? He told me he was Gil Mettler."

The man laughed. "Sometimes Darryl likes to play little games. But his name is Darryl Porter."

"Mr. Mettler, you don't have to do this if you don't want to. But, if you don't mind, would you show me your ID?"

He laughed again, reached in his back pocket, and pulled out his wallet. He flipped it open and showed me his driver's license.

I would have blushed if I could. "I'm sorry. It's just that some strange things have been going on lately."

"Yes, I think I know."

"Is Daryl around?"

"No. That's one of the reasons I wanted to talk to you. Darryl didn't come home last night."

I looked at him, waiting for him to continue. I wasn't sure where Temp had spent the night and I was worried, but I didn't think I would unburden myself on a stranger. I didn't understand what Mettler's problem had to do with me.

He must have been reading my mind.

"Darryl left right after your visit yesterday. Didn't say a word, just bolted."

"Mr. Mettler, do you know why I was here yesterday? What I tried to talk to Darryl about?"

"I caught enough of it to know it was about Raymond Johnson."

"You knew Raymond?"

"Yes, I knew Raymond. A long time ago we were very close, but that was a long time ago. I'd gone on with my life since then, but Raymond seemed stuck in a time warp. He was all good times and party. Kept popping in and out of my life, destroying whatever I had going at the time and then disappearing again. Mrs. Galloway, do you understand obsessions? I think Raymond used to be my obsession, now I'm his."

"So he was back in your life?"

"Yeah, he was back."

"What did this have to do with Darryl?"

"Darryl was mine. Raymond saw him as something else to be destroyed. Raymond didn't exactly take him away from me—until last night Darryl always came home—he did something worse. He seduced Darryl's imagination, got him involved in one of his little schemes."

"I suppose you know Raymond is dead?"

"Yeah, I know. That's why I'm worried. I'm scared Darryl may be in over his head in something dangerous."

"Into what? What do you think he's into?"

"Come on, Mrs. Galloway. I'm the one who sent you the negatives."

"That something I'm curious about. Exactly why did you send them to me?"

"I wanted to blow it for them. That's why I sent them to you. I was trying to save Darryl. I knew that if they pulled off whatever it was they were into, Darryl would be lost forever."

"So, what was the scheme?"

"I have no idea. Since you were looking for Raymond, I just thought you'd know what the negatives meant."

"There were three pictures."

"The first two didn't mean anything. They were just a frame of reference so you'd know where they'd come from."

"Who took the pictures?"

"I did. Darryl brought the last one to me not long ago."

"How long ago?"

"A week or so ago."

A couple of customers had come in during our discussion. Mettler looked around as if he was surprised to see them. "I guess I'd better get to work."

"Just one more question."

He paused.

"Mr. Mettler, have you ever spent any time in the South?"

He considered the question. "Just when I was in the service. Why?"

Mother wasn't home when I got there, but she'd left me a note. It read, "Went to the Claridan."

I left immediately, cursing under my breath. I don't

believe in a lot of foul language, but Mother will make you curse sometimes. I just wanted to get to the Claridan in time before anything happened, before Mother made something happen.

I skidded to a stop in front of the Claridan Arms and hurried to the back where Raymond's apartment had been. Mother wasn't there. I walked around to the street side. No Mother. I even checked the little narrow walkway in back between the building and the fence. Mother wasn't there. I went back out front and scanned the street in both directions. Still no Mother. I had absolutely no idea where she could be. Well, yes I did, but I was trying to think positive. And I was starting to get scared.

I got back in my car and drove slowly down the street. When I got to the bus stop in front of the coin-operated laundry, I realized that I'd started to despair a little too early. Mother stood at the bus stop, presumably waiting for a bus.

I pulled over, and she opened the door and got in as if she had been expecting me.

"Mother, what are you doing here? What's going on?"

"I was afraid I'd be too late. That they'd already be gone."

"Who?"

"Not who. What."

"Mother, I'm not going to play word games with you. What're you talking about?"

"The barn pictures. I was afraid they'd be gone."

"Wait. Hold on. Maybe you'd better start somewhere a little closer to the beginning."

"I kept wondering why that boy's place was so dark. Why he had the windows boarded up. Then when I

took the mattress off the bed and I saw those planks
we put underneath to keep it from falling through, it
kinda dawned on me. But you wasn't there, and I
couldn't reach Cleotis, so I had to get there and make
sure I was right."

"Right about what?"

"Right about the boards."

"Boards?"

"Those boards Laura painted on. You know how
Jimmy's bed was always falling through the frame
'cause we didn't have any slats. I used a couple of
those boards, those old barn planks Laura had painted
on, for slats. That's what was holding the mattress up
in Raymond's room. When I took the mattress off to
turn it over this morning, there they were."

I pulled over to the curb. I couldn't process what
she was telling me and drive at the same time. "You
mean we had the paintings all the time?"

"Uh-huh, they the ones Laura sent that time instead
of a smoked ham."

I couldn't get over the fact Mother had the paintings
all the time.

"I have a couple of them. The other ones are nailed
up on the boy's windows."

I couldn't wait to get to Mother's and see the famous work by Aunt Laura, aka Blind Lula. Mother
kept cautioning me to slow down. Mother of all people. I skidded to a stop in front of the house and
hopped out of the car. Mother struggled, disengaging
herself from seat belts and bucket seats bent on holding her hostage. I returned to the car to help her.

"Come on, Mother," I urged.

She bristled at my barely disguised impatience.

"Just hold your horses now. I don't know what you're so anxious for. It's just an old piece of wood. My piece of wood, I might add."

I dragged her through the yard and up the couple of steps leading to the front door. I had my key in the door and had turned the knob when Mother grabbed me from behind and shoved me out of the way with such force I stumbled down the steps, falling to my hands and knees. Stunned, I found myself looking up at her from the ground like a toddler who still hadn't gotten the walking thing down.

"Run!" she hissed under her breath, her face contorted into an evil mother mask. I stared at her, dumbfounded.

She kicked at me. "Run!" she spat and raised her hand as if to hit me. "Go on. Get outta' here!"

Dazed, I climbed up from the ground and started toward her. I don't know what I was thinking. I just wanted to go to her, touch her, calm her. She whirled around, opened the door, and stepped into the house, slamming the door in my face. Everything happened so fast, it was almost as if she'd vanished, leaving nothing but a trail of evil-smelling liniment behind.

Walking backward, I stumbled to the front gate, my impulses telling me to obey Mother and run. But I didn't. At least not until I flashed back on last night at my house. Then I ran. I ran as if I was racing the devil. Still, I left the yard reluctantly, knowing that my mother was behind locked doors with a killer.

Chapter Twenty-one

I ran out of the front gate past my car. I could have driven around the corner to the Tyler place, but it was quicker by foot. It was broad daylight, and I was running through the neighborhood, trying to save my mother's life.

I yelled to a woman sitting on her porch, "Call the police." But she just looked at me as if to say, "Call 'em yourself. You the one carrying a Dooney Burke bag. You better have a phone in there." I'd forgotten I even had the phone. I stopped, ripped open my purse, and fumbled around in it. The phone was like a live fish in my hands. I flipped it open and punched at buttons, but it skittered out of my hands and landed on the walk. I didn't have time to deal with it. I ran off and left it.

I passed kids playing and a man trimming his hedges. I rounded the corner at Fourteenth Avenue, and the 72 bus pulled up to let passengers out. The kids, the man trimming his hedges, the bus—such ordinary things, but they seemed out of place as I ran a footrace with evil. I hit the Tyler yard and headed straight to the backyard, climbing over debris the movers had left to mold in the damp and bake in the sun for so long that it was unrecognizable. I waded through thigh-high weeds without regard for broken glass and wet things. I had to get as close to Mother's house as possible without being seen, and I had to find something to fight with too.

I crept to the spot in the back fence where I had confronted Lyle and craned my neck to get a view of Mother's house. Mother's back door popped open. I ducked down. Mother came out first.

"Ain't no use making all this fuss. I told you. You can have the mess. It ain't nothing but junk, anyway."

Mother was talking unnaturally loud, even for her.

Lambert came out after her.

He was holding a gun. He looked pale and wan. For once he wasn't wearing that ratty down jacket. From as far away as I was, I could see that his face was shiny with sweat and his shirt was stuck to his body in places. His movements had a nervous, jerky quality to them as he looked over his shoulders and cast his eyes about the yard. He nudged Mother in the back with the gun, and she whirled around to face him.

"I've told you, now. Don't be sticking that gun in my back."

Lambert told her to shut the fuck up and get on to the garage.

I had no plan. I had no weapon. That didn't matter. Lambert had used the "f" word to Mother, and somebody was going to die. Lambert had a gun, but I was taking no bets. I dropped my purse, hoisted up my skirt, and started over the fence.

The noise I made attracted Lambert's attention. He looked away from Mother for just a second. A second too long. Mother bit her lower lip, sucked in her breath, and shoved Lambert with the heel of her hand against his left shoulder. It was a hard shove with a lot of force behind it, but the way Lambert screamed and dropped to his knees was totally out of proportion. I was almost over the fence. Another second and I would have made it, had Lambert not regained control of himself and aimed the gun at me.

"Mrs. Barkley, ah do believe ah'm gonna have to shoot your little pickaninny here if you don't cooperate," he said with a forced southern accent and a gritty smile.

Mother had headed for the front yard after shoving him, and she was just about there. She turned slowly and came back. The look on her face just about broke my heart—it scared me too.

I dropped down into the yard. Lambert stood up. There was blood on his shirt where Mother had shoved him. He didn't even bother to look at Mother. He didn't need to. He had the gun trained on me, and he knew Mother would do whatever he said.

"Now," he said, "I want you to get your rusty old ass over here and open this garage."

Mother went to the garage and fished in her pocket until she found a key. She unlocked the garage, and I helped her swing the overhead door up.

"Now, where is it?" demanded Lambert.

"In the loft space in the back," answered Mother.

"Get it."

I moved to help.

He motioned at me with the gun. "No, you stay where you are. Let the old broad do it. Then I'm going to show her how a gunshot feels."

Mother moved slowly. She got a ladder and leaned it against the back wall. Then, arduously, she climbed up to the loft. She fumbled around, tottering on the

ladder until she located a large flat wrapped in burlap.
She slid it along the loft until she could get a grip on
it, then she grabbed it with both hands.

"Here it is," she announced.

She turned slightly on the ladder, and it started to
wobble one way and Mother wobbled the other. A
couple of small objects tumbled down to the garage
floor. Lambert's eyes grew wide, then they tightened
down to mean little slits, and he dashed into the garage to save Laura's painting and his fortune. But he
was too late. The burlap-wrapped package came crashing to the floor. Dust rose, more things fell, and by
the time I made it into the garage, Lambert was writh-
ing on the garage floor, clutching his throat, and
Mother was standing over him, the canister of Power
Punch in her hand.

I grabbed her and we got out of there, locking the
garage behind us.

"Where's the gun?" I asked her when we'd secured
the door.

We looked around us on the ground.

"It's in there with him," said Mother.

We listened. We heard retching sounds and then
silence.

"Come on," I said, dragging Mother toward the
house.

Lambert was stirring. I heard cursing and then an
explosion. I looked back to see a hole as large as a
tennis ball splintering the wood near the lock. There
was another shot. Splinters of wood and plaster exploded around us. We ducked our heads and ran. We
got into the house and locked the door as Lambert
took three more shots.

But we weren't safe. If Lambert could blast through

the garage door, he could blast through this one too. I grabbed the phone to call the police. The doorbell started to ring. I dropped the phone. Had he gotten out and gone around to the front door? Was it some kid who stood a chance of getting caught in a cross fire?

Mother started toward the door.

"Don't open it!" I yelled. But she paid me no mind.

I dashed into the kitchen and got the largest knife I could find. I had no illusions about it holding its own against a gun, but at least it was something. When I got back to the living room, Brother Cummings was standing there with his shopping bag. I have never been so happy to see any man young or old as I was to see him.

"It's about time you got here, Cleotis."

"Oh, sugar pie, I got here as soon as I could."

Sugar Pie? Did he call my mother "sugar pie"? My head was reeling. My life was in danger, and all I could think of was he called my mother "sugar pie."

"He's here. The one I shot, he's come back."

Brother Cummings took off his felt fedora and handed it to Mother. He peeled off his coat and handed that to her too. Then he reached in the shopping bag and pulled out the shotgun.

"You ladies stand back," he said as he removed the pom-pom cover from the gun's barrel, folded it neatly, and stuffed it in his pocket.

Mother moved back.

I dropped the knife and grabbed the phone again. "Police! Police!" I screamed into the receiver.

There was another loud explosion, this time at the back door. It shook the house. I heard glass breaking.

Brother Cummings moved swiftly to the kitchen. I dropped the phone and followed him.

"Maybe we'd better stay back here," said Mother, "and let the men finish this up."

Lambert had stopped shooting and was trying to beat his way through the door with something metal. I heard more glass breaking and the scream of wood splitting and Brother Cummings's voice calm and clear over it all.

"Go away and leave these women alone. I'm warning you, I am armed."

Lambert screamed, "Fuck you, old man."

I heard Brother Cummings say, "Satan get ye behind me." Then he stepped onto the service porch, pumped the shotgun, and fired both barrels into the back door.

Chapter Twenty-two

The police carted Lambert off. I caught a glimpse of him as they wheeled him out on a stretcher, his face frozen in a bug-eyed stare of disbelief. At first I thought he was dead, but then I realized he was probably in a state of shock. Besides, if he had been dead, they would have covered his face.

The police separated us into different rooms of the house and took our statements. I told them everything I knew, and I believe Mother and Brother Cummings did too. I also told them what I'd been able to piece together about Raymond and Lambert's plot to relieve Mother of some valuable art she didn't even know she had. It wasn't until the next day when I read the paper that I learned that Darryl Porter's body had been found in an old VW bus parked in an unofficial camp along the American River near Discovery Park. The van was registered to Lambert.

As soon as I could, I called Temp, reaching him at home.

"Honey—everything's okay now—but there's been some trouble here at Mother's."

"What? I'll be right there."

"Wait. What about the house? Was everything okay when you got home last night?"

"Everything was fine. What's with all those weird messages you left with everybody?"

I was sure somebody had been in there when we got home last night. I couldn't believe everything was fine.

"The doors were all locked?"

"Yes."

"The windows too?"

"T, I told you everything was fine."

"I guess I just got spooked last night, that's all."

"There was one thing. Shawn been doing some more of his experiments?"

"What do you mean?"

"There was this weird smell in the house. Like some kind of chemical."

"A medicine? An ointment or something?"

"Yeah, it could have been."

"Lambert. He was in there last night. He's the one Mother shot. He was too smart to go to emergency. He knew the police would have alerted all emergency rooms to be on the lookout for him. I guess he was treating it himself. I remember that weird smell. It was some kind of unguent or something, like that Absorbine Daddy used to use."

Temp said, "I'll be damned. The bastard was in my house." Then he got all proprietary about the kids. "Where are my children? Are you sure they're all right?"

"They're fine. They're with Rob and Anita. I checked on them this morning. They're not ready to come home yet."

Brother Cummings had called the brothers from his lodge. They came in their old battered hats and faded overalls. They came with their pickup trucks and tool belts. By nightfall they had all the damage Lambert had done cleaned up, patched up, and painted. While they worked, Mother, Brother Cummings, Temp, and I sat around Mother's dining-room table and tried to make a little sense of the whole mess.

"So that's what all this killing was about?" I said, studying the third picture of the *Devil's Gonna Get You* triptych that Temp and Brother Cummings had taken off Jimmy's bed and leaned against the dining-room buffet.

"Doesn't look like much, does it?" said Mother. "How much did you say it's worth?"

"The magazine article said the high six figures."

"Like one hundred thousand dollars."

"Up to nine hundred thousand dollars."

"Lord, have mercy."

"What are you going to do with it, Mom?" asked Temp.

"I'm going to put it back under my mattress and sleep on it. Child, get real. I'm going to sell it."

"This Lambert, how did he know you had the paintings, Mom, when you didn't even know you had them yourself?"

"Theresa can answer that."

"I can?"

"Yes. Remember Tyree."

"Yes . . ."

"Well, didn't he tell you he sold all of Laura's stuff lock stock and barrel to some white man?"

"Yes . . ."

"And knowing Tyree as I do, he's a lazy child. I bet he didn't even sort her papers out. Just sold the man everything."

"The pictures and the money orders. That's how he got them."

"That's what I think. He must have seen something in her stuff, maybe one of her paintings. So he buys it all. That way nobody knows what he's really after. And Tyree was all too willing to sell it to him. He had to get rid of Laura's things and pocket the money before Walter Lee got there."

"And he meets up with Raymond and cooks up a plan to get the rest of them."

Mother nodded.

But I wasn't going to let her get off that easy. "And you fell for it."

"No."

"Yes, you did."

"I knew he was lying when he said Walter Lee wrote those letters."

"Oh, you did, did you?"

"Yes, I did."

"Tell me how."

Mother allowed her eyes to settle briefly on each of us. But when she started to speak, she spoke directly to me. "Walter Lee was put out to work when he was eight years old, and he worked hard every day of his life up and till he got so he could work no more."

Temp listened politely. I couldn't figure out what Mother was getting at, but Brother Cummings nodded in understanding.

"Your daddy didn't write those letters. The only thing Walter Lee could write was his own name."

"That's not true. There you go again, Mother. Always putting Daddy down."

Temp reached over and took my hand. I was fighting back tears.

Mother leaned forward. She spoke with uncharacteristic gentleness. "Listen to me, baby. Your daddy couldn't go to school. He was too busy working, trying to put food in his mouth and clothes on his back. It's true your daddy couldn't read or write. He was ashamed of it, and he hid it from your kids. But Walter Lee was not dumb. He was smart enough to see to it that each one of you got an education."

I leaned across the table and took Mother's hands in mine. We sat like that for a few moments. After a while Brother Cummings got up and went to the kitchen. I could hear water running and the refrigerator closing. He was preparing to boil water and crack ice. Temp and I left to go get the kids and go home.

There was just one more thing for me to do. I took out my cell phone.

Temp glanced over at me as he drove. "Now what, T?"

"I just have to check in at the office."

I started to punch in Brenda's number, but thought better of it and called my own number instead.

Brenda answered crisply on the first ring. "Personnel Office. Brenda Delacore speaking."

I could have sworn she said "personnel officer."

"Brenda, this is Theresa."

"Theresa, I was hoping you'd call. I got some good news for you. Gardner withdrew his complaint."

I was instantly suspicious. "He did? Why?"

"He realized it had all been a misunderstanding."

"He did, did he? What else?"

"What do you mean, what else?"

"There's got to be more, Brenda. When do you get to the part about the horse's head in his bed?"

She ignored me, then went on. "Also, Heather is no longer on your tail. She's leaving."

"Heather? Leaving? Now, that is good news. When did all this happen?"

"The Senate Office of Research called for her personnel file today. I sent it right out. But don't worry sister-girl, I fucked up a few things in it before I did."

"You did what?"

"I screwed around with her file a little. Took some of those bogus, inflated evaluations out. Salted it with a few private citizen complaint letters from my secret stash."

I put my head in my hands.

"Theresa, Theresa. You there?"

"Brenda, we want Heather to go. They won't take her when they see all of that."

"They'll take her. It's not about all of that. They'll take her. Just watch and see."

This time Brenda was right.

The next evening Mother invited us over. She said she had an announcement to make. Temp insisted Shawn and Aisha go too. They agreed under the condition that no corns were to be trimmed. I went as reluctantly as the kids. I was afraid of what the announcement might be.

We got to Mother's and knocked twice before Brother Cummings pulled the door open. He had on a burgundy smoke jacket. My stomach tightened when I saw him. Mother came out of the kitchen, carrying a tray of finger food.

"You all come on in," she sang out. She was wearing a pink dress with a lace peplum.

After we'd noshed a bit and I'd fought down a rising tide of nausea, Mother looked at Brother Cummings.

He nodded slightly, and she stood up and cleared her throat. I nearly bolted from the room when I saw that.

"Everybody," she said, "I have an announcement to make."

Shawn held his fist to his mouth as if it were a herald's trumpet and gave a flourish of toots. I started to sweat profusely.

"Temp, you come up here with me."

Temp stood up, grinning widely. He walked over to Mother and put his arm around her shoulder.

"Everybody," she said, "I'd like you to meet my new business partner. As of today I am now a twenty-five percent owner of Second Generation."

We all applauded. Brother Cummings opened the sparking apple cider, and we toasted the new partnership of my mother and my man.

Don't miss the next
terrific mystery by
Terris McMahan Grimes

Other Duties As Required

coming soon from Signet

My name is Theresa Galloway. Theresa Nicole Galloway, to be exact. I am of sound mind, all things considered. I do not smoke. I do not do drugs. And, except for a little white zin now and then, I don't drink. I'm gainfully employed. I attend Mount Pleasant Baptist Church. I'm married. I have children. And I am scrupulously honest. It's important that these things be known about me. I have a lot at stake here.

You see, there's a dead man in my office. He's dead and cold and he doesn't have on any underwear. I know, I checked—on all three counts.

Let me back up a little here.

I came to work this morning at the State Department of Environmental Equity, where I'm the personnel officer, just as I've done for years. The only difference being the hour. I had an important report due today, and that accounts for my 6:30 A.M. arrival. My office door was slightly ajar as I'd left it. I pushed it open with my shoulder, dropped my case on the small conference table near the door, and walked around behind my desk to turn on my computer. And tripped over a body. A dead man.

There was no blood or anything, but the man was dead. Thanks to my mother, I've seen enough dead folk in the last couple of years to know a dead man when I see one. My first thought wasn't CPR. I wanted to bolt from that room, make another door if necessary, just get as far away as I could from that pitiful form on the floor. And I would have if something hadn't held me there. Even today I can't explain why I didn't. It's just that there was something about the dead man. He was an older man in his late fifties or early sixties, from the looks of him. He was balding. He wore a lightweight plaid shirt and a well-worn pair of khaki pants. Nothing exceptional. But what kept me there staring down at him was the way he'd collapsed. He was in a sort of half crouch, as if just before he'd died he'd been scrabbling around on his hands and knees under my desk furiously looking for something and had simply run out of steam—or time, or some important element needed to sustain life—and had just dropped where he was. His position was so natural yet unnatural at the same time. I knew he was dead, but somehow I still wanted to reach down, shake his shoulder, and ask him if he was all right. I found I had extended my hand to shake him before I caught myself. Then I saw he was clutching something in his left hand—a scrap of paper. Without considering the consequences I reached down and gently tugged the paper loose from his grip, kind of like pulling the fortune out of a Chinese fortune cookie. I smoothed the paper out and read its contents out loud. "TFAGS." The password to my computer.

The rest of my brain kicked in then, and I finally reacted appropriately—I got scared. I mean, really scared. And the questions I would have asked had this been some decent hour and I'd been fully awake bogarted their way to the front of my mind.

Excerpt from OTHER DUTIES AS REQUIRED

Who is this man? How did he get in here, the personnel office, one of the most secure places in the department? He certainly didn't work for me. I'd know him if he did. Of the thirty employees in the personnel office, only two are men. I'd used my electronic key card to get in. Did he have one? If he did, how'd he get it? And my password—what was he doing with it? I studied him closely. His hands were rough and callused. They were not the kind you'd expect to see poised at a keyboard. He wore soft leather slip-on shoes with crepe soles that were more house slippers than street shoes. The heel part was almost worn completely off. They were scuffed and dirty. A thin coating of fine dust clung to them and the cuffs of his pants. One shoe had come off, revealing a naked white ankle and a bony, hammer-toed foot. He wasn't even wearing socks. How had he died? Had somebody killed him? Why?

Those last two questions seemed to echo through my office, bouncing off the walls, ricocheting off windows, getting louder and louder until they just about drove me from the room. I might have been exaggerating just a little when I said the rest of my brain kicked in. If the whole thing had been fully functioning, I don't think I ever would have gotten it into my mind to search his pockets—roll a dead man, so to speak. But that's just what I did. He was, after all, in *my* office dead, with *my* computer password in his hand. At least I had the right to know who he was. Chances were, he wasn't trying to tap into the latest version of computer solitaire, and he just didn't look like a hacker to me.

I pushed my sleeves up, way up past my elbows. Then I lifted his pocket out from his body with one hand and gingerly stuck the other one in. My fingers almost instantly came into contact with flesh—cold, prickly flesh. I jerked my hand out. The pocket was one big hole all the way through—to him. I'd touched a dead man, and all I'd found out was he didn't have on any underwear.

I straightened up from my sorry inquiry, and another sector of my brain kicked in. "Sure is quiet in here," it seemed to be saying. It *was* quiet. Unnaturally quiet. Public office buildings don't get that quiet on their own. There should have been a janitor around somewhere, and maybe a few early arrivals should be showing up soon. But how soon? I looked down at the body. How long, I wondered, had it taken him to die?

Fortunately, self-survival requires very little brainpower. My survival instinct kicked in and demanded that I get out of there, that I put some distance between me and the dead man and maybe even his killer. I backed up slowly until I got to the door. Then I turned around, walked out, and carefully closed the door behind me. I stood there with my back against the door, trying to see through the hodgepodge of mix-and-match cubicles that made up the personnel transactions unit. It's funny the demands we make on ourselves in times of stress. Finally I got up enough nerve to walk around front to the reception area. I picked up the receptionist's phone and dialed 911. I forgot to dial 9 and had to redial. The dispatcher or whoever it was I talked to wanted to keep me on the line until the police got there, but I hung up and went outside and waited at the front of the building where the smokers stand. When the police got there, I was washing my hands in the ornamental fountain. Spray had gotten in my hair and on my clothes, and I was just about soaked but I didn't care. There was a dead man in my office.